THE SWORD AND THE JUNGLE

Further Titles by Christopher Nicole from Severn House

Black Majesty Stories

BOOK ONE: BLACK MAJESTY
BOOK TWO: WILD HARVEST

The Dawson Family Saga

BOOK ONE: DAYS OF WINE AND ROSES?
BOOK TWO: THE TITANS
BOOK THREE: RESUMPTION
BOOK FOUR: THE LAST BATTLE

The McGann Family Saga

BOOK ONE: OLD GLORY
BOOK TWO: THE SEA AND THE SAND
BOOK THREE: IRON SHIPS, IRON MEN
BOOK FOUR: WIND OF DESTINY
BOOK FIVE: RAGING SUN, SEARING SKY
BOOK SIX: THE PASSION AND THE GLORY

BLOODY SUNRISE
CARIBEE
THE FRIDAY SPY
HEROES
QUEEN OF PARIS
SHIP WITH NO NAME
THE SUN AND THE DRAGON
THE SUN ON FIRE

The Russian Saga

BOOK ONE: THE SEEDS OF POWER
BOOK TWO: THE MASTERS
BOOK THREE: THE RED TIDE
BOOK FOUR: THE RED GODS

writing as Alan Savage

THE SWORD AND THE SCAPEL
THE SWORD AND THE JUNGLE

THE SWORD AND THE JUNGLE

by

Christopher Nicole

writing as

Alan Savage

This first world edition published in Great Britain 1996 by
SEVERN HOUSE PUBLISHERS LTD of
9–15 High Street, Sutton, Surrey SM1 1DF.
First published in the USA 1997 by
SEVERN HOUSE PUBLISHERS INC of
595 Madison Avenue, New York, NY 10022.

British Library Cataloguing in Publication Data
Savage, Alan
   The sword and the jungle
   1.English fiction – 20th century
   I. Title
   823.9'14[F]

   ISBN 0-7278-4964-6

Typeset by Hewer Text Composition Services, Edinburgh.
Printed and bound in Great Britain by
Hartnolls Ltd, Bodmin, Cornwall.

'He knew that the essence of war is violence, and that moderation in war is imbecility.'

Macaulay
Lord Nugent's 'Memorials of Hampolen'

Contents

Part One

Retreat From Hell

'But wherefore thou alone? Wherefore with thee
Came not all hell broke loose?'

John Milton
Paradise Lost

Chapter One

Debacle

The twin-engined aircraft's wheels hit the runway, bounced, and then settled, the pilot managing to avoid the bomb craters that scarred the tarmac before the plane came to a halt before the wand-waving aircraftsman. The pilot looked over his shoulder. "Welcome to Rangoon," he said.

The door was already being opened. "Come on, come on, hurry up there!" the aircraftsman was bawling. "The Japs'll be back any moment."

"Listen," said the medical attendant. "Go fetch transport. I have casualties."

The aircraftsman peered past him at the two people seated on the floor of the otherwise empty Dakota; the plane had been stripped of seats and all interior fittings so that it could be used for transport, in normal circumstances. "They don't look sick to me," he commented.

"He's an officer," the attendant hissed. "Move it!"

The aircraftsman gulped, and hurried off.

"Sorry about that, Captain Brand," the attendant said. "We'll sort it out."

"Just one almighty fucking flap!" the pilot remarked, coming aft from the flight deck. "Begging your pardon, Mrs Brand."

Constance Brand gave a faint smile. She was a tall, slender woman, with fine but cold features; her complexion had suffered from the excessive sun- and windburn to which it had recently been exposed. Her

3

hair, escaping irregularly from her headscarf, was long, loose and black. At least she presumed it was still black; since her rescue from the shattered hulk on which she had been floating she hadn't dared look too closely at the roots. Her clothes matched the general picture of a woman who had been through the mill; she wore a man's shirt, belted over a pair of white men's drill shorts, and cut down sandals which were thonged around her ankles. "Actually, we can walk," she said, her voice a low contralto.

"You're an army wife, Mrs Brand," the pilot reminded her. "When my manifest says two casualties, my duty is to deliver two casualties. Right, Captain?"

Harry Brand nodded, and grinned at his wife. His somewhat craggy features too had been burned raw by the sun and and the wind during the past month, and in addition he was still weak from a leg wound, which, although treated and bandaged by the navy doctor, and thus had healed better than he could possibly have expected or hoped, was still apt to be painful. His fair hair was as tousled as his wife's, and he too was wearing obviously borrowed clothing. "Let's be VIPs, while we can," he recommended.

A car had been driven on to the runway, and some more orderlies were waiting, commanded by a sergeant. "Captain Brand? The General is waiting."

"General Hutton?" Harry ventured.

"No, sir. This is General Alexander," the sergeant said, opening the rear door for Constance. She was glad to escape the noonday heat. The aircraft had been relatively cool, following the enormous heat of the small boat, and before that, of Singapore. Now the heat was back, and more than the heat, an enormous sense of deja vu. Rangoon was packing up. There were crowds at the airport, being restrained by relatively good-natured MPs, and other crowds already beginning to trail to

4

the north. Some drove cars, at a snail's pace because of the throng; some pushed carts or had them drawn by donkeys; most had bicycles. All were laden with children and pets and all the household goods they could carry, and were accompanied by barking dogs, clucking chickens, braying donkeys and plaintive sheep. Behind them, parts of the city were burning. Constance had not seen anything like this before: in Singapore there had been nowhere to go, on land.

But Harry had. "Just like Belgium," he muttered. "A refugee is a refugee is a refugee, as Gertrude Stein might have said."

"Do we know General Alexander?" she asked, as Harry settled himself beside her.

"He had a division in France, before Dunkirk," Harry said. "I believe he was the last British Commander off the beach, so I may have met him. I don't remember much about it."

He himself had been carried off the Dunkirk beach, badly wounded and half out of his mind, Constance knew. It was not a subject she wished to pursue, as his dementia had been caused by the death of the woman with whom he had been in love . . . when he had already been married to her! But that had been more than a year ago, and surely their recent experiences had recreated their marriage – although she knew that was as much up to her as to him. She took refuge in mundane matters. "I really would like to have a bath and brush up, and maybe find some decent clothes, before meeting a general," she said.

"Generals, my love, are always in a hurry," Harry commented, and looked at the crowds on the road. "Maybe this one has more reason than most to be in a hurry."

A Burmese newspaper reporter forced his way through the throng, peering through the windows as the sergeant

5

started the motor. "Is it true you have escaped from Singapore?" he shouted. "Both you and the lady?" He had been chatting with the aircrew.

"No comment," Harry replied. It was what he had been told to say.

"He'll print that you said yes, sir," the sergeant remarked. "And by tonight you'll be a hero. *Did* you escape from Singapore, sir? Madam?"

"Yes," Constance told him, and looked at the empty waste of Dalhousie Street, populated only by armed police. "But not many people are going to read about it. There won't be anyone here by the time that newspaper goes to press."

Constance realised she was more frightened than at any time since the war had begun, even the European war. Poland, and then even France, had seemed remote from the perspective of England. The Blitz had been fought above them, and for all the frightful bomb damage and the casualties, no human enemy had ever come among them, machine-gunning and raping, murdering and pillaging. Singapore had simply been too crowded with events, both physical and emotional, as she had sought to resuscitate her marriage. The collapse of the island's defences, so utter and so final, had come with startling suddenness; it had been too overwhelming for fear. And the escape had been a wild adventure, a defiance of the gods. Following which the problems of survival, adventuring, imminent daily catastrophe, were surely things on which she could turn her back, perhaps to tell her grandchildren. But here it was, all over again, only a few weeks later, the same burning buildings and cratered roads, the same terrified people, the same grim-faced soldiers patrolling the streets in a vain attempt to prevent looting, the same collapse of civil authority, of civilisation itself.

She remembered reading, before the War, a short story entitled *Leiningen and the Ants*. It told of the march of a huge army of soldier ants across a portion of Brazil destroying everything in their path, and of the efforts of a coffee baron to resist them. She felt that the Japanese were the soldier ants of Asia, always pressing onwards, irresistible, implacable, utterly destructive of anything a European might call civilisation. Leiningen had stopped the ants. Did the British in Asia have a Leiningen?

General Alexander was a brisk, dapper, somewhat little man – at least when standing beside Harry Brand's bulk – who wore a conventional military toothbrush moustache and had a habit of looking at one as if he did not truly believe what he was hearing. Well, in this case, perhaps he was justified. "Sit down, Mrs Brand," he invited. "And you, Brand. Any news from your Dad?"

"I'm afraid we've been rather out of touch, recently, sir," Harry said. Everyone in the army knew his father, the famous Sir George, once the youngest brigadier in the British Army, and now a general.

"I'm sure he's thriving. You'll take some tea?" He nodded to the hovering aide-de-camp, who in turn snapped his fingers at the white-jacketed Burmese waiter. The military headquarters was a spacious, airy, verandahed building in its own palm-shrouded grounds. It was far removed from the screaming, terrified mob they had seen outside the airport, or even from the deserted and sinister town centre. Save for the craters in the grounds and the ever-pervading smell of death and destruction, it might have been a thousand miles from the nearest war.

"I must apologise for our appearance, General," Constance said. "We were cobbled together by the

7

Navy, God bless them. I was starkers when they picked me up."

Alexander surveyed the bare, sun-burned legs, and the woman's clothing which inadequately concealed a very full if slim-hipped figure, and perhaps reflected on how fortunate the Navy could be. "I think they did a very good job, Mrs Brand. But, if possible, we will find you some more suitable clothing." He turned to Harry. "I know you were picked up drifting about the middle of the Bay of Bengal, but I'm not going to ask you for any details on how you got out of Singapore, Brand. Others may want to try the same way. I had you brought here instead of sending you direct to Calcutta because I want you to tell me how it was. I mean, eighty-six thousand men. . . . I know the newspapers are claiming you were overwhelmingly outnumbered, but my intelligence reports do not credit the Japanese with any more than that."

"We were overwhelmingly outnumbered in morale, sir," Harry said. "The speed and ruthlessness with which the Japanese struck, again and again and again, the way they did things we thought were impossible . . ."

"We have the same problem here," Alexander said. "Morale." He walked to the window and looked down at the garden, where his staff were piling documents to be burned. "I only arrived here yesterday, you know. The situation is extremely critical. Every man in this army expects to find a Japanese soldier looking over his shoulder when he turns round. Were you in the jungle, Brand?"

"Yes, sir."

"Are they *that* good?"

"No, sir, I don't believe they are. The problem is that we are that bad, at the moment."

Alexander turned, frowning. "You can say that, about your own men? Your own comrades?"

"I assumed you wanted to hear the truth, sir."

Alexander sat down himself. "Go on."

"My battalion, sir, was sent out to Malaya direct from England. In the first place they were raw troops. We were supposed to lick them into an efficient fighting force. They were also lads who had been born and brought up in one of the most civilised countries in the world. I know there *are* poisonous snakes in England, but I have to confess that I have never seen one in England, and neither had any of my men. Neither had they seen pythons or tigers or leeches, and none of them had previously had malaria. I'm afraid they were simply terrified of the jungle, and physically unable to cope with it. And when, in their imagination, and then in reality, the jungle became filled with Japanese, invisible until they bayoneted their victims, well, maintaining morale was a difficult business."

"Were you terrified of the jungle?"

"I was fortunate, or perhaps unfortunate, sir, enough to have fought in East Africa against the Italians. We didn't have much jungle, but we had a lot of unpleasant aspects of nature."

"You were part of an Indian division. Yet the Indians seem to have been as frightened of the jungle as your people."

"With respect, sir, why should they not have been? Like my men, they were mostly recruits. And in any event, why should an Indian necessarily be an accomplished jungle fighter? There are jungles in India, but it is a vast country. Those men were not necessarily recruited from jungle areas."

"There are no jungles in Japan. Are you saying that they are better soldiers than ours? Indian or British? Or Australian, for that matter."

"I do not believe they are, sir. But they were better trained for the job they were required to do. They had certainly been trained, somewhere, to fight in the bush.

9

Maybe in French Indo-China, or southern China . . . They were also trained to move on foot, whereas our people were trying to apply European tactics: take away their transport and they were like fish out of water. And, what is more, the Japanese were required to advance and infiltrate and surround regardless of casualties, and without concern for civilians or property. We were attempting to fight a civilised war. But there is no such thing as a civilised war. The Japanese were, are, fighting a *war*!"

Alexander stroked his chin. "What about the command structure?"

"I am not qualified to criticise my superiors, sir."

"You were there, Brand. You are an intelligent man. And you come from a long line of soldiers. I know your father. I what your observations. I *need* your observations."

Harry glanced at Constance. Her face was tense, but she gave him an encouraging smile. "Well, sir, I am bound to say that our senior officers were not up to the job."

"I'd like some evidence of that."

"I can offer several examples, sir. Political indecision. When we first got to Malaysia we were told that in the event of hostilities with Japan becoming a fact, or even a strong possibility, we would advance and seize the Kra Peninsula, regardless of Thai sensibilities. That idea was abandoned, presumably for political reasons. Lack of determination, of clear objectives. General Percival and Governor Shenton never seemed to be thinking together. The General had a war to fight, the Governor had a civilian population to humour. When it comes to a war, you cannot do both; someone has to be in overall command. Tactical lack of vision. We kept being, officially, outflanked and required to fall back. As you have just said, sir, we were not really outnumbered in the peninsula. Our command must have been aware of this. Yet every time a Japanese force, sometimes hardly more than a patrol, got round behind us, we were required to withdraw to a fresh position. Not only was that bad tactics, but it was catastrophic for morale. I believe that if some of our forces had been told to create a defensive box in various selected areas, and told that they must fight to the last man, or until relieved, we would not have lost Malaysia."

"Would that policy not have involved heavy casualties?"

"With respect, sir, the policy actually followed involved the loss of the entire army."

Alexander gazed at him for several seconds, then grinned. "You are certainly a chip off the old block, Brand. But you have put your finger on several pulses I have already felt out here. Is there anything else?"

"Perhaps the worst of all, sir: wishful thinking. Our senior officers evaluated each situation in the light of what they *wanted* to happen, not the worst that *could* happen. As for example, when we had finally retreated onto Singapore Island, and the Causeway had been blown up, we were told it would be some weeks before the Japanese could attempt to get at us. They crossed two days later."

Alexander nodded. "A tale of catastrophe. Unfortunately, we are having the same trouble, as I have said." He gestured at the wall map. "We took a pasting, along the lines you have just outlined, east of the Sittang River. So we elected to pull back across it and hold that line. Sound strategy, But then there was a flap and the bridge was blown with two brigades still on the east bank. I believe some of them have got across, but think what *that* has done for morale. Then, the command on the ground decided it was impossible to hold Rangoon. I have been sent here to reverse that idea. Rangoon must

11

be held if it is humanly possible. We are trying to block the Japanese advance. I had you brought here because I wanted to find out something of what happened in Malaysia, in order that I can stop it happening here. Now you must be on your way. You and Mrs Brand will be flying out first thing tomorrow morning. I'm sorry to say you will find this flight a little more crowded than the one in from the Andamans." He stood up, and Harry and Constance stood also.

"May I ask where we are going, sir?" Harry asked.

"Calcutta, in the first instance. From there passages will be arranged for you to return home, hopefully together."

"Home, sir?"

"Don't you want to go home?"

"Oh, yes! Please." Constance bit her lip. She hadn't intended to become involved in this military conversation at all. But the thought of seeing her son Mark again, and being out of danger, of being clean and and having decent clothes to wear . . .

Alexander was looking at Harry. "You will, of course, once you have given the Staff a complete report on what happened in Malaysia and Singapore, in the first instance have to go back to the South Midlands, as you are still technically an officer in that regiment. I know there may be some criticism of your abandonment of your men . . ."

"With respect, sir," Harry said. "I did not abandon my men. My company was so badly cut up it was incorporated in what was left of two other companies, and as I was myself wounded, Colonel Harris dismissed me from duty."

"Well, then, I shall put that in my report, and you should have no bother at all." He frowned at Harry's expression. "But you're not happy."

"I feel, sir, that my experience of warfare against the

12

Japanese would be more useful here than at some training depot in England."

"Harry!" Constance protested.

Alexander looked from one to the other. "It seems to me you are a glutton for punishment, Captain," he remarked. "You have been through an horrendous experience, with your wife. Now she needs to be escorted back to England. You are wounded, and thus are entitled not only to convalescent leave, but not to be called upon for active service again, unless you volunteer. And if you go home to England, you are almost certainly going to get a medal and a leg up. I shall recommend you for both. I am told you've got the Military Cross, anyway, for your behaviour at Dunkirk."

Harry grinned. "I never had the time to pick it up."

"Then you have something to look forward to. I suppose, if you were to stay here, you would also get your due reward, but it'll be a darn sight longer in coming. Have you considered all of those points?"

"Yes, sir. And I am volunteering to return to active duty here, just as soon as is possible."

Again Alexander glanced from one to the other. "And your wife?"

"I would very much like my wife to be given a passage home."

"By herself? Don't you think we should ask her what she feels about it?"

They both looked at Constance. So perhaps it had all been a dream after all. Although, when she had married this man, she had understood that it was the Army that was his life, and she had to accept whatever crumbs fell from that table. Which did not prevent her latent resentment from bubbling. They had been through so much, she had really supposed that *they* might have become the most important thing in Harry's life, as it was in hers. But those were domestic problems, not to

13

be divulged to a stranger, even if he was a general and seemed anxious to help. "I think I should go home, General Alexander," she said. "I have a son waiting for me."

"Of course. Well . . . how is your leg, anyway, Brand?"

"Just about as good as new, sir. A fortnight lying in the sun, and being looked after by Constance, would cure any man."

"You'll have to be examined by my surgeon. But if you really are fit and wish to stay, I'll co-opt you on to my staff for the time being with the brevet rank of major, and find you a more useful position as soon as possible. However, ah . . . I shall arrange married quarters for you both, tonight." He cocked his head at the wail of the siren. "Here come the bastards again. I think we should take cover." He held out his hand. "It has been a great pleasure, Mrs Brand. Please report to the airfield at dawn tomorrow. Brand, you will see Mrs Brand on the aircraft and then report here." He gave a grim smile. "If the place is still standing."

There was an orderly waiting to show them down to a bomb-shelter; Alexander apparently had his own. Built only half into the ground, with a lining of corrugated iron, their shelter was clearly not going to keep out much more than the odd splinter. "We can't go deep, you see, sir," explained the orderly. "Or we flood."

Harry and Constance saw what he meant; any temptation to sit down was ended by several inches of dirty water that covered the floor. There were a dozen people here already, clerks and other orderlies. Two or them were English women secretaries, who regarded Constance's outfit with raised eyebrows. "Got it off a midshipman," Constance explained. "He didn't object."

14

"Really!" one of the women commented. "One feels it is one's duty to preserve a sense of dignity among the natives."

Constance squeezed Harry's arm as he would have come to her defence; she had never needed defending. "Are you a native?" she inquired. "One would never have supposed it."

The woman glared at her. "Of course I am not a native. I was born in London."

"Then we've nothing to worry about, have we?" Constance asked with a bright smile.

Any reply the woman might have considered making was obliterated by the crump of the bombs as the Japanese Aichi bombers came in almost at rooftop level. "I'm afraid we don't have anything to send up against them, sir," the orderly shouted.

Harry nodded. "Just like in Singapore." He put his arms round Constance and held her close. This was reassuring. She had no illusions that his arms, or even his entire body, would keep out a flying bomb fragment, but it suggested there was something still there, between them. She looked up at him, and he looked down at her. "Mad at me?" he asked.

"Of course," she replied.

There was so much that still needed to be said between them, to be accepted or rejected, and there was no time. But there had never been any time.

Harry had seduced Constance virtually the day war was declared, simply because they had both felt in the mood to be seduced. *Götterdämmerung* had been in the air, and the devil take the hindmost! Over the few months before September 1939 they had conducted a sort of love-hate relationship. She had been a good friend of the wife of his cousin Hector, now a prisoner

15

of war in Germany. Thus it had seemed natural for her to swim into the Brand tank, that cosy secluded world of soldiers and their wives. All male Brands were soldiers, had been soldiers since the Battle of Blenheim. Officers, of course. And all Brand women had sat at home and waited, their upper lips ever so stiff. Brand men came home with their shields or on them.

Constance Lloyd, daughter of a wealthy stockbroker, had found it all rather nauseating. But undeniably exciting, especially with war looming. And Harry had currently been *the* eligible member of the family. That he was given to outrageous behaviour she had put down to the fact that junior officers and undergraduates have approximately the same points of view. But she had understood from just about their first meeting, when, drunk, he had immediately proposed marriage, that he was really not the marrying kind. Yet she had allowed herself to be seduced, as much by the fever around her as by the man himself. Even after he had gone off to France she had never considered marriage. She understood that she had committed an irrevocable act, taken in the context of her class and her time, an act that would somehow have to be explained away to the satisfaction of the man she eventually *would* marry, but she had never doubted she could do that. Just as, in her innocent arrogance, it had never occurred to her that the act might be far more irrevocable than she had supposed possible.

Constance had never been either a dissembler or a coward. When she had realised she was pregnant she had gone to her parents and confessed the situation. Then things had been taken out of her hands. To her surprise and great relief, everyone had behaved in a most civilised manner. The Brands had welcomed her as a daughter-in-law, just as her parents had welcomed Harry, if somewhat less happily – Harry and James Lloyd

16

had never actually liked each other. She had found, in view of everything that had happened, the prospect of being Harry's wife very attractive. He was an exciting man, and love would surely grow as they entered the delights of parenthood together. She had supposed he felt the same. She had been quite unaware that in the interval between leaving her arms and being informed that he was about to become a father, and therefore, by the conventions of *his* class and time, a husband, Harry had fallen desperately in love with a Frenchwoman he had met and wooed during the long winter of 1939–40, while the BEF had sat in France and waited for something to happen.

He had not told her this until after he came out of hospital following the wounds he had received at Dunkirk. But by then she had understood that their marriage was just about over; it had never really existed. She had reacted badly, she now knew. She felt, she told herself, that she might have ridden the knowledge had it not been that the Frenchwoman had been killed in the retreat. One cannot fight something that is no longer there, a memory which Harry, guilty about what had happened, feeling himself responsible for her death, would no doubt carry to the grave. So she had opted out. By the time she had realised her mistake, Harry was in Malaysia. No one had raised any objections when she had announced her intention of joining him; James Lloyd had by then become an official in the Ministry of Transport, and arranging a passage had been a matter of pulling strings, while in the summer of 1941 Malaysia had seemed one of the safest places in the world to be, certainly safer than blitzed England.

The only problem had been Mark. But here too support had been total. The two grandmothers had willingly agreed to share the little boy during his mother's absence; no one had supposed it would be for

17

very long. Constance Lloyd, the spoiled child who had always followed her own agenda, and taken little hiccups such as unanticipated pregnancies and the breakdown of marriages in her stride! Now she would put her marriage back together again.

Instead she had jumped with both feet into the middle of a war so savage it made what had happened in Europe seem like a garden party. In the middle of that continuous catastrophe the growing realisation that there was not going to be a reconciliation – the presence of another old flame of Harry's, the detestable Marion Shafter, had seen to that – had been irrelevant; she had delayed her departure for too long to get out. Yet when the officers had been informed that the fortress was about to be surrendered, and those who no longer held commands were invited to try to escape if they could, or dared, it had been to her that Harry, wounded and helpless, had turned. She, with her skill at sailing small boats, had embarked them on a three-week adventure which had ended in a typhoon. But it had been more than an adventure. It had been the honeymoon they had never had, as Harry's wound had mended and he had realised that she was more than a pretty face and a willing body who had entirely messed up his life, but a valuable person in her own right – who loved him. As he loved her, she was certain. But they needed so desperately to talk. Because he loved the Army more.

The quarters to which they were assigned were in an abandoned church. Hospital-type railings had been erected and they had a bed, round which a curtain could be drawn. But there were people no more than a foot away on either side, and the toilets and washing facilities were communal. "Makes that little old boat seem like the *Queen Mary*," Constance said, sitting on

18

the narrow bed. Not that she was concerned about the size of the bed; the smaller the better. She was more interested in the dress, underwear and stockings that had been produced for her to wear; she didn't think they had been laundered all that recently.

"But for that storm, we could still be on it." He sat beside her, in turn he regarded the uniform he had been given; it was a much better fit. "I imagine you're still mad at me."

"Of course. I had hoped . . . well, the idea of a long, slow voyage home, the two of us . . ."

"Probably four to a cabin."

"There'd be the deck, and moonlit nights at sea. Do you *have* to stay, Harry?"

"Yes. I want to fight, Connie. If I ever get back to England, with a wound, even a healed wound, I'll have the devil of a job getting back out again."

"And me? And Mark?"

"If you still want to call it off, I won't contest it, Connie. I have behaved very badly to you. I certainly don't deserve you."

She wished he wouldn't make gestures like that; one day she might carelessly accept the offer. And she couldn't stop herself responding. "What do you suppose happened to your friend Marion? You thought she was spying for the Japanese, didn't you?"

"She *was* spying for the Japanese; that's why she was in Changi. But now . . . I imagine she's received some kind of a medal from Hirohito."

"May the worms eat her bloody gut while she's still alive!" Constance said, with an unusual vehemence which left him with raised eyebrows. She picked up her washbag – a present from the Navy – and joined the queue at the ablutions. People attempted to chat with her, but she didn't really listen to them although she endeavoured to smile. She was preparing herself for abasement, and

19

it was very difficult for her to accept. Constance Lloyd had only ever surrendered as a conscious act of will – her will. Well, then, this would have to be an act of will as well. When she got back to their cubicle, Harry was already in the bed and beneath the blanket. "Just what have you got on under there?"

"Shirt and shorts."

Constance stripped, and slid beneath the blanket beside him. "You could at least follow fashion," she suggested.

He raised himself on his elbow. "Are you sure?"

"I'm your wife. And I mean to go on being your wife! Stay and fight your war. I'll be there when you come back."

Constance had an idea that they were the only couple in the converted church who had attempted to have sex that night, and equally that those to either side of them had been aware of it; when they emerged from behind their curtain the next morning they received several old-fashioned looks. She wondered if anyone realised that it had been no more than an attempt. Harry had been, not for the first time, impotent. It had begun after his return from France. The result of his wounds, the doctors had said; it'll all come back. Absolute twaddle! It was the result of watching his mistress die and being unable to help her. It *should* all come back. But apparently not with his wife, which had played an important part in their separation. Yet it had come back, during their escape. Another reason why she had supposed the crisis was over.

But perhaps, during the escape, he had not thought of her as his wife. Now, at the mere suggestion of civilisation – this was civilisation? – the crisis was back. Fortunately, everyone in the church was in too much of a hurry to be over-inquisitive about this very odd couple who had appeared in their midst: the Japanese planes were back at dawn. The crypt was crowded with dank and frightened humanity. "What time was I supposed to take off?" Constance whispered into Harry's ear.

"Right around now."

"Then you could be stuck with me." She wouldn't have been altogether unhappy about that. But while the bombs were still crashing down about them an MP sergeant appeared in the doorway of the shelter and began calling a list of names.

"You must go," Harry insisted.

Constance was reminded of the famous scene from *A Tale of Two Cities*. People found their way towards the sergeant, while a rumble of muttering rose, either in farewells or from those not on the list. "That's you," Harry said.

Constance looked around the terror-filled gloom. At least she didn't have one of those overstuffed suitcases or little cloth bundles that clearly belonged on the end of a missing stick – just the washbag given her by the Navy, and that precious document ensuring VIP treatment back to England. "You were to deliver me."

"I suspect that agenda has been replaced. Off you go now. Give Mark a hug and a kiss for me. Same for Ma and Louise. And your Ma as well." He grinned. "I don't suppose your Pa would appreciate it, from me."

"Mrs Brand? Is there a Mrs Brand?" the MP was shouting, having reached the end of his list and starting again.

Constance bit her lip. "And your Dad?"

"Oh, him as well if you can find him. And Joss and her boy."

"Mrs *Brand*!"

Constance put her arms round his neck and kissed him. "Don't forget to come home." Then she was hurrying for the doorway.

*   *   *

21

The women were herded into a truck for the drive to the airport. The bombers had passed on now, and the all-clear was sounding, but there were more fires and more craters. "They never stop, do they!" stated the woman seated beside Constance. She was in her mid-thirties, Constance estimated, which made her some ten years the older. She had yellow-brown hair, cut properly short, where Constance's, in the absence of anything remotely resembling a hairdresser for several months, had grown almost to schoolgirl length, straight and black. The woman was also sensibly dressed in slacks and a bush jacket, well cut and of good material, with a matching slouch hat. Everything about her, especially the small crocodile-skin suitcase, suggested affluence, and perhaps tough-mindedness. The face was handsome rather than pretty. But she was smiling.

"I suppose not," Constance agreed, feeling like something the cat had dragged in. The dress that had been found for her was ill-fitting and the sandals inappropriate, although, being open and tied round her ankles, they were at least comfortable.

"I'm Joan Allbright," the woman said, and waited.

"I'm Constance Brand."

"From down the coast, are you? I don't recognise the name."

"Ah . . . yes, down the coast," Constance agreed. She didn't want to get involved in being either a heroine or notorious for having escaped Singapore.

"My husband is an oil executive," Joan Allbright said, and again waited.

Constance side-stepped the implicit question. "Is he coming out with you?"

Joan Allbright shook her head. "He's needed to stay. We aren't going to give up the oilfields."

Constance's knowledge of Burma was of the scantiest.

"Where are they?" Joan raised her eyebrows. "We haven't been out very long," Constance explained.

"What bad luck, to run into this! They're a couple of hundred miles north of here. Around Yenangyaung. That's where Alexander really has to hang on to, and stop the Japs. We can't let them have the oilfields." They had reached the airport, and there were several planes waiting to take off. "Stick by me," Joan Allbright recommended. She had clearly put Constance down as an innocent who needed protection. But Constance was happy to obey, for the time being anyway, and followed her new friend into the queue. They had apparently been allotted to different aircraft, but Joan soon sorted that out, and they found themselves seated side by side in a very crowded cabin; most of their fellow travellers were women and children, and some of the children were very small and noisy. In addition, a large percentage were either Indian or Burmese. "Definitely third class." Joan commented, wrinkling her nose. "How did all these people get seats?"

The same way we did, by pulling rank, Constance thought, but decided not to say it. What made the closeness worse was that the windows were blacked out with thick paper stuck to the glass, creating a strong sense of claustrophobia. "You're not going to be sick, are you?" Joan asked.

"I shouldn't think so. I've spent the past week in a submarine," Constance replied without thinking.

Joan shot her another distinctly old-fashioned glance. "You never did say what your husband did," she remarked.

"It's top secret," Constance said, beginning to enjoy herself, especially as they were finally taxiing.

The Burmese steward came down. "Only two hours to Calcutta," he told them. "Ladies, relax."

"Chance would be a fine thing," Joan grumbled, as

they soared rather bumpily through the clouds. "Do we have an escort?"

"No, ma'am," the steward said. "No Japanese right about now. We fly over sea, see?"

"I hope to God he's right!" Joan said.

"As he said, relax," Constance recommended. "There's nothing we can do now about anything." They reached their cruising height, which was a bit higher than recommended, Constance reckoned; the cabin was not pressurised and breathing was a trifle difficult, which brought more wails of complaint from the passengers. Constance began to worry about Joan, who lay back in her seat with her mouth open gasping like a fish out of water. Two hours?

She called the steward. "It is only temporary," he assured her. "As soon as we are well clear we will come back down."

A quarter of an hour passed, just about the longest 15 minutes of her life, Constance thought, and that included her experiences in Singapore. Then there was a sudden tremendous buffet, and the plane did descend, several hundred feet in the space of a second, Constance estimated, wondering where she had left her stomach. It also immediately banked steeply to the right. Now there was panic in the cabin, and the steward was rushing up and down trying to placate people, most of whom were being violently sick. Joan closed her mouth. "We're going to die," she announced. "I know that we are going to die."

"Surely not," Constance said. She didn't feel afraid, merely irritated that she should have survived so much to come to a sudden end in this sardine tin. And without Harry or Mark, but she wouldn't have wanted either of them here with her.

The captain came on the intercom. "I'm sorry to say that we have lost an engine," he said. There was a huge wail of terror. "There is no need to be afraid. This plane can land on one engine. But we cannot now make Calcutta. I am turning back over the land, and will put down at Akyab. From there transport will be arranged to Calcutta. Please go through the emergency landing procedure."

The steward proceeded to explain about things like taking out false teeth and putting one's head between one's legs. "Why did we lose the engine?" Constance asked. She hadn't heard any noise to suggest they had been attacked.

"Plane not good," the steward explained.

"Talk about encouraging," Constance muttered to Joan. "Are you all right, Mrs Allbright?"

"Yes," Joan said, but she didn't look all right.

"I hate to ask you this," Constance said. "But do you have any false teeth?" Joan Allbright stared at her in consternation; she hadn't been listening to anything the steward had said. "You have to take them out," Constance explained. "Because there may be a bit of a jolt when we land, and if you swallowed them you could choke."

"Well, really," Joan said. But she took a handkerchief from her pocket and appeared to cough into it.

Constance stared at the blacked-out window. She felt she would go mad if she didn't know what was happening, where they were, and before she could reflect had dug her nails into the thick paper and pulled violently. It came away and she could see out. Instantly there was a protest from the steward but there was nothing he could do about it; other people promptly followed Constance's example, which brought a fresh chorus of shrieks. Constance looked down, first of all at the sea. Oh, shit, she thought, not again! But a moment later they were flying over land, and she was looking at nothing but trees,

25

but they were clearly coating hilly country; every so often a serrated peak would come through the green, black and sinister. In the valleys were silver streams, threading their way presumably to the sea. Then she saw a road, a good distance away, almost obliterated by the crowded traffic proceeding slowly along it. There was even a railway line, but there were no trains to be seen. Somehow the sight of the refugees made her feel better. There were so many people, all in the same situation. "Can you see the airfield?" Joan asked.

There was nothing remotely resembling an airfield beneath them. Nor were there any other aircraft to be seen. The engine in the wing on her side was functioning, so it had to be the other one that had failed, or had been shot up, and from the shouts coming from the other side of the plane she gathered it was a pretty ghastly sight. "Must be ahead," she said. Because now they were definitely coming down, whether voluntarily or not she couldn't be sure.

The pilot came back on the intercom. "I'm afraid we cannot make Akyab," he said. "I will set down on the beach."

The steward was jumping up and down in the doorway to the flight deck, trying to get everyone's attention. "We land soon!" he bawled into his mike, the words almost lost behind the continuous crackle. "Bumpy, eh? You put head between knees!"

Constance had no idea how many people obeyed him; she certainly did. So did Joan, but a glance to her right showed that the older woman was also being violently sick. It was certainly terrifying, for the plane was dropping very fast. My God, Constance thought, if we hit something going down at this rate . . . and suddenly realised that they were actually crashing – she was going to die without ever seeing Harry again, or Mark. They would never know what had happened to her if, as seemed obvious, they were crashing into the jungle. Mark would never even remember what she had looked like!

There was a tremendous tearing, crashing blackness.

Chapter Two

Retreat

Constance realised she was hanging upside down in her seat belt. She couldn't be sure whether she had for a moment lost consciousness or not; she was surrounded by confused noise and movement. But she knew she had to get out of this situation just as rapidly as possible. She twisted her head to her left and gazed through shattered glass at a mass of foliage. Shattered glass! Was she cut? She looked at the seat in front of her, and at the cabin roof, which was now below her, and at the blood gathering there. Oh, my God! she thought. But, although she was a mass of pain and discomfort, there was nothing sharp, as she was sure there would have been had she been cut. Then she looked to her right, and saw Joan Allbright, also hanging from her seat belt, and dripping blood; her throat had been slashed by a sliver from the imploding window, which had miraculously missed Constance herself. "Mrs Allbright!" she gasped. "Joan!"

There was no response. Constance grasped the woman and shook her, but that only caused her to bleed more freely. Now she became aware of what was happening in the rest of the cabin, the screaming, shouting, gasping bodies straining to reach the exits. And also of the smell of escaping aviation fuel!

Joan Allbright was dead, or dying. Constance released the other woman's belt, and she fell in a heap onto the cabin roof. Constance released her own belt, landed half on top of the woman's body, wasted a precious moment to try to find some sign of life, then joined the throng pressing for the doorways. She burst out in the midst of a mass of bodies, and only then discovered the plane was hanging in the trees which had broken the first impact and saved her life and others.

She fell some 8ft to soft earth, landing with a jar that winded her. For a moment, as she felt a sharp pain, she thought she might have broken something, but she knew she couldn't wait to find out. She staggered to her feet and lurched through the undergrowth, regardless of the thorns which tore at her. She supposed she must have covered about 50 ft when the plane exploded. The blast hurled her forward and left her stretched on the ground, only half conscious. But again the trees had broken the worst of the blast, and she was alive.

If she was going to stay alive in the middle of the Burmese jungle. That was another matter.

"Ah, Brand," Alexander said. "Wife get off all right?"

"As far as I know, sir," Harry said.

For all the disastrous situation in which he found himself, and early in the morning as it was, General Alexander appeared as spotlessly cheery as ever. That could not be said for his staff, who all seemed to have slept in their clothes, and were looking somewhat askance at the sudden appearance of a new face, wearing a very obviously borrowed uniform, and walking with a limp.

"This is Major Harry Brand," Alexander said. "I won't go into all the names now, Brand; you can pick them up as we go along. Major Brand is an escapee from Singapore, gentlemen. He has fought the Jap in the jungle of Malaysia, and will, I believe, be of value to us in fighting the enemy here." He paused to look around the faces, as if daring anyone to disagree with him. "Now," he went on, "as you all will know, our attempt to mount a counter-offensive to hold Pegu has failed. Not only are the Japanese advancing from the east, but since the Sittang Bridge disaster they are well on their way to coming in from the north-east. I am afraid there is no hope for Rangoon, so we are going to pull out, now. We will retreat north to Prome, and Toungoo, and set up a new defensive line there."

This time the officers exchanged glances, and Harry understood what the general had meant during their meeting yesterday; these men's morale was shattered – they did not believe they could hold a defensive line anywhere. He himself was more amazed at the way the commanding general, having announced yesterday his intention of holding Rangoon if it was humanly possible, had now accepted the inevitable; but rather than be downcast by the failure of his first objective, was coolly choosing and implementing his next best option. "Final demolitions will commence now," Alexander went on. "And the garrison will pull out, now. Make it orderly, gentlemen. I am afraid quite a few of you will have to walk with your men. Brand, as you have a gammy leg, you will come with me. Thank you, gentlemen."

They hurried off to their respective commands, leaving the general with only his immediate staff. "Cheer up," he told them as he looked around their gloomy faces. "I have done this sort of thing before."

Outside was all the evidence of a city about to be abandoned; huge explosions were taking place and the oil storage tanks a few miles away at Syriam were blazing and gushing great clouds of black smoke into the air. In the harbour, the engineers were bulldozing the cranes into the water with enormous splashes. It was a relief to leave the doom and destruction behind.

But the march north was hardly less traumatic. The

railway had been bombed in several places and was unusable, and the garrison, which included 7th Armoured Brigade, found their way blocked by thousands of refugees, some actually fleeing, others just squatting and waiting, for what, no one seemed quite sure. The headquarters staff were also disconcerted to discover that they had several women with them. "I thought I gave orders that all white females were to be flown out?" the General demanded.

"Yes, sir. But these simply refused to go."

"Why not, for God's sake?" The staff officer shrugged and rolled his eyes, leaving Alexander to make his own judgement as to whether they had boyfriends or husbands they did not wish to leave – or were just afraid of flying. "Well, I suppose we can't leave them to the Japanese. But keep them out of trouble, Mitchell. What a relief it must be to you, Brand," he remarked. "To have a sensible wife."

He and Harry were the only two who had also experienced the retreat through Belgium in 1940. They shared a common memory, of refugees and collapsing morale, of utter frustration . . . and of fear, not personally, but for the people they commanded. Behind them they could still hear the explosions in the city, but out here on the road the only sounds were human. Yet they felt compelled to scour the skies looking for enemy aircraft. And only an hour out of the city a messenger arrived from the advance guard, panting with excitement. "The road is cut, sir."

"What the devil do you mean?"

"The Japanese are in front of us, sir. Just north of Taukkyan. They have erected a road block, and have extended their defensive position to either side."

"Holy shit!" muttered one of the staff officers.

"We must force our way through," Alexander said. "Use the Armoured Brigade. This isn't jungle, gentlemen." He gestured at the rice plantations to either side.

31

"This is relatively open country and a blocked road. We could be in France or England, or North Africa, dammit! And the enemy can't be there in force. We'll drive through them." The orders were given, and the rest of the column halted, while the few tanks that remained in the armoured brigade went forward, supported by infantry. Alexander himself went up to oversee the fighting. Harry would have gone too, but permission was refused. "You're still limping, Brand. I'm putting you in charge of the domestic front for the moment. You find a good place for headquarters until this business is finished. We shan't be long."

Finding somewhere to park the headquarters vehicles and set up some kind of communications network wasn't difficult; Harry chose the nearest rice plantation. It had been abandoned, but the manager's house had not even been looted; there was even beer still in the icebox.

"I've been out here for tennis," a voice said. Harry, standing with hands on hips surveying the lavish entry hall, turned his head. He estimated the woman was in her early thirties, which made her somewhat older than himself – he had not yet reached 30. She was short and a trifle chunky, wore her yellow hair cut in a pageboy around her ears. Her face was also chunky, but not unattractive. As she wore slacks and a bush shirt it was difficult to estimate her figure, but he thought there might be quite a lot of it. "I'm Susan Davies," she explained.

"You're not Welsh?"

"My husband is."

He hadn't noticed the wedding band. "And your husband is where?"

"Yenangyaung. I'm hoping to join him in a couple of days. Do you think there is still water? I'd love a bath!"

"Why not have a look?" He left her to see to the unpacking of the gear, principally the radios on which their entire command structure rested. The plantation, he was happy to discover, had its own generator, and he soon had this working: the fuel tank was nearly full. Next thing was to see if there was any food to supplement the rations they had brought out of Rangoon, all the while listening to the sound of firing from a few miles to the north. Then he had to post sentries to control the refugees, quite a few of whom, having followed the retreating army, now simply sat down in the plantation compound, waiting to be fed. And, no doubt, protected.

Harry decided to get to the top of the house and see if he could find out what was going on. He climbed two flights of stairs, passing paintings of racehorses and English scenes, and listened to a splashing noise. Without thinking, he drew the revolver he had been given and opened the door, looked at a bedroom, and beyond, the open door to a bathroom. And in the tub was Susan Davies. He had forgotten about her! "Oops!" she said. "There was water when the generator started."

She was making no great attempt at concealment and, as he had surmised, she had a lot to offer. He turned round. "Enjoy it while you have it," he suggested, and then hurried back down the stairs, alarmed by the roaring of motors, to find that 7th Armoured Brigade was back, the crews sullenly despondent, and missing two of their tanks. With them was the Army Commander.

Harry didn't have to ask what had happened. "Get Sixty-Three Brigade," Alexander snapped, "and tell them I want the Frontier Force Rifles up here, and fast. The armour couldn't get through, and the paddy is too soft for vehicles to outflank the enemy. If we don't break through that block we are going to be overrun."

Harry hurried off to give the order, and the Frontier Force Rifles duly assembled and advanced. But they

33

too failed to make any impression on the withering machine-gun and mortar fire coming from the roadblock, and they too were unable to force their way round. Casualties mounted and the entire lower floor of the plantation house became an impromptu hospital as the surgeons got to work. The staff gazed at the General, anxiously; it was now late afternoon, and they were still only some ten miles north of Rangoon, which they had to assume was by now occupied by the enemy. It was unlikely the Japanese would stop advancing, they must know what was happening up here.

"Right," Alexander said. "I don't think there would be much to be gained by trying to launch a night attack. But at dawn tomorrow we either get through or we die right here. I want all of Sixty-Three Brigade concentrated, both to guard our rear and to force that block." Staff officers hurried off, and the General grinned at Harry. "That wouldn't be a whisky decanter on that sideboard, would it? I think we could all do with a drink."

"Yes, *sir!*"

The General's confident demeanour was invigorating, even if no one needed to be a military genius to know that their situation was desperate. Most of the army in Burma was already lost, so far as anyone knew. For the commanding general also to go into the bag – *another* commanding general, after the Singapore debacle – would be sheer catastrophe. The Burmese cooks were already preparing supper, happy to have the run of an elaborate kitchen. They were being overseen by the women, among whom Harry discerned his little friend. "All clean and correct?" he asked her.

"As a matter of fact, yes." She jerked her head, and he followed her into the corridor. "Are we really stuck?"

"We're going to break through tomorrow."

"Is that the truth?"

"Well . . . we're going to try."

"And if we don't succeed?"

"Then the Japanese are going to have another general in their bag. Together with staff and hangers-on."

She gave him a long stare. "Is it true what they say about them?"

"They're soldiers, Mrs Davies, fighting, watching their comrades die. If they get in here, they'll be on a high. All will depend on how much control their officers have."

She gave a little shiver. "I've never been raped. And by . . . well . . . the whole idea gives me the creeps."

"Maybe it won't happen."

He made to leave her, and she held his arm. "Are you married?"

"Yes. Sort of."

"What kind of answer is that? Where is your wife?"

"Calcutta. She's on her way back to England. As are you, Mrs Davies."

Another little shiver. "I'm going to Yenangyaung."

"Don't you like England? Aren't you English?"

"No. Yes. Sort of." She smiled. "Do you follow me?"

"And your marriage?"

"Oh, very definitely sort of." She has ants in her pants, Harry thought, at the idea of being raped. And I don't know where I stand as regards Connie. It had been a magnificently romantic gesture, coming right round the world to look for him. Only a woman like Connie would ever have considered doing that, much less actually done it. But had it worked? The reappearance of Marion Shafter had meant that Constance had definitely called off their marriage in Singapore. Their fortnight on the boat, forced on them by circumstances, had been idyllic, but the very moment they had regained contact with the human race, with human realities, doubts had begun to creep back in, and with them, that terrifying impotence, recurring to haunt him. And once Connie

35

regained the comparative sanity of England . . . By this time tomorrow, this woman and I may both be dead, or at least, mentally dead, he said to himself. Her tongue came out and circled her lips. "Do we have . . . allotted sleeping places?"

"I imagine it's doss down where we can."

"Well . . ."

"I have to get back to the General, now," he told her, and looked at his watch, another gift from the headquarters staff. "I could be here at ten o'clock. Or thereabouts."

"I'll wait," she promised him.

It was 10.15 before the last sentry had been checked, the last disposition made. The generator had been closed down and the night was surprisingly quiet, save for the constant jungle hum with which they were surrounded; there might not have been an enemy within a hundred miles. "You'd better try to get some sleep, gentlemen," Alexander told his staff. "Tomorrow will be a busy day."

Harry smoked a cigarette before finally making up his mind. Last night's sexual disaster was a misfortune that had afflicted him, over periods of time, ever since his return from France in June 1940. It had had nothing to do with his wounds, although it had been convenient to give them the blame. The real reason had been the death of Nicole, the way she had died, the abiding memory of her. That even more than Marion had caused the split with Constance. He wondered what Susan Davies's reaction would be if he couldn't make it tonight?

He went along the corridor outside the kitchens, using his torch as there were no lights available. Susan was sitting on the floor, exactly where he had left her three hours before, but he didn't suppose she had actually

36

been there all that time. "Hi," she said. "I've done some reconnoitering."

She got up and held his hand, led him along the corridor, then through a doorway and a couple of other rooms. There were people all around them in the darkness, snoring or sighing or muttering to each other in low voices, the wounded groaning or occasionally crying out. But Susan knew where she was going, and after another doorway she squeezed his hand. "In the corner," she whispered. Then squeezed his hand again. "Kneel."

There was some kind of mattress on the floor, and a blanket. "You are a very efficient woman," he told her, inhaling a strong smell of stale food; he gathered they were close to the kitchens. They knelt together, and she turned against him, her mouth open. Her tongue was hungry, and her hands more possessive than any woman's since Nicole. He wondered just what the state of her marriage was. She seemed desperately anxious to get back to Yenangyaung, but equally anxious to fit in some outside sex on the way. But if she could roam, so could he, pulling her shirt out of her slacks to slip inside and caress the surprisingly cool flesh. "That feels good," she whispered into his ear, and unbuckled his belts, laying the revolver holster softly on the ground. "I don't think there is anyone else in here," she said. "But we don't want to attract anyone, either."

He unfastened her belt in turn, and their hands found flesh together. She held him while he slid his hands over her buttocks. He felt himself erecting as they kissed again. Then she released him and lay down to kick her slacks right off, while he pulled down her knickers. Then did the same for himself, and went down on her. But he was gone again, as he immediately knew. "It's a tough war," she said into his ear.

"For some."

"You really are done. But we'll fix that!"

"You won't, you know." He put his hands back under her shirt to hold her breasts again; they were large and hard-nippled and titillating, but even they weren't going to help.

"You mean it's happened before?"

"Regularly."

"Then you do have a problem. But nothing Mummy can't fix." He pulled his head back to gaze at her in the darkness. "What we have to do is find something which will take your mind off your own problems. Listen, squeeze my ass – hard!"

"But, I will hurt you!" he protested.

"That's it. You have to hurt me. You have to know you're hurting me. But you can't really do me any damage, not like if you were to squeeze my tits, one in each hand."

It seemed the most absurdly simple piece of psychological stimulus, but the fact was that he was hardening at the very idea; not even Nicole had been so earthily provocative. She moaned in a mixture of discomfort and pleasure, he felt, while still stroking him. Then she said, "Now!" and rolled on to her back, carrying him with her.

He surged into her, again and again and again, and he felt her lifting herself to meet each thrust. "Oh, boy!" she murmured. "Oh, boy!" They subsided together, and she bit his ear. "You know, Major, there is nothing the matter with you that a good woman can't cure. It'll be much better the next time."

"Will there be a next time?" he asked. "With you?"

"You mean if we don't break through tomorrow? Maybe not. But at least I won't feel quite so much a victim of the Japs."

"And if we do break through?"

"Then there'll be a next time. I promise!"

*　　*　　*

38

Harry awoke to a touch on the shoulder and gazed at a sergeant-major, who stared at Susan without changing expression. "Time to move out, sir. Ladies will form up in the rear, madam."

Harry sat up and looked around what turned out to be a larder, in which they were alone. "Didn't I do well?" Susan asked.

He dragged on his trousers, strapped on his belts. "Listen. No matter what happens now, I'll never forget you."

"Snap!" She stood on tiptoe to kiss him. "But we have a date, remember? Now you'd better get along."

Relationships, Harry thought. He had had a few. But this chance encounter at such a time in each of their lives, would have to rank very high. Maybe just because it was such a time in each of their lives.

The troops were already moving out. "Do I pack everything up, sir?" Harry asked Alexander, who looked as spruce as ever,

"We must maintain a communications centre. Remain here, Brand, and keep in touch with Brigadier Cowan. He is still holding just south of us. As far as I know he has not yet been attacked. But when we break through he must bring his men up as rapidly as possible. Once that is done, you will also follow as rapidly as possible. Put the seriously wounded in the trucks, but anyone who can walk must do so. Destroy anything you cannot carry." He gave a grim smile. "That does not include the ladies." He peered at Brand. "And do try to have a shave, old man; you look like something the cat dragged in!"

Harry duly found some water and a razor and scraped at his chin, while Susan arrived to grin at him. "Going on parade, are we? Oops, bandits!" He had been shaving in the porch; the morning was already bright and warm and the plantation hummed as the men assembled all the materiel they could carry Now he ran outside to look up at the Zeroes dropping from the sky. Men and women scattered in every direction. Harry threw himself to the ground, carrying Susan with him. "Oof!" she gasped, and rolled on to her back. "I don't think they're looking for us."

The planes, although flying hardly above tree-top level, were not firing as they zoomed northwards across the plantation, but a few minutes later they did hear the sound of firing, overlying the earlier shooting as the Brigade had approached the roadblock. "Jesus!" Harry commented. "Well, that's it. You'd better get with the other ladies, Sue."

"So we can all lie down in a row with our legs apart? I think I would rather have you use that revolver. Last bullet, and that sort of thing."

He realised that she meant it. "I have no orders to shoot anybody, yet. Except Japanese."

She held his arm. "Promise me, if they break in, you will do it, Harry. Or give me a gun of my own."

They stared at each other. "I'll do it," he said. "Now go and behave yourself. It could be the last time you'll have a chance to do so."

Once again the attack on the block failed, the British and Indian troops being scattered by the marauding planes. "Oh, to have a squadron of Spitfires available," Alexander said, when he returned to the plantation, "What is the situation with the rearguard?"

"Brigadier Cowan reports that he has not yet been attacked, sir."

"I wish I could understand the Japanese strategy. Tell me, Brand; you have experience of these people. They must know they are holding up the Rangoon garrison.

40

They must know they have us in a trap. But they're not really doing anything about it. Why?"

"It could be they're waiting for reinforcements, sir. That block may be a powerful defensive post, but it is possible there are not sufficient men to attack *us*."

"And the rearguard?"

"There again, sir, they may have run out of steam, or they may just be making sure that they do have Rangoon. I imagine they expected us to fight for it to the last man. I know we assume the Japanese don't have lines of communications, that they exist on a handful of rice a day, but the fact is, sir, while the food assessment may be accurate, to fight they do need logistical support as regards guns and ammunition."

"I'd still have a go, if I were their commander," Alexander said. "After all, there's me, waiting to be gobbled up. They must understand what a coup that would be."

"Well, sir, do they know that you are here? You landed in Calcutta only three days ago, sir. I am sure Japanese intelligence reported that. But do they know you immediately took off and flew in to Rangoon? I would say not, as their intelligence in Rangoon must have been part of the refugees fleeing the city." Alexander stroked his chin.

"So, from their point of view," Harry said. "There is half a brigade trapped in this pocket with nowhere to go, and of very little importance taken in the context of the war as a whole. They're more interested in what they can accomplish farther north, knowing that we must fall eventually. They're probably going to leave things as they are, until we let them know we wish to negotiate a surrender. They're becoming quite used to British forces asking for terms."

"I wasn't sent here to surrender to anybody, Brand. So you would estimate that we may yet have a little time."

"Another twenty-four hours, perhaps, sir."

"Right. We keep banging away at that road-block. It has to give eventually."

"Yes, sir," Harry said doubtfully. The field officers were even more doubtful; they were concerned as to whether their troops had the morale to carry out another attack. Alexander assembled the men and addressed them, the Jap aircraft having returned to base to refuel. He had Harry speak too, stressing that the Japanese were in no way superior soldiers, and that it was time to show them what British, and Indian, troops could do. He also called up the rearguard. This was to be all or nothing, now, and before the enemy planes came back.

"Very impressive," Susan told Harry, as the women were also assembled; with the wounded they would follow the main attack in one of the few trucks remaining – Harry could not help wondering if she had confided to any of them how she had spent the night, but they all seemed quite normal in the way they regarded him. "You should go into politics, after the war."

The signal was given and the tanks moved out, followed by the infantry, and then the headquarters staff and the domestics. Harry was again chafing at being given a relatively minor position, although he reckoned that they would all be up to their ears in it soon enough. Then to his amazement, the General himself came on the radio from his position just behind the Armoured Brigade. "The block is gone. We're through. Move it!"

When Alexander rejoined the headquarters staff, Harry asked him what had happened. "Damned if I know," the General said. "Looks as if you were right after all, and they had no idea they had me in the bag. So the troops blocking the road north must have been called away for more important duties, as their commanders read the situation. I wonder if we'll ever know the truth of it?"

Prome was some 150 miles north-west of Rangoon, and the British kept on the move all night and into the next day to reach there. The town was vital to Alexander's plans, for it was situated on the Irrawaddy, and there was a ferry. "We can get the women across there," he told his staff.

"I think most of them have husbands in the oilfields at Yenangyaung, sir," Harry suggested. Which was another 100 miles farther north, although also on the Irrawaddy.

"They'll have to get out at Prome," Alexander said. "I don't know what conditions will be like in the oilfields."

"Ah . . . there's the small matter of where they go, sir," ventured Major Mitchell. "After crossing the river."

"According to my map, there's a road from the ferry to a place called Taungup, on the coast. I imagine they can get ships out of there?"

"Yes, sir. But it's a track rather than a road, and leads through some pretty rough country, up and down hills and what have you. And there is no transport."

"Well, we'll give them a small escort, but they'll have to walk. How far is it?"

"Fifty miles, sir."

"Damnation!" Alexander said. "But it's still their best bet, Major. Have it done. The situation is pretty grim," he confided to Harry that night, as they sat together in the command truck, for the column was keeping moving throughout the 24 hours. "We've got the remnants of the Pegu garrison holding Toungoo, which is roughly parallel to Prome. That is the line we simply have to hold, but I don't have the men to do it. Our only hope is the Chinese."

"The Chinese?" Harry was aghast,

"Chiang Kai-Shek seems willing to help. Well, if we get kicked out of Burma, we could lose control of the Burma Road, and that would be a disaster for him. So he is sending us two divisions. They should be coming out of Yunnan about now."

"But that's great, sir," Harry said. "Two divisions! That'll make all the difference."

"It's not as good as it sounds. A Chinese division is not the equivalent of one of ours, or one of the Japanese, either. I'm informed it's more like a brigade; what we would call a division, they call an army. In addition, the local experts I met in Calcutta tell me that they're no good as soldiers. Well, maybe the local experts are wrong; I seem to remember reading before the war that it was expert opinion the Japanese were no good as soldiers, either. And these Chinese are our only hope. I suppose the best thing is that they have an American general in overall command, chap called Stilwell. I'm going up north to meet him and co-ordinate our efforts as soon as we have a line established. You'll come with me; I don't think Stilwell has any experience of fighting in these conditions."

The army straggled into Prome two days later. Alexander had sent orders and liaison officers on ahead, and camp sites were fairly well organised. In Prome too they made radio contact with units of the Pegu garrison, who were occupying Toungoo, just over 50 miles due east, and on the Sittang. This was the line Alexander was hoping to hold while he re-grouped, brought up whatever reserves were available, and, hopefully, got the Chinese into action. But a glance at the map told

Harry it was not going to be easy; the two railheads were separated by a massive mountain range, not all that high but difficult enough, their serrated peaks covered in thick jungle. Ideal country for Japanese infiltration tactics. But it was his business to convince these men that the Japanese were not superhuman; if a Japanese soldier could scale a succession of jungle-covered hills, then so could a Britisher or an Indian.

While he was still considering this, Susan appeared. She looked considerably the worse for wear, her clothes sweaty and dust-stained, her hair matted, and she was clearly very tired, as were they all. But she was also very angry. "We're told we're being sent across the river, here," she announced. "To walk fifty miles to some seaport."

"The General thinks that's best."

"Well, you're his pal. You can tell him it's not on!"

"It is on, because he says so. Sue, you just have to face facts. If we can't hold the Japanese here, we can't hold them at Yenangyaung. If we can't do that, we won't hold Mandalay. We won't hold any part of Burma. And if we do have to pull out of here, all hell is going to break loose. I imagine your husband is going to be pulling out himself in a couple of days. You can meet up with him in Calcutta."

"I want to go home," she said. "Even if it's for an hour. I have things there . . ."

"Which you wouldn't be able to carry out, anyway," he pointed out.

She glared at him, and he almost thought she was going to stamp her foot. "And what about our second round?" she asked.

"Maybe it wasn't meant to be."

"Well . . . the least you can do is kiss me goodbye."

"Ships that pass in the night," he said, as he obliged. "But listen, as I said, I'll never forget you."

"We're still going to have that second round," she assured him. "Some time, some place."

Constance was not at all sure how long she lay face down in the undergrowth. She seemed surrounded by a vast noise, but gradually she realised the noise was mostly in her head. She pushed herself up. She was covered in dirt and leaves and her dress and stockings had been reduced to several strips of material. At least her borrowed petticoat and underclothes were intact, but she had lost her shoes and her headscarf.

Holding on to a tree she dragged herself to her feet, suddenly aware of the heat from the fiercely burning aircraft. Instinctively she took a step towards it, and then checked; there was nothing she could do to help anyone in there, and there were sufficient people needing help out here; the forest was littered with weeping women and screaming children, all Indian or Burmese. When she went towards them, moving slowly and painfully, they merely gaped at her, and went on with their wailing. "Doesn't anyone speak English?" she shouted.

"I am here, lady." It was the steward. He had lost his white jacket and his hair was singed.

"Do you know where we are?"

"I think it is Arakan, lady."

Constance thrust her hands into her hair, which was a tangled mess. "Where is Arakan?"

"Is this piece of land running up the side," the steward explained. "Over there . . ." he pointed west, "is the Bay of Bengal. Over there . . ." he pointed at the mountains rising to the east – they had actually crashed into the foothills – "is Burma."

"Right. We need to get some place where there is food and shelter, and hopefully an airstrip. Which is the nearest town? We passed over a road and a railway just before we crashed. Down there." She pointed south.

"That was the railway from Bassein, lady. But that is a long way. And it is towards the Japanese. I no think we should go there."

"Okay. So where do we go?"

He scratched his head. "I think that must be Taungup."

"How far?"

"Oh, not far. Maybe ten miles."

"Ten miles!" Constance looked at the mountains rising and falling.

The steward grinned. "Not up there. Taungup along coast."

"Is there a road?"

"No road, lady. Until Taungup. Then there is road to Prome."

"Right! Where is Prome?" He pointed north-east. "How far?"

"Maybe fifty miles. But you no want go Prome. Maybe Japanese in Prome by now. We should go Akyab."

"And where is that?"

"Akyab is on the coast, north of Taungup. They have an airstrip at Akyab. And it is closer to Calcutta. All on the same way, you see, lady."

"And how far away is it?"

"Maybe a hundred miles."

Constance looked around herself at the other survivors. There were about 30 of them, including ten children, of whom she had, quite without intending to, assumed leadership. She and the steward, but she knew he was going to do whatever she decided. But there was only one decision she could make, initially. Ten miles, without shoes, certainly in her case, food, or water? "Will there be food in Taungup?"

"Oh, yes, lady. Taungup is a town. People. And food. You know what, maybe boats, too. It is on the coast."

47

"Right, Taungup it shall be." Time enough to make a choice between Prome and Akyab when they got there. "So, lead on Macduff! Do you think you can get these women moving?"

"Who is this Macduff?" the steward asked. "My name is Bom See."

"Oh, right. I am . . ." she felt like being sufficiently democratic to tell him to call her Constance. But she still had to be the leader. "I am Mrs Brand."

"Yes, yes, lady. You Mrs Brand."

"Now, these women."

Most of the women just seemed to want to sit there and wait. Nobody could say for what. But Bom See patiently explained that this was not like an ordinary plane crash – supposing there was such a thing as an ordinary plane crash – that there was not going to be any search party looking for them, and that if they were not prepared to walk to Taungup they would die, and their children would die with them. While he argued with them, Constance went back to the aircraft to see if there was any sign of life, or if there was anything to be salvaged. The flames had abated but there was still a considerable heat. And there was no sign of life. Poor Joan Allbright; she could only hope the woman had died instantly. There was also no hope of retrieving anything worthwhile from the wreckage. Sadly she turned back to join the little band of survivors.

Chapter Three

Prisoners

The survivors made their way down to the beach, and then proceeded north, sometimes on the sand and sometimes, when the rocks were too sharp for their feet or there was a headland to be climbed, just inland. Constance, lacking shoes, found the going very hard; the Burmese women appeared more able to cope, while the older children found it great fun, in the beginning. But they soon grew very tired and both hungry and thirsty. Fortunately Bom See, who was also equipped with a large knife, was able to climb a coconut tree and provide them with some ready sustenance. "Can one live entirely off coconuts?" Constance asked him.

"Oh, yes, Mrs Brand. But soon we come Taungup."

Water was the real problem, for while the coconut milk assuaged their initial thirst, it was not really a substitute. But soon they came to a stream, and lay on the bank to drink. God knows what germs we're taking into our guts, Constance thought. She was even more concerned when, sitting on the bank to bathe her cut and aching feet, she discovered a leech attached to her left big toe. "Don't pull out!" Bom See shouted. "That way is bad sore. I fix."

The women crowded round, apparently offering advice, while he smothered the toe and the creature in dust made into mud by the addition of water, packing it very tightly. When he removed the caked mud the leech went with it, to Constance's great relief; the thought that she might have swallowed one of them made her want to vomit.

Then, to her consternation, Bom See proceeded to take her toe into his mouth and suck it, pausing every few seconds to spit. To do this he had to push her knee up, leaving her sitting in a very unladylike position, especially in view of the fact that all she really had on was her borrowed underwear. She looked at the women in alarm, but they did not seem to find anything unusual in what the steward was doing. Or in the sight of the white woman, wearing nothing more than slip, bra and knickers and a few strips of tattered cloth, her stockings in rags, sitting in their midst to be tended. To be sure, most of them were hardly more properly dressed; several had lost their sarong-like skirts, or *longyis*, and they apparently did not indulge in underwear at all. But if anyone had told me I would be in a situation like this, this time last year . . . or even six months ago, Constance thought she would not believe it. She could not imagine what her mother, or even more, her father, would say if he could know of it.

The Lloyds had always been a very gentile family, lost in a world of "spending pennies", "the curse", "*that* sort of thing", "passed away", "unfortunate condition", and so on. How absurd it all seemed now. She had had to pee in front of all these people, she expected to start menstruating any day now, she had had sex, unsuccessfully, with her husband the previous night, she had just seen some 50 people burned alive . . . but at any rate she wasn't pregnant, as far as she knew. Harry hadn't been impotent on the boat. Poor old Harry. She had meant what she had said, that she would wait for him to come home, with no very clear idea of what would happen then. But suppose he didn't come home? That did not mean he would necessarily have been killed, but he might easily be taken prisoner by the Japanese. The important thing was, did he *want* to come home? At least, home to her. The evidence of last night did not suggest that.

"We go, now," Bom See suggested, "Not far, now."

It was dusk before they straggled into Taungup, which was a much larger place than Constance had expected or dared hope. They were greeted outside the town by a small army of children, who escorted them in with shrieks and yells and questions, which Bom See answered as best he could. Then there were people emerging from their homes to stare at the ragged refugees. Again questions were asked, and then to her enormous relief, Constance found herself facing a white man. "I am the District Commissioner. Is it true that you were shot down?" he asked.

For the first time all day Constance tried doing things with her arms to protect herself, although he was resolutely attempting to keep looking into her eyes. "I don't think we were shot down," she said. "I think one of the engines caught fire. Please . . ."

"My God, my manners!" he said. "You look done in. Your feet . . ." Constance hadn't dared look at her feet for the past couple of hours. She was certain only that they were agony, yet she had had to force herself to take step after step. Now she looked down at the bloody mess on which she was standing, and her knees gave way. The District Commissioner caught her neatly and swept her from the ground. "You need looking after," he said.

"Those others . . ."

"They'll be cared for."

She had to suppose he was right, as the entire community seemed to have turned out and was surrounding the refugees. Bom See came towards her. "You all right, Mrs Brand?" he asked. "I bring doctor."

Constance looked up at the man accompanying the steward. He wore a beard, red streaked with white,

51

but the hair on his head was dark, although also with white streaks. His eyes were blue, and he was big and obviously strong. He wore bush clothes as if they were part of him. "Yes," she said. "I am all right, thank you, Bom See."

The District Commissioner surrendered her. "I'll come over and have a chat later," he said.

The doctor lifted Constance into his arms, and she gave a little sigh of relief. "The steward told me your name is Brand," he said, carrying her up a short flight of steps from the street into a comfortably furnished bungalow, where lanterns glowed softly, and insects hummed at the screening in an effort to enter. Two female Burmese servants were waiting there, and they came forward with exclamations of concern.

"Constance," she said. "Constance Brand. And you're an American." She had at last identified his accent. But she had expected to be taken to a hospital.

"John Wishart." He carried her down a corridor, the girls scurrying ahead of him to open a bedroom door. He spoke to them in Burmese, and they hurried off, then he carried her into the room and laid her on the bed.

I should be resisting this, she thought. I simply cannot allow myself to be carried into a bedroom by a man I have only just met, when I am already virtually naked. But it was so good to feel his arms round her, and she was so tired. "I'm filthy," she said.

He nodded. "I have told the girls to draw you a bath. I think you should have that first, then I will look at your feet properly and dress them. But you will need to spend the next few days in bed."

"Here?" She sat up. "I can't do that!"

"Why not?"

"Well . . ." she flushed. "Do you have a wife?"

"As a matter of fact, yes. But I sent her to India the moment the Japs moved into Burma. All the white women

52

resident here have been evacuated. We shall try to do the same with you."

"But you stayed."

"It is my business to stay. I am the doctor."

"Oh! I'm sorry."

He smiled. "For me being a doctor? The fact is, the hospital is full and will now be fuller, as we look after your fellow refugees. You wouldn't enjoy it there. Have your bath, and we will find you something appropriate to wear. My wife left quite a lot of her stuff behind. You are somewhat taller than her, but I'm sure we can manage something."

Nothing had ever felt so good, Constance thought, as she soaked in the hot tub, while one of the girls washed her hair and another scrubbed her back. She had, quite literally, fallen on her feet, and if they still ached and burned – taking off her torn stockings, which seemed to have melted into her cuts, had been agonising – the rest of her was feeling quite good. Of course, the brandy was helping, as it traced its way down her chest, and she could smell the most delightful aromas arising from the kitchen. Suddenly the war and all the horrors she had experienced over the past few weeks, culminating in the crash, seemed very far away. A dressing-gown had been found for her, and in this she was wrapped and returned to the bed. John Wishart came in a few minutes later, sat beside her feet. "These are badly swollen, as well as being cut," he said. "I am told you, and the people with you, were involved in a plane crash."

"Yes. But I wasn't injured in that. I'm not going to lose anything, am I?" She spoke light-heartedly, but it was a very real fear.

"I don't think so." He was bathing her toes and insteps in some kind of ointment, which burned even

53

as it soothed. "However, would you object if I gave you a thorough physical examination? You look pretty done up."

"Be my guest," she said, and closed her eyes as he released the tie for the robe.

"Just how long have you been on the run, anyway?" he asked, using a stethoscope.

"Since the surrender of Singapore."

He raised his head in surprise. But he had also noticed her wedding band. "Do you have a husband with you, or did he have to stay behind?"

"Oh, he got out with me. He's in Rangoon."

"I hope not. The Japanese are claiming on the radio that Rangoon has fallen. However, they also admit that the garrison has retreated north, so we must hope he is with them. What unit is he with?"

"He is on General Alexander's staff."

"Ah! Then he should be all right. Roll over." She obeyed, and the dressing gown was entirely removed. She felt his hands on her flesh, very gently. "Do you realise you have a quite severe case of sunburn? All over. Doesn't it hurt?"

"Everything hurts. I've become used to the sunburn."

"Any internal problems?"

"Not so far as I know. A little dysentery, I suppose."

"You weren't raped, by any chance?"

Constance rolled on to her back again. "I escaped with my husband, Dr Wishart."

"Point taken, even if question not answered." He smiled. "Well, as I said, I don't think you can walk for at least a week."

"You mean there's no other way of getting out of here? You said something about boats."

"All those capable of putting out to sea and making Calcutta have gone with our refugees. We are hoping to have some return, when they have unloaded their

54

cargoes. But whether they will, or how soon, depends on the military situation along the Irrawaddy, I imagine."

"Isn't there a road from here to Prome? I could rejoin my husband."

"I think you would find it difficult to persuade anyone to go with you, as that would be moving towards the Japanese. I think it would be a good idea to wait until we know just what the situation is on the other side of the river. And that will give your feet time to recover. I understand your flight was to Calcutta."

"And then England. Among my other problems, I also happen to be a mother."

"You hardly look old enough." He stood up. "Feel like dinner? The girls will bring it to you."

"Here? *Shouldn't* I be going to hospital?"

He stood above her, looking down at her. Slowly she pulled the covers over herself.

"Wouldn't you rather stay here?" he asked.

"Would you take offence, General, if I say that this proposal stinks?" General Stilwell inquired. Harry had learned, from brief chats with junior officers who had been in Mandalay before they had arrived, that this man was known as 'Vinegar Joe', and he could understand why. It had been obvious from the moment of their first meeting that he had not taken to Alexander, the American's presumably deliberate lack of smartness contrasting strongly with the British officer's. He also clearly held the British Army in total contempt. When Harry had been introduced and his presence explained he had almost snorted. "What do they say about sinking ships?" he had inquired. Alexander had had to put his hand on Harry's arm to prevent an international incident.

"And that ship sure was full of holes, eh, Major?"

Stilwell had continued, apparently oblivious that he might have given offence, although the various staff officers present were shuffling their feet uneasily, save for the Chinese, who did not appear to speak English. They were very smart, and the most junior of them had as many medal ribbons as Alexander himself, but to Harry they looked disconcertingly like the odd Japanese he had personally encountered. Now Stilwell had been studying the map and Alexander's proposed dispositions. "You want me to take my men down here, east of the hills, and defend Toungoo. That's not a problem. While you try to hold on to Prome. Maybe that's not a problem either. But when we're both established, what do we have? You can draw all the lines you like on the map between Toungoo and Prome, but we still won't be able to communicate with each other, save by radio. And there sure as shit is no way we can give each other mutual support."

"We have reinforcements coming," Alexander said. "I know that we are obliged at this moment to stand on the defensive. But we must always bear in mind the other fellow's problems. His line of communication is very long, and very thin. There is the monsoon on its way . . ."

"In another month or so."

"The longer we can delay them the better. Do you have a better idea?"

"Sure," Stilwell said. "Pull back above Yenangyaung. Make right here, Mandalay, your strong point. We can give you better assistance here, and our lines of communications become even shorter."

"You mean abandon the oilfields?"

"Look, General you're not going to get any oil out of those fields anyway while a battle is going on just south of them. Cut your losses. Or are you scared of losing face to these guys?" He glanced at the various Burmese officials who were sitting in on the conference. "For Crissake, what face do you have to lose, after Singapore?"

Now Alexander was as angry as Harry. "General Stilwell," he said. "Your troops of the Chinese Fifth and Sixth Armies were offered to me by Marshal Chiang Kaishek. It is my decision how they are to be used. And my decision is that they should garrison Toungoo and defend it for as long as possible. I hope that is understood."

Now Stilwell was equally angry. He stood to attention. "And I shall carry out your orders, General. Under protest."

"What a way to fight a war," Alexander said, as he and Harry had a whisky before dinner. "Still, as long as he does fight . . ."

Harry was looking out of the window at the massive walls of Fort Dufferin, within which were their quarters, and where the meeting with Stilwell had been held. Dufferin was above everything else the symbol of past British triumphs in Burma. But then, so had been Singapore, in Malaysia. Dufferin was an exceptionally interesting place, containing within its perimeter the old royal palace together with all the amenities required by the British, including even a polo field. "Any chance of having a look at the city, sir?" he asked. "I've never been to Mandalay, and some of those temples are out of this world."

"Yes," Alexander agreed. "But you'll have to leave them for your next visit, Harry. I'm seconding you to the new commander, who will be here in a day or two. Sadly, I'm to go back to India. To take the broader view, eh? I hate to abandon you, but GHQ have really got the wind-up over that narrow escape we had at Taukkyan. I'd take you back with me, but I think you'll be more use where it matters, if you're still prepared to volunteer."

"Yes, sir." Harry was content with that; he still wanted to fight. "May I ask who the new commander is, sir?"

"Bill Slim. He's been doing well in places like Iraq. He's tough. He'll fight." Alexander gave a brief grin. "Maybe he'll make sure Stilwell fights as well. Do you know him?"

"No, sir."

Alexander nodded. "You'll like him."

Supposing he likes me, Harry thought. He could hardly expect General Slim to welcome a member of his predecessor's staff, even with the glowing recommendation Alexander gave him. On the other hand . . . "I know your father," the new commander remarked, on his arrival the following day, and after Alexander had introduced the immediate staff.

That was inevitable. "Yes, sir."

Slim looked him up and down, and Harry did the same in return, while endeavouring not to show it. The new commander was a stocky man with a lantern jaw and piercing eyes. He certainly looked as tough as Alexander had claimed. "So you're an expert at jungle fighting," Slim remarked.

"I've had some experience, sir," Harry said.

Slim nodded. "Good! I hate self-professed experts."

"Tell me what you think of these dispositions, Bill," Alexander said, indicating the map. "I have to tell you that not everyone likes them."

Slim studied it for some moments. "My orders?"

"Hold as much of Burma as you can, while we build for a counter-offensive."

"Which cannot now be until after the monsoon, so we are talking about next year."

"The monsoon should also hold up the enemy."

Slim considered again. "I need a positive directive. Which is of more importance to the war effort: Burma, or Burma Corps?"

"You don't think you can hold Prome?"

"I've never fought with the Chinese before," Slim pointed out. "And according to the dispositions I studied on my way here, more than half of our lot are composed of Burmese. Give me the Brigade of Guards and one of tanks, and I will hold Burma. As I do not have either, I'm not certain I can hold Mandalay, much less Prome. Or the oilfields. I need to know whether I go down fighting with my people, or whether, if it comes to it, I salvage what I can."

Alexander stared at him for some seconds. "The decision to evacuate Burma must be a political one," he said. "I will back your recommendation, should it come to that. But yes, I would rather have an army capable of defending India than an indefensible piece of territory and no army to fight for it. But, Bill, that is a last resort. Make it good."

Slim nodded. "Well, Major Brand," he said, "I think the sooner we get down to Prome the better."

Slim's arrival made an immediate difference to the British, Indian and Burmese troops at Prome. Alexander had been an inspiring leader, but he had also been somewhat distant. Slim got down among his men, inspecting every position, listening to every problem. Prome had not yet been attacked, but there were definite signs of Japanese activity just to the south. "What's on the other side of that ferry?" the General inquired.

"There's what these people call a road to a little village on the coast, Taungup," explained one of the staff officers.

"We sent our non-combatants across," Harry explained, "a few days ago."

"You reckon they'll be safe in this Taungup? Have we any troops across the river?"

"There is a small garrison in Taungup itself, sir," explained Brigadier Halstead. "We simply don't have the men to defend it adequately."

"The women were supposed to get out by boat," Harry said.

"Well, I hope to God they did," Slim said. "I want a report on the situation, just as quickly as possible. Brand, you were given to me as an expert on the jungle. Take a patrol of twenty men, with one other officer, cross the river, and make south to find out what is going on. The last thing we want is for a large force of Japanese suddenly to appear on the west bank. Start first light tomorrow. I need that report in a hurry, Brand."

"More refugees have turned up," Wishart told Constance. "Including seven white women. Walked all the way from Prome, poor devils. They began with adequate footwear, but now they're nearly in as bad shape as you were."

She was sitting up in bed, wearing one of his wife's nightdresses – that it was far too short for her hardly mattered as her lower half was beneath the covers. Apart from the continuing pain in her feet, she was actually feeling a new woman after a week's rest; she had not truly realised how exhausted she had been. And even the swelling was subsiding. Throughout that time she had been waited on hand and foot by the two Burmese girls. She had not seen all that much of the doctor, for which she had been grateful, because she had not yet made up her mind how to take him. Quite without warning she had been thrown, literally, into his bed. Well, he was a doctor, and he seemed to be devoted to his wife; there were photographs of her about the house. But she had wanted to have the time to think, without distractions. Not that her thoughts had got her very far. She was sure she loved Harry – or she was sure that she *could* love

60

Harry. But if she was going to be separated from him for God knew how long, without any certainty that he loved *her* . . . she just had to get on with being Mark's mother, and living her own life, and see what pieces were there to be picked up when this mess was finally sorted out. Thus her first duty was to get out of here, get to Calcutta, and thence to England. Maybe, with the arrival of these other women, something would be organised.

Bom See had come to see her, and reassured her that all the other survivors had been well cared for. "All we need now is boat to reach Calcutta," he said. "They speak radio, and it come soon, they say. You well soon, Mrs Brand?"

"Soon," she promised. But now she was excited. "More refugees? Where from?"

"Prome. They were sent here by the British. Seems they have indeed evacuated Rangoon, and have retreated to Prome."

"Do you think they might have news of my husband?"

"I'll surely find out, Mrs Brand." Presumably, she thought, it was added protection for both of them that he would not use her Christian name.

That afternoon a woman came to visit her, standing rather nervously in the doorway of her bedroom. "Mrs Brand?"

"That's me," Constance said.

The woman came farther into the room. She was a somewhat short, chunky woman, in her thirties, Constance estimated, and not at all bad looking. but showing all the signs of the nervous exhaustion invariably introduced by flight. "Dr Wishart said you wanted to know about your husband," she said, standing by the bed and looking more nervous than ever.

"Yes, please. Do you know anything?"

"I . . . spoke with him, three days ago. My name is Susan Davies."

"Oh, how splendid! If you spoke with him . . . you mean he's in Prome?"

"He was leaving, with General Alexander, to fly up to Mandalay for some high-level meeting, when I left."

"Was he all right?"

"Sure. He said you had gone to Calcutta."

"My plane crashed. I'm lucky to be alive."

Susan Davies considered this. Then she said, "It's odd, isn't it, that you should be here, and him just fifty miles away."

"You said he was in Mandalay."

"He went there. But I think he was coming back. To Prome, I mean."

It was Constance's turn to consider. "There are radios here. I wonder if I could get in touch with him? As you say, it's ridiculous that we should only be fifty miles apart. He thinks I'm in Calcutta. If he hears about the crash, and doesn't know that I'm all right, he'll be worried stiff."

"I'm sure he will be," Susan said. "But I imagine you'd have to talk to Dr Wishart about that."

"Are you going to Calcutta?"

"As soon as there is a boat available capable of making the trip. It's a long stretch, you know. But I suppose you know all about that." Constance raised her eyebrows. Susan flushed. "Your husband mentioned how you had got out of Singapore."

"Did he? He seems to have had a good time to chat, while fighting the Japanese."

"We were in the same truck, you see. Retreating from Rangoon." She hurried on. "Some people here are saying it would be better for us to take the coast up to Akyab. Then we wouldn't have to put out into the open sea, and there's an airstrip at Akyab."

"Sounds a good idea," Constance said, but she was anxious to be rid of the woman, who pretended to know so much about her affairs. But the point was, she *did* know a lot about her affairs, and she could only have got the information from Harry. But Harry, of all the men she had ever met, was the least likely to confide any of his personal business or background to a stranger.

"Well . . . I suppose we'll be going together," Susan said, and retreated to the door.

Wishart came home soon after. "They're in surprisingly good shape," he said. "Did Mrs Davies have anything worthwhile to tell you?"

"Quite a lot. Do you think you could get a message to Prome for me? To my husband?"

"How do you know Major Brand is in Prome?"

"Mrs Davies said he was. Do you know her?"

"Her husband is someone fairly big in the oilfields at Yenangyaung. I've never met either of them, though. I'll see if I can get through to Prome." He went to the door, and checked there. "There's no chance he can get down here, you know, Mrs Brand. He has a war to fight."

"I know," Constance said. "I just want him to know that I'm all right."

"Of course. Leave it with me."

He was back in half an hour. "I got through, and Major Brand is there. But he isn't there right this minute, if you follow me. They say he's out on a reconaissance. I left a message that you were here and all right. I told them you, and all the women were hoping to be moved on in a week or so."

"Do you think he'll be able to get a message back when he returns from this patrol?"

"I should think so."

"It would be wonderful if he *could* get down here, if only for a day," Constance said.

Wishart nodded. "Yes, indeed." He didn't want to tell her there was almost no hope of that.

*   *   *

63

"What do you reckon, sir?" Captain Keeton asked, when the patrol – 20 men from the Burma Rifles – was assembled on the west bank of the Irrawaddy. "Start at Taungup?" He was looking longingly at the road, and then distastefully at the jungle-covered hills to the south of it.

"I don't think there is any point in that," Harry said. "If the Japanese were anywhere near Taungup, it would have been reported by radio from there. Same goes for Sandoway and Bassein. We need to look more directly south, and find out if they have crossed the river west of Rangoon."

They probed through the forest, up and down the hills, for three days, without finding any sign of the Japanese, although from their various hilltop vantage points they could see considerable movement on the east bank of the river; they were more interested in, and alarmed by, the evidence that there were tigers in the vicinity, but although they could hear them from time to time they did not see any of the great beasts. Keeton, indeed, was in a state of some agitation; he was not long out from England, and found the jungle as terrifying a place as did most people with no knowledge of it, watched in amazed admiration as Harry led his men through the thick bush, ignoring chattering monkeys and excited birds, shrugging off leeches, mosquitoes and knife-edged leaves and thorns, himself dealing with an inquisitive snake with a single blow from his machete.

They picked up the railroad to Bassein on the second day, although this had been blown up in several places, which included the bridge across the Bassein River. Up till now they had maintained the strictest radio silence, but it was while they were camped on the banks of the river that night, preparing to cross the next day, that they were called from Prome. "Return to base immediately," the message ran.

"Jesus!" Keeton muttered. "What's happened, do you think?"

They had heard no sustained firing to indicate that the Japanese had launched a major attack. "We'd better go find out," Harry decided.

They made better time going back, as now there was no suggestion of finding any enemy. But when they assembled the next morning, there were only 12 men present. "What the hell . . .?" Keeton glared at his sergeant.

The sergeant shuffled his feet. "They have gone home, sir."

"Gone home? Just like that?"

"They think it is finished, for them. For us too, maybe."

"Well, they are going to be court-martialled and shot," Keeton declared. "For desertion in the face of the enemy. And that goes for anyone else who runs away." The sergeant looked sceptical. "What a mess," Keeton remarked to Harry. "What do you reckon?"

"That more than half the forces under Slim's command are Burmese," Harry replied.

They regained the ferry the next day; at least there had been no more desertions. But Prome was in a flap. "My orders are to destroy this ferry the moment you're across, sir," said the engineer sergeant who greeted them.

"What's happened?" Keeton asked.

"It's those Chinks, sir. They've 'scarpered'."

Harry went immediately to find Slim, who was issuing orders for the withdrawal to Yenangyaung. "Glad you got back, Brand," he said, hardly looking up from the maps spread in front of him. "See anything?"

"There are no Japanese west of the river, sir. At the moment."

"There soon bloody well will be. They've stormed Toungoo."

"But . . . Stilwell had two divisions."

"Had two divisions. He's pulling one out. The other has disappeared."

"Disappeared?" Harry was incredulous. How could a division, even one at only brigade strength, just disappear?

"Melted into thin air," Slim told him. "Anyway, Stilwell is taking his other division back north, and we don't have a left wing."

"Bombastic twit!" Harry muttered,

Slim grinned. "You are entitled to your opinion, Major Brand. However, it is obvious that our position here is untenable, as the Japanese can either come in from behind us or now concentrate all their people in a direct assault. I have already given orders for a position to be prepared before Yenangyaung, and we will hope to stop them there. If we can't, the oil wells will have to be blown. There's a sapper captain, Scott, up there, waiting for my orders. I am giving them to you, personally, because I don't want anything to go up until I say so; we need that oil for just as long as we can get it. When you do receive the order, however, I want everything which could possibly be of any use to the enemy to go. So it's up to you to check Scott's dispositions. You will leave now, and go on ahead and make sure all is as I require."

"Yes, sir." Harry hesitated, "And you?"

Another grin. "Oh, I shall be along, Brand. But I shall bring my army with me."

Harry saluted and went outside to where a car was waiting. He just had time to gather up his scanty gear, when a signals sergeant hurried up. "Major Brand! I have a message for you. From your wife."

66

"Glory be! You mean we're in touch with Calcutta?"

The sergeant looked at his paper. "No, sir. She's in Taungup."

"What did you say?"

The sergeant handed him the paper. Harry could hardly believe what he was reading. Constance, in an air crash? But apparently all right. But . . . in Taungup? Keeton had wanted to go down there, and he had seen no reason for it. He had not wanted again to become entangled with Susan Davies. Now she and Constance were together, and hopelessly exposed to the Japanese advance, once Prome was evacuated. And he could do nothing about it, save by deserting the Army. He just had to believe that she and the other women had already left by boat, or would do so before the Japanese got there. "When did this come in?" he asked.

"Four days ago. Just an hour after you'd left on patrol, sir."

Damnation, he thought. One hour! He could easily have included Taungup in his sweep. But there was no use crying over spilt milk. And four days! They had surely got away by now. But if they hadn't . . . he had to make them understand the urgency of the situation. "Can you send a message back, Sergeant?"

"I can, sir. Supposing there is anyone there to receive it."

"Just send: *Get out now. Use any means, but go. I love you, Harry.*" The sergeant hurried off, and Harry nodded to the driver. "Let's go."

"Still no sign of any of those damned boats coming back," Wishart said, as he and Constance drank tea on the back porch of his house, looking out over the rather sparse garden.

"Have you tried calling?"

"The DC has, but it's rather far to Calcutta from here. We've raised Akyab; they don't know anything. But at least the airstrip up there is still in use. We're beginning to wonder if you ladies shouldn't forget Calcutta, at least in the first instance, and trek up there. I know it's some hundred and fifty miles, but you could probably do it. There's an airfield at Akyab, but even if there are no planes, from Akyab you would make Cox's Bazaar easily, and once you reach Chittagong, you're laughing; there's a railway into Calcutta from Chittagong. And your feet are just about as good as new again."

"What about you?"

"I'll hang on here."

"You don't think the Japanese are going to get here?"

"I have the utmost confidence in people like your husband, Constance." It was the first time he had used her Christian name.

"But if they do get here . . . when you think of all the atrocity stories . . ."

"There are atrocity stories in every war, in most cases proved to be false when the war is over. I wouldn't like to put money on your safety, at least from rape, which is why I think you should get out. But I don't think they are going to trouble any doctors; they need us as much as anyone."

"I hope you're right. I owe you a very great deal."

"It's been a pleasure, entertaining a beautiful woman for a week. Can't think when I've enjoyed myself more."

She flushed and poured some more tea, while he cocked his head. "There's my receiver. Someone must be trying to raise me. Could be your husband, replying to your message. Want to come and listen? You might even be able to talk with him."

"I'd like that." If only to keep me from temptation,

she thought. He was right about her feet; she could move quite easily now, at least when wearing soft slippers. The idea of having to walk 150 miles filled her stomach with lead. But there was really no necessity to walk.

"*Get out,*" Wishart repeated. "*Most urgent, get out now. Use any means. I love you, Harry.*"

"Is it possible to speak with him?" Constance asked.

Wishart put the question, then shook his head. "Major Brand has left Prome on assignment. "Get out. Most urgent." That can only mean the Army is evacuating Prome. I must inform the Commissioner."

Who already knew. "Once the Japanese have Prome," he told the assembled townspeople, which included the survivors of the air crash. "They will undoubtedly use the road to come down to the coast. Here. Now, apart from the police, and the company of soldiers in the garrison, who will of course have to surrender, we are all civilians, so I do not consider that we are in any great danger from the enemy, but there will obviously be severe restrictions upon our movements, and upon what we can, or cannot do, once we come under Japanese military rule. If there are any among you who wish to leave while you can I shall give them every possible assistance, but I should advise you that the decision must be made, now. Thank you."

Singapore all over again, Constance thought, having attended the meeting, only this time without Harry. But why was she feeling so pessimistic? She had been the leader in the escape from Singapore; Harry had been too badly wounded at that time to be more than a passenger. If only she wasn't so mentally exhausted. There was a great deal of chat going on all around her, and a few minutes later Susan Davies joined her. "What are you going to do?"

Constance made a face. "Start running again, I suppose."

"May I come with you?"

"Of course. What about your companions?"

"They're pretty divided. Better the Japs than either the jungle or the sea. Can't say I agree with them."

"I'm going to get out by boat. That's the way we got out of Singapore."

Susan frowned. "You mean, try to sail to Calcutta? That's four hundred miles of open sea. And there are only small boats left in the harbour."

"I know. I'm going to sail up the coast to Akyab, as you suggested. That's only a hundred and fifty. Wishart says it might be possible to get a flight there, or if not, to reach the railhead at Chittagong."

Susan considered. "When you say sail, you mean sail as in sail? Who's going to do this sailing?"

"Me."

"You know about boats?"

"Of course. Beats walking," Constance pointed out. "I've tried some of that."

Wishart arranged a boat for them, whereupon they suddenly became very popular. "That thing will only hold ten people," Constance said, peering at the rather ancient timbers. But if they were always going to be close to land . . . the trouble was that the triangular lateen sail looked even more ancient, and she had never handled one before. But the principle had to be the same.

"Well, you wouldn't catch me putting to sea in that," Alice Ogilvie remarked. "I think you'll drown."

"I can come, Mrs Brand?" asked Bom See.

"Oh, please," Constance agreed. She was sure he would be an enormous help, if only to keep them supplied with coconuts.

Three of the Indian women also wanted to come,

which involved two children. "How long do you think it'll take?" Wishart asked.

"There's a bit of a breeze, and it's from the south," Constance said. "A hundred and fifty miles . . . we should make about four knots, over twelve hours of daylight . . . say three days. If the breeze holds."

"We'll fit you out with food and water for five, just to be sure," he said. "But watch the water."

"We'll put ashore every night, so we should find the odd stream. John . . ." she rested her hand on his arm. "Please come with us?" She forced a smile. "We may need medical assistance."

"I'm going to pack you up a first-aid kit as well," he promised.

"But you're staying?"

"I don't think I have any choice." She sighed, and kissed him. For a moment they clung to each other. "Maybe you'll meet up with your husband," he said gently.

The whole town seemed to have assembled to see them off; Constance gathered that several others were considering doing the same thing, as it now seemed quite clear that the sea-going boats were not returning. Others, including the remainder of the white women and the other survivors of the plane crash, were preparing to leave by land, equipped with as much as they could carry. "Better them than me," Susan remarked, as she settled herself amidships in the small boat.

She was clearly regarding herself entirely as a passenger, Constance thought. She wasn't bothered about that. Bom See also knew about boats, more than her, as it turned out, at least of the lateen-sail variety, and the two of them were quite sufficient to handle the small craft. The wind was fresh without being boisterous, and soon they were gliding along, just outside the reef, the Indian women and children chattering contentedly. Wishart had found some of his wife's bush gear for Constance to wear, and with a matching slouch hat she was as well protected from the sun as she could be, as was Susan. "I suppose we'll look back on this and say what an adventure," Susan remarked, when they put in to an empty beach for the night.

"I think I shall remember the mosquitoes most," Constance said, slapping.

Bom See, in his element as the only male in the midst of so many attractive women, lit a fire, which helped to keep the mosquitoes off, but did little about the sandflies. "Do you think that's wise?" Susan asked. "It can be seen for miles."

"Only from the sea," Constance assured her, pointing at the dark forest wall a few feet away from them.

Next day the wind had dropped, leaving the morning shrouded in a looming heat haze. The Indian women gabbled, and Bom See had a long face. "What we do now, Mrs Brand?"

"May as well stay put," Constance said. "And wait for it to come back. You could cut us some coconuts."

But while he was doing this they heard gunfire. This set the women to chattering more vigorously than ever. "Came from the south-east," Susan said.

"That's where it would come from," Constance pointed out. "And not all that far away. I reckon the Japanese have reached Taungup."

"So what do we do."

"Sit it out. There is nothing else we can do. The wind will be back."

They sat together on the sand, eating coconut and gazing at the little wavelets. The firing had stopped, but now they knew there was an enemy out there. "Have you ever been . . . well, raped?" Susan asked.

"I'm afraid not."

"Or . . . had an affair?"

Constance grinned. "I am one of those terribly orthodox and boring women. I have only ever had sex with my husband."

"Oh," Susan said. She was obviously feeling extremely guilty.

"But I don't have anything against people who are . . ."

"Promiscuous?"

"Well, I was going to say something like 'liberated'. I suppose they are promiscuous. But it's whatever you're made like. It's just not me."

"Anyone can see you're a lady," Susan said.

"Are you trying to say that you're not? Because you've cheated on your husband? I don't think that necessarily follows. If even a bit of the history I've read is true the word promiscuous covers an awful lot of queens and princesses."

"I suppose so," Susan said.

Bom See stood beside them. "We go now, ladies?"

"I don't see much point, Bom See," Constance said. "There still isn't enough wind to move the boat. We're better off here."

"People come," Bom See said.

Constance and Susan both stood up, turning to face the forest, and heard voices, high-pitched, excited, and not speaking Burmese. "Quick!" Constance snapped. "The boat!" Which was anchored in the shallows just off the beach.

Bom See waved at the Indian women, who went chasing the children, playing farther down the beach. Heart pounding, Constance waded into the shallow water, her arms full of gear, but she had only just dumped it in the boat when she was checked by a rifle shot. She turned, and saw the men on the beach, little

73

men wearing green uniforms, but armed with rifles and bayonets, She looked at Susan, who had fallen to her knees, in the shallow water, staring at the Japanese, and then at Bom See and the women and children, another 50 yards away. Constance knew she was caught, and so was Susan. But the others . . . "Run for it!" she shouted.

And immediately regretted what she had done. For as the women turned the Japanese opened fire. Two of the women and one of the children fell in an explosion of blood. The other woman and child checked, and waited for the Japanese to go up to them. Susan vomited. Constance gazed at the soldiers who came down to the water's edge, increasingly aware of a curious feeling of lightness, as if her body was filling with air, to such an extent she thought she might float away. Oh, please let me just float away, she prayed.

One of the soldiers spoke to her, and when she did not move, jabbed at the air with his bayonet. Maybe it'll be that way, she thought. A quick, clean thrust. She raised her hands into the air and began to wade ashore, checked as she saw that four more of the soldiers had dragged Susan from the water and laid her on the sand and were tearing off her clothes. Susan was staring at the sky and screaming in a high-pitched voice.

The man closest to her stepped into the sea and grasped Constance's shoulder to jerk her forward. She lost her balance and found herself also lying on the sand. She raised her head at another scream, and saw that the Japanese had tied Bom See to a tree, and were thrusting at him with their bayonets, the points slicing through the flesh while blood spurted and he shrieked and writhed. Other soldiers were raping the surviving Indian woman; the child was already dead. Someone put his toe into Constance's ribs and kicked, rolling her on to her back. It was the man who had pulled her ashore, and he still had his rifle and bayonet. He stood above her, grinning at her, and suddenly thrust downwards. Constance tensed every muscle in her body, waiting for the burst of agony that would mean she was dying, but the blow was aimed to pass neatly between her legs, which had fallen apart when she had been rolled over, thudding into the sand so hard that the haft actually hurt her crotch.

She gasped, her breath releasing in a huge gush of air. The soldier grinned some more, and withdrew the bayonet. Then he laid down his rifle and knelt between her legs. Constance desperately wanted to hit him, or at least close her legs on him, but she felt paralysed, the realisation that she was actually still alive being overtaken by the understanding that she was now about to be raped. She closed her eyes, so that she would not have to look at him, felt his hands tearing open her slacks, which were buttoned up the front like a man's, and then heard another voice, also high-pitched, but sharper than any of the others,

The hands left her, and she opened her eyes, to look at a Japanese officer standing above her. "Get up," he said, in English.

Constance sat up, and then pushed herself to her feet, hastily grabbing her pants as they would have slid past her thighs, and rebuttoning them, drawing the belt tight. The officer had stepped past her to stand above Susan, who was also lying on the sand. But her slacks and knickers had been torn right off, and he had been too late for her. Susan's eyes were shut, and she was moaning. "Get up," the officer said again.

Susan opened her eyes to stare at him, then gave another shriek. The officer turned to Constance. "She is hysterical. Attend to her."

"She has been raped," Constance said. "She has every right to be hysterical." She felt pretty hysterical herself, as she looked at Bom See's dead body, pierced time and again by the bayonets, and at the other women, and the children, all now dead.

"You bow," the officer said, "when you speak to me. Bow."

Constance could not believe her ears. "Bow? To you?"

"You bow, or my men beat you. Now." Constance bit her lip, then bowed, quickly. "You go more deep," he told her, "and more slow." Constance obeyed. "Now," he said. "You say to her, get up."

"I will have to help her."

"You no bow." Constance felt that she was taking part in some ghastly pantomime. But she bowed again. Survival was the key. And thus far she was better off than any of the others. "You help her," the officer said.

Constance knelt beside Susan, who had stopped screaming but was still moaning. "Come along," she said. She inserted Susan's legs into her pants, trying not to look at the trickling blood, then pulled them up and buckled the belt. "You must get up," she said. "It is over now." At least for the time being, she thought. Slowly Susan's sighs subsided, and she allowed Constance to help her to her feet and finish dressing her. Constance bowed to the officer. "Am I allowed to ask what is going to happen to us?"

He grinned. "You go camp. You walk, eh? Long way."

Constance shuddered. She put her arm round Susan's shoulders, and helped her across the sand. "Oh, Constance," Susan whispered. "They raped me! Oh, Constance! Did they rape you too?"

She was desperate to share her ordeal, and now was not the time to pretend to any superiority or better fortune; they were going to share whatever other ordeals lay ahead. "Yes," Constance said. "They raped me too."

Chapter Four

Flight

Yenangyaung was a rather typical Burmese village, straggling beside the broad, fast-flowing waters of the Irrawaddy, dominated by the oil derricks and storage tanks which were scattered about the sparse bush around the settlement. That it was a relatively wealthy part of Burma was both to be expected and obvious; there were several extremely up-market bungalows, freshly painted offices, mostly bungalows too, and even the native houses looked well-to-do. The war had not yet reached it, save by rumour, and although people looked anxious, there was none of the panic Harry had observed in Rangoon, or in Prome. However, he found that Yenanyaung was garrisoned, for want of a better word, by fewer than 200 men of the 1st Gloucesters, who had already been heavily engaged earlier in the campaign and were hoping to enjoy some well-earned rest and recuperation. Their commanding officer had been taken to hospital, seriously ill, but Harry located a somewhat anxious major. "You mean Prome has gone, just like that?" McRae was horrified.

Harry surveyed the situation without pleasure. Pleasant and peaceful as it appeared, Yenangyaung was a bottleneck. The town straggled beside the Irrawaddy to the west, while to the north the area was turned virtually into a peninsula by the Pin Chaung, a broad stream which flowed west into the main river. To complete the third side of the rectangle was the Paunggwe Chaung, which flowed into the Pin Chaung; this last was virtually dry at the moment, but it was still an obstacle to any rapid movement of troops. There was no ford across the Irrawaddy if one wanted to go west, and only one across the Pin Chaung, supposing one wanted to go north – which one did. He could envisage the entire Burma Corps being trapped in this small area of land only about three miles across, and began to understand Slim's worst possible scenario. "I'm looking for Captain Scott," he told McRae.

The engineer officer was found, and given Slim's instructions. He clearly did not like them. "The whole shitting shebang?" he inquired. "They'll hear it in Calcutta."

Harry grinned. "Certainly in Mandalay."

Scott went off to prepare his charges, Harry to have a primitive bath, shave and a meal. For the moment all was peaceful, but the time to reflect started him worrying about what might have happened to Constance. Everything depended on how fast the Japanese advanced into Arakan, and his memory of their methods in the Malay Peninsula were not reassuring. He wondered if Constance and Susan had encountered each other, and what they would have to say to each other? He was in fact heartily ashamed of the way he had succumbed to Susan's urgency. But at that moment they had been two people utterly adrift, she too terrified of the Japanese to think straight, he aware only that after his relationship with Constance had been looking so promising, at their first contact with civilisation they had flown apart, all over again, compounded by his confounded sexual problems.

He had just had to seek reassurance on that front, and Susan had provided it. Now he discovered he had fresh problems of his own as his limited privacy was invaded.

*   *   *

78

"The name is Davies," said the obvious Welshman in the sun topee and white suit; he wore a fashionable toothbrush moustache, had a brick-red, drinker's complexion, and was overweight, which explained a great deal to Harry. "Am I to believe that you mean to blow the oilfields?"

"If we have to, Mr Davies." Harry was dressing as fast as he could.

"That oil," Davies pointed out, "is the only source of supply in Burma, or for the Burma Corps."

"I know that, Mr Davies, but we also have to bear in mind that should we be unable to hold the Japanese, your oil will become *their* principal source of supply in Burma, and that would be unfortunate."

Davies harrumphed. "Were you in Rangoon?"

"Briefly." Harry knew what had to be coming next.

"Did you hear anything of my wife? Susan Davies? She was down there on a visit. Hasn't been able to get back yet. Worried, don't you know."

"Your wife, together with several other Englishwomen, was with us on the retreat."

"Then where is she? Was she all right? *Is* she all right?"

"She was all right when last I saw her, Mr Davies. But she was sent across the river from Prome to Taungup. That was when we assumed we could hold the line, Prome-Toungoo. As we are now evacuating Prome, Taungup has become vulnerable, I'm sorry to say."

"You mean she may have been taken by the Japs?"

"We must hope she got out in time. If it is any comfort to you, my wife was also in Taungup, when last I heard."

"My God!" Davies muttered. "Those devils . . ."

"As I said, we must hope and pray, Mr Davies." He wondered if Davies would ever see his wife again. Susan

Davies had declared that she would rather die than submit to a Japanese rape. What would Constance's reaction be to such a situation? It was something of a shock for him to realise how little he truly knew about his wife. But he had only spent a total of about four months in her company in the two and a half years they had been married, and for three of those months he had been recovering from severe wounds, a patient rather than a husband. But he could not imagine Constance killing herself.

Next day the command came to blow the oilfields. Already the advance guard of the retreating Burma Corps was straggling into Yenangyaung, their morale having undergone another shattering experience. Not only had the Japanese frontally assaulted Prome, in what had turned out merely to be a holding action, they had infiltrated through the hill country and continued to chase Stilwell's Chinese army up the railway track to Mandalay, undoubtedly with the idea of enveloping the British troops.

"They're like bloody water," Keeton complained, having come with his new command – he had been so fed up with his Burma Rifles, who had largely disintegrated anyway that he had obtained a transfer to the Gurkhas. But this was another aspect of the British problems; each unit, and especially units like the Gurkhas, had their own way of doing things, and Keeton, with his military moustache and his Sandhurst background, was still learning about his men – in the midst of a collapsing situation. "Anywhere there's a gap, they're in it, only unlike water they can flow uphill. How do we get out of this place, Sir?"

Conversation was temporarily halted by the exploding oil wells; Scott had been quite correct when he had

80

estimated the bangs would be heard a good distance away. Harry watched the huge clouds of black smoke filling the sky and reckoned that any Japanese within 20 miles who had not heard the noise of the explosion would know that the British were planning to abandon Yenangyaung. "There's a ford," he said, when he could hear himself speak. "But you had better wait for orders."

Slim himself arrived later that day, with a battered headquarters staff. "It's grim," he told Harry. "I have had to tell Alexander to beg Chiang to commit some more troops to protect our left, but I don't know if we're going to get them; Chiang, educated by Stilwell, I suppose, seems to feel that we just don't have the guts to stand and fight. Damnably, he's at least half right. I'm not talking about our British and Indian troops; they're doing all they can. But those blasted Burmese – I have lost forty per cent of my strength in the past week. They've simply packed it in and gone home. Trouble is, once they take off their uniform and put on a longyi, it's impossible to tell whether or not they were once soldiers."

"So what do you reckon we are going to do, sir?"

"I have told Alexander that I do not consider holding Burma is practical, in the present circumstances, unless the Chinese are prepared to give us massive assistance. As he said in Mandalay, that has got to be a political decision. Until that decision is made, our first business is to get out of this mess, and that means getting out of Yenangyaung. But I'm not even sure we can do that." He gave one of his sudden, and charming, grins. "But we're sure as hell going to try."

* * *

In fact, Chiang Kai-Shek recovered very rapidly from his fit of contempt, no doubt realising that the British and the Indians were fighting as hard to keep open the Burma Road as were his own people. Next morning, Slim sent a patrol across the Pin Chaung ford to discover the exact situation north of the river, while the Army prepared to fight its way to Meiktila if necessary. Harry was in command, because of his experience of jungle warfare. Not that there was a great deal of jungle involved, as once across the ford there was a reasonably good road leading north-east to Kayakpadaung and thence Meiktila. But this was actually more dangerous than the jungle, as they did not know if the enemy had cut the road as they had outside Taukkyan, and Harry well-remembered his first encounter with the Japanese on the road beyond Kuala Lumpur, which had involved as desperate a shoot-out as he had ever known. Nor had they gone very far when movement was discerned ahead of them, and this was a considerable body of men, wearing khaki, but small and with yellow faces.

"Back up," Harry snapped at his driver, signalling the other vehicles to do the same, and then saw that the leaders of the approaching men were carrying their rifles high in front of them, with their caps on the ends of the barrels. "Stop," he said, and got out, walking slowly towards the strangers, hand resting on the butt of the revolver in his holster, although he was well aware that if they were hostile he was a dead man.

Now a man stepped out of the approaching ranks and came towards him. He was a tall man, for either a Japanese or a Chinese, and most remarkably handsome, while as with most Chinese officers, as Harry now recognised him to be, he was immaculately dressed. "I General Sun Li-jen," he announced in halting English. "You General Slim?"

"Ah, no," Harry said. "But I will send you to General Slim."

"You take me," Sun told him. "I am General Thirty-Eight China Division."

"And I am very glad to see you," Harry said. "But I must make sure the road to Meiktila is clear."

"Road clear," Sun said, and gestured over his shoulder. "My men have road." He grinned. "At present. No Japanese, now. We cover your retreat. But you must hurry. Tomorrow, who can say?"

Slim was equally impressed by the Chinese commander. "For the first time I feel we have our flank protected," he told Harry. "But we have still got to get the hell out of here." It was a grim business. They were again surrounded by a huge mass of refugees, all as usual attempting to take all of their livestock with them, who had followed the Army north and who were now joined by the suddenly terrified inhabitants of Yenangyaung itself, and were constantly attacked by Japanese planes, to which the RAF in India had no answer. Each raid was accompanied by a fresh panic, with people scattering in every direction – there were no adequate shelters – and ended with pitiful little bundles of what had once been human beings scattered everywhere; just as pitiful were the dead or dying animals.

The Army itself was strung out over a considerable area as it found its way north; there was room only for the guns and the tanks to use the road, so that the infantry units were forced to travel across country, and almost every hour brought a frantic call for help from some unit or other which had either lost its way or had 'bumped' a probing Japanese force; on one occasion a whole brigade had to be committed to rescuing stragglers. Harry was kept busy with Keeton's small and mobile force of Gurkhas, feeling their way through the bush to the aid of various parties; Keeton was glad to have

Harry, as he had developed a considerable respect for him since their patrol in Arakan.

Now, again, their orders were not to become engaged with anything larger than Japanese patrols in case they might need rescuing themselves, but it was a nerve-wracking and exhausting business, as in the jungle one never really knew what was on the other side of the next bush, while the temperature seldom dropped below 90 degrees, even at night, so that one's clothes were never dry and hands were inclined to slip on rifle butts. And they came across more than one example of the ferocity with which this war was being fought; in one village there were the naked bodies of three Indian soldiers who had been tied to uprights and bayoneted to death. "Swine," growled Keeton. "I hope we're going to do the same to them."

Harry preferred not to make a decision on that, but when the next day they encountered a Japanese patrol of half a dozen men, who they managed to surround and smother with rifle fire, he did not interfere when his men shot out of hand two of the Japanese who had only been wounded. We are becoming an army of animals, he thought. Because that is what we are, as are they.

Their task was also complicated by the presence here too of refugees, begging for food and medical help. But Harry could not help but wonder if they were genuine refugees, or fence-sitters who would tell the next Japanese force to come along just where the British could be found? Yet some of them were in appalling condition, obviously not having eaten for several days. He could only direct them, through his Gurkha sergeant who spoke Burmese, to the nearest road and hope that it was still under Chinese control.

Meanwhile, Burma Corps continued its retreat, and the Japanese continued their advance, and once again the Chinese did a disappearing act. This time it was 55

Division which fell apart. General Sun and his 38 Division were still doing their best, but when Meiktila fell everyone knew the game was up. "Next stop Mandalay," Slim told his officers.

There, Alexander was waiting for them. "Your orders are to get your people out of Burma," he said. "Chiang is pulling his men up north, and some wag has put it about that Burma Corps is going with him and leaving India to fend for itself. You can imagine how Delhi reacted to that. So you are to pull back across the Chindwin River to Imphal on the Indian border. Leave the enemy nothing of value here." He pointed out of the window at the huge Ava Bridge spanning the Irrawaddy some five miles downstream of the city. "Particularly that."

Slim nodded. "You say all the Chinese are going north?"

"Don't tell me you'd like some of them to hang about?"

"I surely would. That fellow Sun is good. And good commanders usually have good troops."

"I'll see what can be done." Alexander took Harry aside. "I am terribly sorry about your wife, Brand."

Harry frowned, while a lump of lead began to gather in his stomach. "You have news of her, sir?"

It was Alexander's turn to frown. "You did not know her plane crashed?"

"Yes, sir, I did. But I also know she survived, and made Taungup."

"Good God! No one reported that to GHQ. Well, then, my best congratulations. Where is she now?"

"There's the problem, sir. Nobody knows. And we must suppose the Japanese have gone into Arakan."

"Yes, they have. I'll see what I can find out, and let you know. Meanwhile, good hunting!"

85

Hitherto the population of Mandalay had felt fairly remote from the war. Panic had only commenced when Burma Corps turned up, in full flight from the advancing Japanese. It escalated as it became clear that there was no intention of fighting for the ancient city. Harry had never seen anything like it before. Always, in his considerable experience of retreating armies, the refugee movement had been underway before he had arrived on the scene. Fleeing people had been clogging the roads in Belgium when the BEF had crossed the frontier in 1940; they had already started to abandon Rangoon when he and Constance had landed there a week earlier. In Singapore there had been no refugees because there had been nowhere to go; the city had merely seethed in despair and resignation.

The inhabitants of Mandalay were divided into two. There were those determined to stay put and make the best deal they could with the Japanese; and there were those determined to get out just as rapidly and as far as possible. India was the dream, as if the frontier would, in some magical way, bring the enemy to a halt. But whether it could do that or not, the borders of Manipur State were 200 miles away, and there was no transport save for the Army. Mizoram was closer, but between Mandalay and Mizoram lay the formidable Rookhlang Range of mountains, some of them more than 4,000 ft high.

"There is nothing we can do either for or about those poor devils," Slim told his officers. "Our job is to get the Army to Imphal. I'm afraid there is going to be many a tragedy, but this whole bloody war is a tragedy." As usual, he managed a grin at the end. "So far, gentlemen. But if we can get a fighting force out, reasonably intact, then hopefully within a year or so we can come back – and make it a Japanese tragedy."

"I don't want any foul-up here as there was at the Sittang," Slim said. "See that everyone who intends to leave is out before the bridge goes up." Harry was one of the officers left behind with the rearguard, as the main body of the Army crossed the bridge on the afternoon of 30 April. By now Japanese units were reported to be only a few miles south of the city.

"Time to go," said Brigadier Clark. "You'll join your commands, gentlemen, and when the time comes to move out withdraw your men in good order, if you please. Major Brand, I understand you're taking the very end?"

"Yes, sir," Harry said.

"Well, good luck. I look forward to seeing you on the other side." He grinned. "Of the river, I mean."

They were standing in the courtyard of Fort Dufferin. "You going to blow this place, sir?" asked a major.

"I'd like to," Clark conceded, "but I don't have enough dynamite to destroy this pile and, if I did, the bang would be so big all of Mandalay would probably go with it. Let's move. Brand, it's all yours."

The price of experience. Harry actually still had transport to join Keeton and his Gurkhas at the road block south of the Government Farm Buildings, from which fortunately all the animals had been withdrawn; situated not far away was the Leper Colony – that also had been emptied although no one knew for sure where all the inmates had gone. "Kind of makes the skin crawl," Keeton confessed.

The Japanese advance was in the main up the road from Meiktila and the block had to be held until the last of the defenders were across. Machine-guns were emplaced, together with a cocoon of explosives; if they were overrun they would all have to go together. But they also had several mortars, and Harry felt they would do the trick.

Soon it was dark, the light disappearing with typical tropical suddenness, aided by a heavy bank of cloud to the west. It was not quiet. Behind them the city seethed, with a good part of the remaining population by now drunk and letting off fire crackers, while around them the cicadas whirred and various other insects hummed or clicked. In the near distance they could hear the clatter of the retreating army. "They seem to be taking their time over it," Keeton grumbled.

Then it was utterly quiet. Even the jungle insects seem to have left. And in front of them nothing but darkness.

The voice made them all jump. "Hi, Johnnie!" it called. "I am hurt, man. Let me come in, man."

Keeton stood up, and was immediately pulled down again by Harry, who remembered these tactics from Malaysia.

"They want us to give away our position," he said.

Keeton scratched his head. "Hi, Johnnie!" the voice called again. "Why you won't help me, Johnnie? I am hurt and bleeding, Johnnie."

The Gurkhas rustled, restlessly. But they had all engaged the Japanese at close quarters before, save for Keeton. "There," said the sergeant.

Harry peered into the darkness, and saw movement, men coming up the road. "Fire!" he said. The machine-guns crackled in time to the rifles, and there came shrieks of pain and dismay from in front of them. "Cover the jungle to either side as well," Harry snapped, although he guessed the Japanese would need to use the road if at all

88

possible, as to take Mandalay, supposing it was defended, they would need tanks and guns; thus they would have to clear the block before they did anything else.

"Jesus!" Keeton muttered. Now the moans and cries for help were genuine, and they were not in English. But the Japanese were also returning fire.

"People behind us!" the sergeant said.

"Jesus!" Keeton said again.

Harry swung round, revolver thrust forward. "Scott here," the engineer said. "If you fellows would care to come with me, we can get rid of one bridge."

Harry had his men send several more volleys and bursts of Bren-gun fire into the darkness, then said. "On the double."

They gathered up such of their weapons as they could carry, set the timed detonator to destroy their heavy gear, and fled into the night, following Scott. Five minutes later there was a huge explosion from behind them, and 15 minutes later they were on the bridge, and 10 minutes later on the west bank. By now the Japanese had recovered and were in close pursuit. They were firing blind into the darkness, but they knew where the bridge was, and two of Harry's men were hit. Neither was killed, and the wounded were carried across. "Here's hoping some of the bastards are following," Scott said, and himself pressed the plunger.

The second explosion was far more impressive, although it could not match that of the oilfields. The bridge was too large to be entirely destroyed, but it was certainly severed, its centre a mass of twisted girders. "That ought to give them something to think about," Scott remarked.

Over the next few weeks Harry realised that he had never really understood the meaning of the word flight before,

89

although he had been unlucky enough to have partici-
pated in two of the saddest withdrawals experienced by
the British Army. The retreat to Dunkirk had taken
place over less than a week, while on the withdrawal
from the Thai border to the Strait of Johore they had
been given a series of positions to hold, and then been
forced, or required, to withdraw from them, always with
the apparent intention of holding the next. Thus the fact
that they were actually running for their lives had not
been apparent. The retreat from Mandalay to Imphal
contained no such illusions.

Equally, the retreat down Malaysia had been to the
east of the hill country, and over mainly flat land. To
get from Mandalay to Imphal, certainly after they left the
good road at Shwebo, Burma Corps found themselves in
the Mingin Range, which in places went up over 3,000
ft. Thus although the actual distance to be covered was
shorter by about a third, on the map, than that in
Malaysia, it was somewhat longer in terms of required
energy, while at the same time they had to make their way
along narrow and uncertain tracks through jungle every
bit as dense and unpleasant as that of Malaya. On top of
all of this, the retreating army, and their accompanying
refugees, were only about halfway to the Indian frontier
when the monsoon arrived.

Slim had been waiting for them in Shwebo, his staff
counting units as they turned up; his main concern,
naturally enough, was to get as many of his tanks and
guns out as possible – everyone knew the monsoon was
due. The monsoon was, in fact, regarded as a very useful
defensive weapon, as it was calculated to bring even
the Japanese to a halt. But Burma Corps had no wish
also to be brought to a halt while still in Burma. The
General listened to the report on the destruction of the

Ava Bridge with grim satisfaction, and issued his orders for the march. "You've done your bit, Brand," he told Harry. "You get on with the guns."

"With respect, sir, I've grown somewhat attached to the Gurkhas," Harry said.

"I need them to cover the retreat."

"Yes, sir."

Slim gazed at him for several seconds, then nodded. "I'll see you in Imphal. By then I'll hope to have some news of your wife."

Although the Japanese continued to control the sky, and raids were daily occurrences, it was at least reassuring to discover there was going to be no close pursuit by major ground forces, which confirmed Harry's conviction that they were not fighting either supermen or commanders who had no regard for the rules of war, but men like themselves who, however ruthlessly and indeed brilliantly led, still needed the sinews of war to fight. Not that the British and Indians could afford to be laggard. And they continued to be hampered by the huge numbers of refugees slowly making their way through the hill country to supposed safety, mostly in conditions of total destitution which increased daily. "What are we to do with all of these people?" Keeton asked.

"There is nothing we can do about any of these people," Harry told him, still convinced that for every ten people clearly fleeing for their lives there was one fellow-traveller, secretly a supporter of the Japanese or at least of Burmese independence: in the reality of the British defeat, the two points of view were synonymous.

But even he was taken aback the morning they overhead a radio plea for help, from an English voice claiming to be that of a Doctor Stevens. "People are dying here," he said. "If there is any unit with medical supplies available in the vicinity, we are begging for your help. We are in the village of Madaw. For God's sake, help us."

The Gurkhas, with the rest of the rearguard, were in Pyingaing, on the road from Yeu, and thus within about 50 miles of the Chindwin River, on the far side of which Slim was prepared to hold off the Japanese long enough to enable the last of his beleaguered army to reach safety. Radio silence had been enjoined on the troops for fear of revealing their exact positions to the Japanese, and Keeton and Harry looked at each other in mutual dismay and concern. "Sounds pretty grim," Keeton said.

"Let's have the map," Harry decided. Madaw was located some 20 miles farther north, and there appeared to be a track of sorts. "Let's find out if anyone knows how to get there."

"You're not serious? Your racism is showing!"

"It's a medical unit," Harry pointed out. "There may be British wounded up there."

Keeton rubbed his nose. "You'll have to square it with the Brigadier."

"Not necessary," Harry said. "I am an observer from headquarters. It is my duty to observe. That's what I'm going to do." He grinned. "All I want from you is all the medical supplies you can spare and permission to ask a few of your men to volunteer."

"You know they'll all do that," Keeton protested.

"I only want three, and a guide."

Keeton was absolutely right about the calibre of his men, and the entire company volunteered. Harry selected Sergeant Lenzing, because of his knowledge of Burmese, and two privates. Finding a Burmese willing to lead them into the bush was somewhat more difficult, until they

92

heard the ringing of a bell. "Seems to me I've heard that before," Harry sad.

"It is a monk, sir," Sergeant Lenzing explained. "His name is Ba Pau, and he is a member of the Nicheren sect, that is, he is an itinerant beggar. But he knows the country, and is willing to guide us," Lenzing rubbed his nose. "He will expect to be paid."

"Half now and half when we find Madaw," Harry said.

"I wish there was some way we could keep in radio contact, or at least let Dr Stevens know you're on your way," Keeton said.

"Mum's the word," Harry reminded him, and led his men north.

It was this day that it started to rain really heavily, and the track rapidly disappeared. Ba Pau was certain he knew the way, however, and Harry had no choice but to trust him, although he did insist that the monk stop ringing his bell; there was every chance that a Japanese patrol might have penetrated this far. Ba Pau was reluctant to do this. "Tell him there is no one to beg from, out here," Harry suggested to the sergeant.

"Ringing the bell is not to attract alms, Major," Lenzing explained. "It is of religious significance. The alms are incidental."

"Well, we do not have the time for religion right now," Harry said. "If he doesn't stop ringing his bell, I am going to take it away from him." Ba Pau agreed, although he was clearly not pleased.

The Gurkhas used their kukris to hack their way through the dripping foliage, and progress was surprisingly steady, but even with only the briefest halts for food or sleep – neither was very attractive in the steady downpour – it took them more than 24 hours

93

to reach the village. They knew it was there some time before they saw it. The men looked at each other as their nostrils were assailed by the stench. They hacked their way through the last tree fringe and looked at the collection of huts, sodden in the rain. But the rain did nothing to alleviate the stench of decaying bodies. Harry had his little party halt on the edge of the clearing while he surveyed the situation, but there was no sign of any Japanese. Sergeant Lenzing touched his arm. "They have cholera, Major."

Harry frowned, "How do you know?"

"I have seen it before, sir." He gave a grim smile. "And smelt it."

Harry left cover and walked into the village. It was easy to tell that there was no one and no thing left alive, but some of the deaths had been quite recent. He pulled his handkerchief from his pocket and tied it round his face and over his nose. As he had only had the occasional wash over the past week and had not changed his clothes in that time the handkerchief was a long way from being clean, but it was cleaner than the air.

He gazed at the contorted limbs, the mouths open reaching for water even as the victims had died from dehydration, the trails of faeces and vomit which surrounded each body. Ba Pau was gabbling, and rubbing his bell in his anxiety to start ringing. "He say we must leave this place, or we die," Lenzing said. "It is in the air."

"Nothing is in the air," Harry told him. "It is in the water and the food. Do not touch any of the corpses, and no one will be ill."

"But what we do now, sir?"

Harry knew what he should do: burn the village. But he dare not do that and tell every Japanese in the vicinity where they were. A hasty search revealed no white bodies, and no radio, either. Clearly the medical team

94

had determined to abandon those who were obviously dying in an attempt to save those who might still live. It must have been a terrible decision, Harry knew. But it had been the only correct one. And they would still need help, he did not doubt.

"We follow," he said.

The Gurkhas were not happy with his decision, but they were soldiers and obeyed orders. Ba Pau was even less happy, as he clearly did not regard it as part of his religious vows to tend the sick, and Harry did not doubt that he meant to abandon the second half of his fee and run off just as quickly as he could, which he did that evening when they bivouaced in a steady drizzle. But he was no longer necessary; the trail taken by the medical team was clearly discernible, and indeed the next day they came upon a dying Indian woman. She still hugged her child to her breast, but it was already dead.

The Gurkhas regarded her with stoic compassion. Harry knelt beside her, poured a little water from his canteen into a tin cup, and held it to her lips. She was past speech, but her fingers closed on his wrist like talons as she gulped at the liquid. "It would be a kindness to shoot her, sir," Lenzing suggested.

"No shooting," Harry said, telling himself that was a military decision because of the noise. "She is going to die soon, anyway."

An hour later they came upon an Indian man, already dead, and later that morning yet another, but this was a white man, his clothes filthied both by mud and by excreta, his eyes staring. But like the Indian woman, he was still alive, and he could speak. "Water," he begged. "For the love of God, water!" Harry used the same cup as he had for the woman, reckoning the man had nothing more to catch. "Have you medicine?" the man asked eagerly.

"I'm afraid not, old man," Harry said. "How many are left?"

"A dozen." The man's face convulsed as a series of spasms raced through his body. "God! I'm dying, man! I'm dying!"

"I can give you a sedative," Harry said.

"Anything." His anguished mouth cracked into a grin. "Maybe I won't wake up." Let's hope so, Harry thought, and swallowed as he placed the pill in the man's mouth. "Listen," the man said. "My wif . . ." he gave another series of gasps.

"Your name," Harry said.

There was no reply. "He is dead," Lenzing said. And I have wasted a pill, Harry thought.

An hour later they came to a stream. "We need to fill our canteens, Major," Lenzing said.

Harry looked at the water. It was beautifully clear; he could see fish wriggling about at the bottom. But he thought of winding up like those poor creatures behind them . . .

He tried to remember everything he knew about cholera. He had begun adult life intent upon becoming a surgeon, and had spent a couple of years in Edinburgh before flunking out and, reluctantly, following the family tradition into the Army. But in between the two he had served as a volunteer with the Red Cross in Ethiopia, in the midst of their war with Italy, and he had seen something of the disease at first hand. Cholera, as he recalled, was in the main caused by contaminated water, and the contaminent was usually raw sewage following a breakdown in sensible bodily hygiene. So surely, he told himself, there would be some evidence of filth to be seen. He had never seen water so clear. The men were watching him, anxiously and thirstily. He nodded. "All right, Sergeant. Fill your canteens."

He did so himself, watched the Gurkhas drinking from the stream as they filled their water bottles, and followed their example. The water was cool, almost cold, and nothing had ever tasted so good. Well, he thought, as he corked his canteen and restored it to its place on his belt, we could now be dead men.

Next morning they emerged from the jungle into a small clearing where there was another stream. Scattered in front of them were eleven people. They were all alive, but hardly capable of movement, they lay beside the water trying to drink, so exhausted and debilitated that they hardly raised their heads at the approach of the Gurkhas. Six of the fugitives were Indians, four men, and two women. Three more were children, all girls. And the remaining two were white people, a man and a woman. Harry knelt beside the man. "Dr Stevens?"

Stevens raised his head. He was remarkably young, or had been quite recently, Harry reckoned. Now he looked old, and there were streaks of grey in his stubbled beard. His hair was black and lank, his eyes bloodshot, his lips caked. But there was no stench: his bush jacket and shorts were torn and muddy, but his bowels had not yet collapsed. Harry gave him water to drink, and then moved to the woman. She was about the same age as the man or perhaps a little older. Harry thought she might be quite good-looking were she cleaned up and given some decent food to eat: she had a fine bone structure and auburn hair, which had apparently been worn fashionably short quite recently, but was now growing out in a a series of red-brown rat tails. She wore a skirt below her bush jacket, and these were as torn and mud-stained as those of her companion but she also had not yet contracted the cholera. He gave her water to drink as well; the Gurkhas were tending the other people. "Any chance of a fire?" he asked Lenzing.

"I do not think so, Major. Anyway, a fire would reveal our position."

"These people have to eat," Harry said. "Or they are all going to die." He left the Indians to the care of the Gurkhas and dragged the white woman into the comparative shelter of a tree, did the same for the man, opened his pack and found a bar of chocolate, half melted in the heat which persisted despite the downpour. But being soft it was the more useful. He broke off a segment, opened the woman's mouth, and placed it on her tongue. Her mouth closed almost with a snap, and he could imagine the saliva burning. He did the same for the man, but his reaction was less positive.

"Are you an angel, or a devil?" the woman asked.

"I suspect most people would go for the latter," Harry said. "Brevet Major Harry Brand, late of the South Midlands Light Infantry, now seconded to Burma Corps headquarters."

She gazed at him from clear blue eyes. "Then you are an angel."

"I won't argue with your assessment, ma'am. Are you Mrs Stevens?"

"I am Anne Chisholm, Dr Stevens's staff nurse. Is he . . ."

"He's alive."

"Have you any more water?"

This time Harry held the canteen to her lips, and when he realised that she was strong enough to hold it there he turned his attention to Stevens. "We did not know you were coming," the doctor muttered.

"We couldn't reply to your message without letting the Japs know where we were," Harry explained.

"But we came as rapidly as we could. What happened?"

It was Stevens's turn to drink deeply. "I have a clinic in Wuuth." His face twisted. "Had, I suppose. We were told to get out because the Japs were coming. The railway had been blown up. Anyway, that led to Myitkyina, which was going towards the Japs. So we decided to take the trail west, for Imphal. We had two vehicles, but these got bogged down. Then the first signs of cholera came. So we went to that village looking for help. It had been evacuated. It was from there I called. Then we set off again, but we had left the trail and couldn't find it back." He shook his head. "I don't think we are going to make it."

"Of course you are going to make it," Harry said. "We are all moving out as soon as you've had something solid to eat. The Japanese are coming this way as well."

They had to drive the survivors to their feet and forward, but it was amazing what some food could do, when coupled with Harry's assurances that it was only a few miles now to the Chindwin. Actually it was 35 miles over appalling country, but none of the refugees had any idea how fast they were travelling. "I suppose you think we behaved very badly, abandoning the sick," Stevens said, as he stumbled along.

"I think you did the only thing you could," Harry assured him.

"If only this rain would stop!" Anne Chisholm said.

"I think it's keeping us going," Harry said.

They sat beside each other that evening as they ate sodden food. They were all so uncomfortable it was difficult to remember that any of them had ever worn clean, dry, clothes and had a roof over their heads. Nurse Chisholm sighed. "I suppose you're right. Do you think it's as bad for the Japanese?"

"I'm quite sure it is."

He asked them about the dying man's wife, and was reassured to learn she was safely in England. In return, they wanted to know what had really happened, and also about his part in it; he told them. "God," the nurse said, "to have got out of Singapore, and come to this! Is your wife all right?"

"I'm hoping someone is going to be able to tell me that when we reach Imphal," Harry said.

"Are we ever going to come back?" Stevens asked.

"I think we mean to," Harry said. "As to what we'll come back to, now that is another question."

There were, indeed, so many questions he wanted to ask, about Stevens, but also about the nurse, young, good-looking, but delving into the Burmese jungle to earn a living? But he decided against it until they reached civilisation; he could tell that both Stevens and Nurse Chisholm were close to complete breakdowns. Next day they reached the river. "Shit!" Stevens commented. "How do we get across that?"

Harry surveyed the west bank through his binoculars. "We signal those fellows," he said, picking out the khaki uniforms.

That same afternoon they were in Imphal. Here Harry took farewell of Stevens, and Nurse Chisholm. "What are your plans?"

"To link up with some medical unit or other. What are yours?"

"To fight the Japanese," Harry told them. He had a bath, while his uniform was laundered; he had no other. But to his delight he was visited by Keeton, who had brought the rest of the Gurkhas out safely. "So what happens now?" Harry asked.

"You'll have to ask the General."

Harry duly reported to Slim, who greeted him with a long face. "I am very sorry to say, Brand, that your wife did not get out."

Harry swallowed. "You mean she's dead, sir?"

Slim sighed. "I don't know. But I think you must anticipate the very worst. Most of the women left Taungup and tried to make Akyab, as soon as they learned that we could not hold Prome. But the Japanese moved into Arakan very quickly. We have had reports of several massacres, involving women, and children. And we have had absolutely no word of your wife, or the women who were with her."

Harry sat in silence. He could not believe it. He had never been sure just how Constance and himself were going to work out all the many difficulties and problems that lay between them, but he had never doubted that they would *have* to work them out, after the war. The concept that there might not be an after the war for either of them had just never entered his mind. Constance was surely indestructible, in her courage, her determination, her sometimes almost manic sense of humour. "I am most terribly sorry," Slim said.

"Thank you, sir."

"Now, I understand that you have a son. In all the circumstances, your wound, your escape from Singapore, your exceptionally valuable service to both Alexander and myself in Burma, and now your bereavement, I consider that you are entitled to a lengthy period of rest and recuperation, and with your family. I am confirming your rank, and making some other recommendations as well. You'll go from here to Calcutta, and then home."

"Am I allowed to decline, sir?"

Slim raised his eyebrows.

"I want to fight the Japanese, sir. I can only do that here. I don't care where you post me, so long as it is a fighting unit."

"And if I tell you that we don't have a hope in hell of getting to grips with the Japanese, as an army, until next year?"

"I'll wait, sir. But here, not in England,"

Slim grinned at him. "You may not have to wait, that long. There's a chap I would like you to meet. Name of Wingate."

Part Two

Going Back

'. . . Every warrior that is rapt with love
Of fame, of valour, and of victory,
Must needs have beauty beat on his conceits.'
Christopher Marlowe
Tamberlaine the Great

Chapter Five

Chindits

"Major Brand," Orde Wingate said. "I've been hearing a lot about you." As I have heard a lot about you, Harry thought. Wingate was regarded as one of the most brilliant as well as most unorthodox soldiers in the British Army. They shook hands. Harry had been given a new uniform, and was every inch the staff officer, with flawlessly pressed khaki tunic and breeches, polished brown boots, suitably adorned cap, gleaming crowns on his shoulder straps. The brigadier, in the strongest contrast, wore a bush tunic and shorts, no identifying badges at all, and on entering the hotel room had removed a solar topee, high-domed rather than the more usual flattened crown; it looked like a relic from the Battle of Omdurman in 1897. But he had piercing eyes and a compelling presence. "Sit." He indicated a chair and took one himself.

This was the first time Harry had been in Calcutta, and he did not much care if it was to be his last. The past couple of weeks had been as traumatic as ever before in his life, and he had not really expected to be able to say that again, or wanted to. The Army, all India, it seemed, was in a state of shock; the events of the past six months had simply been too devastating for most people to grasp, especially those born and bred to imperial majesty in south-east Asia. The Japanese had always been regarded with paternal admiration by the British. They were a hard-working, frugal nation of little people, the accent being on the word little. Trained by

British sailors, they had developed a considerable naval ability, and as such had even been considered worthy allies of the world's greatest sea power at the turn of the century. But they would of course never be able to match their instructors at an art built up over centuries of total blue-water supremacy.

As for the Japanese Army, it too was industrious and frugal, and successful, but the only people it had ever fought were the disintegrating Russians of the last days of the Tsarist Empire, and the equally disintegrated Chinese, who would rather fight each other than any foreign enemy. The war with China had been accompanied by atrocities on a scale forgotten in Europe's history, and that had lessened the respect with which the Japanese were held. But of course, again it had been Japanese raping and murdering Chinese, and Asiatics were by definition barbarous to each other: it was well known that the Chinese spent much of their time raping and murdering each other – even their judicial process of publicly beheading anyone convicted of almost any crime was barbaric. The Japanese would never have the irresponsibility to vent such brutishness on the British, their traditional friends and mentors. In any event, when it came to fighting the Japanese would never dare take on the British. Every Englishman in south-east Asia knew they were inferior soldiers. Sadly, that opinion was also held by the British Supreme Commander, General Wavell.

Over the past six months all that had changed, except, even more sadly, for Wavell's opinion. The Japanese had gone to war with a deliberation and panache, and ruthless determination, the British had been unable to match. Wavell might be unable to understand how the British-Australian-Indian forces in Malaysia had been beaten and evicted in a month, how Singapore should have surrendered in another fortnight, and now how

106

the British had been driven out of Burma. He had sacked generals left and right in the belief that they had not done their best. But the fact remained that it had happened. That English women had been raped in Hong Kong and marched off to humiliating captivity after Singapore. That an army of 86,000 men had laid down their arms in the greatest catastrophe ever to overtake British arms; at Yorktown, in 1781, Cornwallis had only given up 7,000. And now they had been driven out of Burma in a matter of weeks. As at Dunkirk, they had been forced to leave nearly all their guns and tanks behind. But at Dunkirk they had been beaten by the Germans, the most professional soldiers in the world. On top of all that, the Japanese had also sunk two of Britain's finest warships.

And on top of all *that*, Harry thought, they have either murdered or captured my wife! That personal blow had been the most devastating he had had to bear. He had known defeat. He had known catastrophe. With his life blighted by the death of Nicole, he did not know if he had ever loved Constance, if he would ever be able to love her. But he could not forget that when the chips had been absolutely down she had found a boat and sailed them out of Singapore, and at the same time nursed him back to health. To think of her raped and murdered made his blood curdle . . . and then boil. If this man could offer him a fighting appointment . . .

"You were in East Africa," Wingate remarked.

"In 1936. With the Red Cross."

"In 1936 I was in Palestine, trying to separate Jew and Arab. I was in East Africa, though, with Cunningham, last year."

"I envy you."

"I understand you've had a pretty busy war yourself, Major. Tell me about the jungle. Is it as grim as they say?"

107

"That depends on who's doing the saying, sir."

"Good point! But you're not scared of it."

"Not if I can find a Jap in it."

Wingate raised his eyebrows. "Personal?"

"One wife, sir."

"The men I want can't be obsessed with personal feelings."

"I am not, sir. I want to fight the Japanese, that is all."

Wingate studied him for several seconds. "We have been turfed out of Malaysia and Burma," he said. "Obviously, next on the Japanese agenda has to be India. They conquered both Malaysia and Burma because the population weren't on our side to begin with, and as soon as we started losing battles and retreating even those who *were* on our side began to consider making fresh arrangements. Can't blame them, really. Now, the same thing obtains in India. Oh, I have no doubt that the vast majority of the Indian population just want to be left alone to get on with their lives and, equally, I have no doubt that the more intelligent Indian politicians understand that we have done them a bit of good over the past hundred years, certainly more than the Japanese are likely to over the next. But there are mavericks, like Subhas Chandra Bose, and it only takes one or two mavericks of his calibre to stir up public opinion. That public opinion is only going to come back to our side when they understand that not only are we not going to lose this war, but that we are going to take back all the territory we have lost. Do you agree?"

"Well, of course I do, sir. But . . ."

"Quite. That can only be demonstrated by military success. And *that* is not going to be easy. I know Slim is hoping to mount a counter-attack in Arakan as soon as the monsoon is over, but frankly, that is something the Japanese will be expecting, and I wouldn't bet my pension on his success. Launching a counter-attack from Imphal, into Burma, is equally a non-starter. We don't have the men or the materiel, and what men we do have are still suffering from the morale-shattering effects of both fighting in the jungle and the apparent Japanese ability to penetrate that jungle at will. Am I right?"

"Sadly, yes."

"That opinion has got to be set to rights, Brand, before we have any hope of beating the enemy on a large scale. We have got to prove, to the world but more importantly to our own people here in India, that the Japanese soldier is not unbeatable, that the jungle is not terrifying, and that we can exist in it, fight in it, and win in it, as well as anyone. Right?"

"Yes, sir. But you have just agreed that any offensive into Burma is at this moment not possible."

"Any conventional offensive, Brand. But this war has already turned convention upside down. Aircraft: there is the secret of this war. It was the German Stukas that really won them the Battle of France. It was the British Spitfire which won the Battle of Britain. It was the Japanese Val bombers and the Kate torpedol-boots, not the Japanese battleships, that sank *Prince of Wales* and *Repulse*. And it was Japanese air superiority that more than anything else sealed the fate of Singapore." He pointed out of the window at an aircraft circling before coming in to land. "Those are the secret."

"You mean, bomb the Japanese out of Burma? I don't think that would work, sir. The country is simply too large, their forces too scattered."

"Aircraft aren't used only for bombing, you know. In my opinion, that is the least important of their uses. It's the ability to support ground troops over great distances, quickly and at short notice that's their true *métier*. And, as you have pointed out, the Japanese troops, a few divisions, are scattered over an area larger than

France." Now he was totally animated, leaning forward, eyes glowing. "I've been given permission to carry the fight to the enemy, Brand. A grand cavalry raid, if you like, only we'll be on foot, a force composed of picked men, men with guts, men who will be trained not to be afraid of either the jungle or the Japanese, men who wish only to kill the enemy, and who are not afraid of being killed themselves. Are you one of those men, Brand?"

"Yes, sir," Harry said, equally fervently.

"Right! As I said, a raid. It will be successful because the Japanese don't think in terms of raids. They aim to conquer and hold what they have taken. The idea of a couple of thousand men just probing into the midst of country they consider theirs, seeking and destroying, will rock them. But there is more: we will have no lines of communication. That will rock them even more. They will naturally, and conventionally, assume that we can only exist for a few days, then we must get out. But we are going to stay for weeks, Brand. Because we will be supplied by air. It's never been done before. That's no reason why it can't be done now. Anything that takes the enemy by surprise is bound to be successful. We are going to tear him apart when and where he least expects it. I call it Long Range Penetration. And we can stay as long as we like, because we'll be supplied from the air. It'll be tough. The toughest thing you have ever experienced. It'll be the jungle. But you know the jungle. We may surprise the enemy, but they won't stay surprised long. There'll be no coming out until I say so. All I need is men with guts."

Harry felt a great glow spreading through his body.

Now began the most exhausting period of Harry's life, but also the most exhilarating. Wingate was given a battalion of Gurkhas and a battalion of British troops,

110

and told to organise his force for Operation Longcloth out of this material. His plan was to create eight columns, four of Gurkhas and four of British, who would operate independently and yet be able to concentrate as and when necessary. He actually did not intend to remain behind the enemy lines for more than six weeks. "That's as long as any man will be able to stand it," he told his officers. "And that even includes you, Major Brand."

The Gurkhas were naturals for such an operation. They knew the jungle and they were masters of the stealthy attack; their endurance was remarkable. To Harry's delight, among the officers who reported for training was his old friend Tom Keeton, who brought with him Sergeant Lenzing. The British were quite the reverse. They were the 13th King's Liverpool Regiment, straight out from England; Wingate had been hoping for battle-hardened veterans of Flanders and Dunkirk. The trouble was that, while Wingate had the ear of Wavell, and, it was rumoured, of Prime Minister Churchill, he was regarded by the main part of the military establishment as an upstart and, worse, a man who did not believe in orthodox military matters. The staff's attitude was that he should, as they all had to do continuously, make the best of what material was to hand instead of seeking perfection.

Wingate knew that for the sort of campaign he was planning only perfection would do. But he did make the best of what he was given. His troops were city-bred men from the offices of Liverpool, Glasgow and Manchester, who had previously been employed solely on garrison duty, soft-bodied and lazy-minded, archetypal non-combat soldiers. They did not like India, they did not like the food, and they did not like Wingate's training methods. They also did not like the weight of the equipment each man, including officers, had to carry at all times; this consisted of a large pack containing

111

personal belongings, two grenades, ammunition for automatics and Bren guns, mess tins, and five days' American K Rations, and of course an ample supply of mepacrine to resist malaria, a total weight of some 75 lb. They did not lack courage. They ran until they dropped, bayoneted sacks until their arms seemed about to fall off, spent hours too long in the sun, ate scanty rations, climbed trees, bridged fast-flowing rivers, walked in the Bengal jungle barefoot to get them accustomed to snakes, leeches and spiders. Unfortunately, they also began to fall sick.

Soon 70 per cent were on the sick list. "They aren't really ill," said the doctor. "They're just playing the old army game: when the going gets too tough, report sick."

"Right," Wingate said. "We'll put a stop to that." He issued orders that any man appearing on sick parade and discovered not to have a serious complaint would be punished. Minor ailments were to be treated by platoon commanders, something they would have to do anyway once the campaign began. Officers were also required to carry out daily inspection of their men's stools, to determine which of them actually did have dysentery. There was considerable grumbling, but Wingate's spirit was, at last, getting to them. But the fall-out was enormous; it included the battalion commander and over 200 of his men. This caused a rearrangement of the original plan, and the eight columns became seven: four Gurkha and three British.

Harry found the going as tough as anyone. But his recent life, both in Malaysia, during the escape from Singapore, and in the Burma campaign, had left him as jungle- and tropical-fit as any man, and he had the personal stimulus of desiring to avenge Constance. To his great pleasure Wingate appointed him to lead one of the Gurkha columns, with Keeton as his second in command. By the time the training was complete the force, officially known as the Long Range Penetration Group, had been nicknamed the Chindits. This was actually a misnomer; Wingate had misinterpreted the Burmese word for a semi-mythical lion, which is *chinthe*. But the Chindwin was the river they were going to have to cross to get back into Burma, and Chindit was easier to pronounce.

There was very little spare time during the training period, and no leave, even for officers, as the operation was top secret. There was incoming mail, however. Harry had written his mother, the only member of his family of whose whereabouts he was certain, to bring her up to date. The last she had heard of either Constance or himself was before the fall of Singapore, and he could at least tell her that they had survived that. But at the same time he had to report that Constance was missing, presumed dead and, if not dead, certainly a prisoner of the Japanese.

This news Helen Brand had had to pass on to the Lloyds, and predictably the letters which came back were a mixture of relief at his personal survival, at least from his mother, and recriminations that he should have allowed Constance to be placed in such danger. As if he had had any choice in the matter! England, and the family, and even his son Mark, seemed very remote in the jungle training camp.

But there was good news as well. His favourite cousin, Hector Brand, had somehow managed to escape from his German prison – there was no information on exactly how he had managed it – and was back in England, reunited with his wife Jocelyn and his young son.

113

Lucky for some, Harry thought. But the news also made him happy.

The training and the organisation, of both the initial penetration and the campaign to follow, took far longer than anyone had supposed it would, and it was not until 14 February 1943 – Valentine's Day – that the expedition began. By then a great deal had happened in the Pacific and south-east Asia. During the previous summer, while the monsoon had raged in India and indeed while Wingate and Harry were having their initial meeting, the American and Japanese fleets had clashed in the Battle of Midway, which had resulted in the sinking of four Japanese aircraft-carriers for one American, and the ending of their hopes, not only of expanding their empire, but even of holding on to their extended perimeter of islands. The Japanese had earlier been checked in a drawn naval battle in the Coral Sea, meant to enhance their invasion and occupation of New Guinea, while on the huge island itself, American and Australian counter-attacks had brought the Japanese advance to a halt, and proved for the first time that 'white' troops could hold their own as well as any in the jungle.

Equally stirring events had taken place in the Solomons, at the very limit of the Japanese perimeter, where American marines had landed on the island of Guadalcanal, and, after several months of fierce fighting, in which both sides rushed reinforcements to the little island and engaged in several bloody battles, forced the Japanese to evacuate after losing 24,000 dead. These were great and heartening Allied successes, but no one supposed they meant the end of the war against Japan was in sight. The Japanese still held most of New Guinea and all the Philippines, as well as the entire Dutch East Indies and British Malaysia and Burma. Thus protected and supplied, Japan could exist forever, growing stronger. Even the four carriers so catastrophically lost at Midway could be replaced, given time. And all the while the Allies were expending men and materiel on a prodigal scale. The Japanese still reckoned that even the Americans would eventually have to come to the peace-table and accept that Japan had established her Greater East Asia Co-Prosperity Sphere.

And Japan had no intention of letting up the pressure. General Ishida's veteran troops, flushed with two successful campaigns in succession, were crouched along the Burmese border, ready for the Invasion of India as soon as the weather was suitable. With them was the Indian National Army of Subhas Chandra Bose, many of them recruited from among the Indian soldiers who had been forced to lay down their arms in Singapore. Subhas Bose and his Japanese masters had no doubt that once they penetrated Assam and streamed towards the Ganges all India would rise in their support, and the British Empire would, to all intents and purposes, come to an end.

The original idea, at least in the minds of the staff, had been that the Chindits would be part of a diversionary move that would supplement a general British and Indian counter-attack against the Japanese forces in Arakan, a pre-emptive strike aimed at the vital communications centre of Akyab, which was intended to put any Japanese invasion of India back to beyond the next monsoon, giving Slim more time to receive reinforcements and train his people for the decisive battle to retake Burma, and, hopefully, Singapore. However, the attack on Arakan, launched in December, as soon as the monsoon ended, was a disaster. Shortage of men, materiel and landing craft meant it could not be mounted on a sufficient scale – Akyab was actually an island – and once again the combination of the jungle and the Japanese proved too much for the British-Indian troops. The offensive achieved tactical surprise, but the advance on Akyab was too slow and gave the Japanese time to bring in reinforcements, while once the British-Indians were checked, Japanese forces infiltrated the apparently impenetrable mountains behind them and all but cut them off. There was another hasty and humiliating retreat, and another resounding defeat to be recorded at the end of it, with Japanese prestige and British-Indian fear of the bush greater than ever.

The question then arose as to what to do with the Chindits? Final training was completed just about the time, in January, that it was realised the Arakan offensive was proving a failure. The Chindits would therefore neither be supporting their own troops nor diverting those of the enemy. It would simply be a raid; would it serve any useful purpose? Major General Irwin, Wingate's immediate superior, felt that they were likely to be chopped to bits by the Japanese, and for a while it seemed as if the expedition would be called off, at least for the time being. But Wingate insisted upon being let loose. "We have trained for six months," he told the generals. "I have honed this brigade to a fine edge. My men are keyed up and ready to go. If they are put off now, you may as well disband us, and accept that all that time, effort and money, have been wasted, because we are going to fall apart. As to what we can do, we can give the Japs a bloody nose, and show everyone else that it can be done."

As usual Wavell, who as Supreme Commander had the last word, was prepared to listen to his brilliant protégé, but even he hesitated, and asked the opinion of the American Lieutenant General Somervell of the Army Air Force: his planes would be dropping the supplies

116

to the columns. "General," the American replied, "if I were you, I'd just let 'em roll."

Wingate was elated, and issued a long order of the day to his men. "The battle," he said, "is not always to the strong, nor the race to the swift. Victory in war cannot be counted on, but what can be counted on is that we shall go forward determined to do what we can to bring this war to an end which we believe best for our friends and comrades-in-arms, without boastfulness or forgetting our duty, resolved to do the right so far as we can see the right."

It was not exactly Churchillian prose, but the men needed no further encouragement; some of them were in tears.

The columns crossed the Chindwin individually, using small boats and in the dead of night; each had a separate assignment. Harry's Gurkhas were directed to a bridge some 40 miles inside Burma, which formed part of a vital road link. The contingent consisted of three companies, a total of just under 300 men. One of the company commanders was a demolitions expert. The going was tough from the very beginning, but so severe had been their training that scanty food, mosquitoes, leeches and exhausting marches, seemed all in the day's work. Even snakes, including pythons 12 ft long, hardly caused comment. The Gurkhas were of course used to snakes, and Harry had seen enough of them in Malaysia and East Africa not to be afraid of them.

What was awe-inspiring was the size of the jungle across which they were operating, and which Harry had hardly noticed in the mad rush from Rangoon to the border. As Wingate had pointed out, Burma was roughly the size of France and consisted of endless ranges of hills bisected by deep, narrow river valleys through which the water flowed with the speed of an express train. And every square inch was covered with the thickest forest of trees, rising from matted undergrowth, that could be imagined. They seldom saw either sun or moon because of the tree screen, and operated by compass, following map co-ordinates as they made for their first drop zone. On the plus side, they didn't see any Japanese, either. "Five will get you ten there's nothing there," Keeton quipped.

But when they reached the zone, they found a huge pile of materiel waiting for them, including fresh food and ammunition. As they still had not encountered any enemy – although by now the Japanese had to be aware of their presence – the ammunition wasn't needed; they buried it to be picked up on their way back. But the relatively fresh food was most welcome.

Such Burmese civilians as they encountered stared at the khaki-clad invaders, by now looking somewhat ragged, in consternation. Sergeant Lenzing was able to talk to these people, and told the officers that there was a considerable number of Japanese in the area. This was confirmed by radio messages from the other columns, several of which had been heavily engaged; at least one had been virtually destroyed – the survivors had returned across the Chindwin. What to do with the Burmese was a problem, as presumably when next the Japanese came along, they would be informed of the presence of a British column in their midst. But they already knew that, Harry reckoned, and the civilians couldn't just be shot. He decided to hurry on, complete his allotted task, and get out as rapidly as he could. Things weren't working out the way Wingate had intended.

A week later they found themselves crouching among the trees on a steep escarpment above the bridge. "It's

118

deserted," said John Chapman, the demolition expert, in disbelief. "There's not even a guard!"

Harry studied both the bridge and the road leading up to and across it for some time through his binoculars to make quite sure that the target was indeed unprotected. "All right, Captain Chapman," he said, when he was satisfied. "Take your company down there to give you close cover, set your explosives, and get back up here." Chapman led his men down the slope. "Captain Keeton, unlimber the machine-guns and cover the road," Harry said. "Captain O'Connor, take your company to the far side of the hill and cover our rear." He stayed with Keeton as the four machine-guns were set up and Keeton's men posted among the trees.

It was just on ten in the morning, and the jungle was still damply steaming. The sun was rising steadily above the trees to the east, having only cleared the surrounding hills half-an-hour before; on the hillside the trees were thin enough for them to be clearly visible. Above, the sky was blue, dotted with puffy white clouds. It was an incredibly peaceful scene. The jungle-covered escarpment on which Harry knelt looked down on the beaten earth road which wound its way through the trees like a snake, clinging to the valley below; the land rose again on the far side. Immediately beneath them, the river, a deep, fast-running tributary of the upper Irrawaddy some 130 yards wide, intersected the road. On the bridge, Chapman and his men were busily setting their charges. They were making no noise that could be heard up the hill, and indeed the only sounds were the humming of insects and the occasional slither of a lizard. Then Lenzing cocked his head. "Vehicles, sir."

Gradually the distant growl became apparent to them all. "I thought it was too good to last." Harry focussed his binoculars on Chapman: the wiring was still not completed. "Tom, we will have to check those fellows

119

until the bridge is blown. Hold your fire until I give the word."

Slowly the noise grew; clearly a convoy of trucks was approaching. Harry did not doubt that Chapman could hear them, but he was continuing his work with deliberate determination. Then he stood up and waved his men back. Thank God for that, Harry thought. But at that moment the first vehicle came round the corner to within sight of the bridge, and this was not a truck, but a tank. There was a man standing in the cupola, and Harry saw him reach for his radio mike. "Open fire!" he snapped.

The machine-guns burst into a deadly racket, and the remainder of the Gurkhas also opened fire with their rifles and Brens. The tank continued to advance, and behind it came another. The lead tank's gun moved to and fro once or twice, then fired at the demolition party, who were running for the trees, scattering them like rag dolls. Chapman, who was slowly and carefully unwinding his wire, still had not taken cover; two men had stayed with him.

The second tank elevated its gun and sent a shell crashing into the trees. This went wide and there were no casualties. "Keep firing," Harry commanded. But bullets were having very little effect on the armoured vehicles, and he was concerned that only two Japanese tanks had emerged. He was quite sure there were more, or at least a convoy of transports. So what the hell were they doing?

The second shot from the second tank came much closer, and a tree came crashing down, trapping several men; below them the first tank was still firing at the demolition squad on the far side of the bridge; the road was covered with little khaki heaps, some lying still, others writhing in agony. The survivors had reached the undergrowth and were returning fire at the tanks as

120

best they could. Harry watched Chapman unhurriedly attach the wires and stand up to depress the plunger. Then he saw that the captain's tunic was stained with blood. Immediately he was hit again, spun round, and crashed to the ground.

Instantly one of the men who had remained with him seized the plunger and thrust it down. There was a huge roar, and a cloud of smoke and dust. Steel girders rose into the air and crashed down again, splashing into the water. The Gurkhas uttered a cheer, but as they did so there was a fresh burst of firing, and several more fell. They had done all that could be expected of them. Harry stood up and waved his arm. "Fall back!" he bellowed.

As they obeyed, a tremendous burst of firing came from behind him. He looked round and saw a line of Japanese infantry coming over the brow of the hill half a mile to his right; warned by the leading tanks, the troops had disembarked from their trucks and now flanked the invaders by advancing through the jungle. They were still separated by the river, which afforded a measure of time for withdrawal, but the enemy firepower was impressive, and Harry knew how adept the Japanese were at crossing even fast-running rivers: he had seen them at work in Malaysia. And this was hardly more than a stream. Even if their tanks and trucks would be stuck for several days until the bridge could be repaired, he had no doubt their infantry would be at his heels within a couple of hours.

He looked right and left. O'Connor, as ordered, had withdrawn his company to the other side of the ridge and was out of sight, but there was firing coming from up there as well. Chapman's company was withdrawing up the hill, still firing at the tanks. And Keeton's men were falling back of their own accord, driven by a withering fire from the Japanese. "Get your equipment out," Harry told the radio operator. "Sergeant Major Bopal, detail a squad to carry out the wounded. Keep those machine-guns firing."

He was surrounded by noise, the beauty of the morning destroyed forever. The tank cannon boomed, and the trees crackled as the bullets tore through them; the rifle and machine-gun fire was continuous. From the hillside there came the shrill cries of the advancing Japanese, accompanied by the blaring of a bugle. They had reached the river now, and were preparing rafts and ropes. They had suffered considerable casualties, and could not be certain of the exact location and strength of the opposing force, but they were not hesitating for a moment. The remnants of Chapman's company were up to him now, and he told them to withdraw into the bush behind his position. Keeton joined him in the midst of his men. "When those buggers get across, we're done," he gasped.

"Like hell we are! Get your men into the bush." Keeton waved his men to follow him; most of them were carrying or assisting their wounded comrades as well as firing their rifles. The first Japanese were now across the water, the rest clamouring to follow; Harry estimated there had to be at least 1,000 of them, and he now had less than 100, without O'Connor. There was no time to dismantle the machine-guns. "Smash them," he commanded, and his men obeyed. Then they too hurried into the jungle.

Harry had anticipated that as they withdrew along the brow of the hill they would encounter O'Connor, and unite to form a solid retreating force. But from the sudden eruption of explosive sound to the south he realised that O'Connor was equally heavily engaged. Harry directed his men towards the firing, and arrived at the little ravine which split the hill, beyond which O'Connor had established his position, just in time to see the Gurkhas overrun by several hundred Japanese, screaming as they charged with fixed bayonets. He realised that yet another enemy force must have forded the river even higher up and advanced unseen through the jungle, and bit his lip in frustration and anger. He could not get his men across the ravine in time to help O'Connor, and he could not fire on the Japanese without hitting the Gurkhas. And behind him there was another battalion of Japanese, screaming for blood – and still blowing their bloody bugle! It was an agonising decision, but he had to save what he could. "We must fall back into the bush behind Captain Keeton," he told Bopal. "Move!"

The retreat continued to be orderly, and the Gurkhas kept up a steady fire into the advancing Japanese. Harry bent double as he scrambled down into the ravine and up the other side. Here he encountered the handful of O'Connor's men who had survived the Japanese change. "Where is Captain O'Connor?" he demanded.

"Dead, sir," a corporal replied. "Together with both lieutenants and the CSM."

"Fall back into the jungle and join Sergeant Major Bopal and Captain Keeton." Harry told them. He himself sheltered behind a tree to oversee the Japanese and discover why they had ceased their advance; to his horror he saw that they were systematically bayoneting the wounded Gurkhas to death. He turned and ran behind his command.

There was no immediate pursuit. The Japanese, having disposed of their prisoners, paused to tend their own wounded, to inspect the Gurkha positions, and to see if anything immediate could be done about the bridge. Harry held a roll call, and discovered that he commanded 134 men, including himself, Keeton, and one of Keeton's subalterns; the other was dead. Twenty-seven men were hurt, eight of them badly. The three officers and the

NCOs did what they could for them, binding their wounds and giving them water, but obviously carrying them much farther was out of the question, and it would have been in direct contravention of Wingate's orders, which were that those unable to walk had to be abandoned. "We'll stay here, sir," one of the wounded men said, "and cover your retreat."

Harry and Keeton looked at each other. Sergeant Major Bopal shrugged and said, "It is the only way, sir."

The men were given a rifle each, 20 rounds of ammunition, and a hand-grenade. Then Harry shook hands with each one, and led his men past them in a final farewell. Each of the Gurkhas in turn saluted his comrades, and disappeared into the jungle. It was some two hours later that they heard a brief crackle of rifle fire, followed by the dull thuds of the exploding grenades. The Japanese had resumed the pursuit.

As they were short of ammunition, Harry's first intention was to return to the drop zone and dig up the supplies they had left there; he knew there should have been another drop of food and medical supplies – both of which they desperately needed – by now. But a direct return march was out of the question; the Japanese were still pursuing and they would have led them directly to the zone. He therefore directed a swing to the north in the hopes of dropping the pursuit.

When they had not seen or heard any Japanese for two days, Harry tried to raise one of the other columns by radio, and managed to make contact with Wingate himself. He reported the situation, that he had blown the bridge but lost more than half his command, and that his men were suffering severely both from malaria and lack of food, but that he hoped to make the dump in another few days. "Forget that," Wingate ordered. "The Japanese have found it and are waiting for you. Head north-west and make for co-ordinates S3 and K4. There you will find some supplies. I'm afraid it's about forty miles from your present position, through fairly heavy country. But it's your best hope of getting out."

"Yes, sir," Harry acknowledged. "And after we've reached the dump?"

"Return across the Chindwin. You have done all you were sent to do."

Chapter Six

The Lost

"This is special meal," announced Sergeant Matsumara. "Very special meal. You ladies eat, eh?" The women stared in amazement at the huge soup bowls from which the guards were ladling the stew. The bowls were the same as were always used to dispense the watery gruel which, with a few bamboo shoots, was the prisoners' staple diet; but the food now waiting to be dumped on their tin plates contained meat and rice. "You not eat too much, eh?" Matsumara advised, grinning at them. "Then you get sick. Not good to get sick."

"It's some kind of a trap," Susan whispered. Constance thought that she would have gone mad without Susan, even if she was not a woman with whom she thought she could ever have been friends, in a civilised society. But she was a woman, and a white, English woman, and the two had become almost sisters as they concentrated upon living from day to day, from minute to minute, while daily growing weaker from lack of proper food and proper exercise, from lack of proper sanitation and proper medication, from mosquito bites and the consequent malarial attacks, and ant bites which festered when scratched, from drinking filthy water which gave them continuous stomach upsets, from ticks and fleas, from being scorched by the sun in the dry season and being unable to get dry when it rained. From the realisation that they had now spent almost a year in captivity. The real world, if it still existed, seemed like a distant planet.

Yet it had been even worse in the beginning, when they had been marched through the jungle back to Taungup. Constance's feet, barely recovered from their earlier ordeal, had again begun to swell, while Susan had stumbled along in an almost catatonic state, shrinking every time a Japanese approached her. On the other hand they had not been raped again; Constance had not been raped at all. In her more light-headed moments she had wondered if she should be insulted about that; she would have said she was a far better-looking woman than Susan, or the Indian woman who had been violated before being murdered!

Taungup had been a shambles of burning buildings, wrecked boats, and unburied corpses. It had not been defended, so far as Constance knew, but the Japanese had not yet carried it by assault. Constance looked for John Wishart, but he was not to be seen in Taungup; his house was a burned-out shell. In Taungup they had been loaded into trucks to be driven over the mountain track to the Irrawaddy. With them now were some 40 women, but Susan and Constance were the only two who were English. Most of the Indian women, who were wives of once prosperous merchants or reasonably senior civil servants, spoke English, and Constance tried to engage them in conversation to find out what had happened to the American doctor, but they were not very responsive. For one thing, the Japanese guards discouraged conversation and were apt to hit first, using their lengths of solid rubber hose, and admonish after, as Constance quickly found out to her cost. The humiliation of being treated like an errant schoolgirl by aggressive little men – not one of them came up to her shoulder – whom she would have expected to touch their caps to her in the old days, was far worse than the stinging pain which took the breath away.

But even when the guards were not in close proximity,

the Indian women were not inclined to gossip with the English prisoners; some of them had been hostile to British rule even before the Japanese invasion, and the rest felt that the British had let them down, by their inability to defend Burma. Thus Constance could not discover what had happened to the doctor, or to the other white women in Taungup. She had to believe that they might have got out in time. As for Susan and herself, equally she had to believe that they would survive, but sometimes it was difficult to be barely confident. In addition to exhaustion and malnutrition, and the recurrent attacks of fever and dysentery which could leave them quite light-headed, there was the constant humiliation of having to perform the most intimate acts under the eyes of their guards, the constant self-disgust at never being actually clean. The fact that all the other prisoners were enduring the same lack of privacy and washing facilities did not make their own situation any better. Constance even dreamed of cutting off all her hair – always her greatest pride – because she was sure it was now a nest of nits, but she had no scissors.

At least they were being given a guided tour of Burma. When they reached the river, they were made to board a ferry to cross to Prome. Here there was more evidence of recent fighting, but this was a place of which the guards were proud. "Big battle here," announced the lieutenant who had taken command of the party, and who spoke English after a fashion. "British get beat, and run for life. Ha ha ha!"

"Ha ha ha!" Constance agreed, because he was addressing her. Indeed he was very interested in her, which was disturbing; she gathered he had paid a visit to England before the war and had found English women most attractive. Not that any sensible man could possibly find her attractive at that moment, Constance reckoned.

She was more worried about Harry's possible fate. He had been with the Army in Rangoon, and this was the Army that had been defeated at Prome, according to the Japanese. "My husband might have been here," she ventured.

There was an instant stinging pain in her right buttock; she had committed the cardinal sin of addressing an officer without being granted permission to speak, and of not bowing. She clutched at the affected part, and received another blow across the knuckles which she thought might have broken a bone. But Lieutenant Ishikawa had given a command in his language and the beating ceased. "What your name?" he inquired.

Constance hated the tears that were rolling down her cheeks; they were at least as much in anger as in pain. "Constance Brand. My husband is Major Harry Brand."

"You want me find out if he dead?"

Constance raised her head. "Could you? Would you? Sir?"

He smiled. He was actually a good-looking young man, and he was even younger than herself, Constance reckoned. "I good to you, you good to me, eh? We friends."

"Oh!" Constance bit her lip. What a terrible mistake! But she didn't dare risk making an enemy of him. "If . . . if you can find out about my husband."

"I find out. You go doctor."

"Eh?" But she did desperately want to see a doctor. "May my friend go too?"

Ishikawa looked at Susan, who was as usual standing silently, head drooping, gazing at the ground. "She crazy, so my people say."

"She is extremely depressed," Constance explained. "Your people raped her. Several times."

Ishikawa considered this, and Constance held her

breath; what she had just said could easily earn her a flogging. Then he said, "She go doctor too."

Constance held Susan's arm to escort her to the makeshift surgery. Here there were several other women, mostly Burmese, but one or two were Indians and some were more Mongoloid; she supposed they might be Chinese. They were all in various stages of nudity, being examined by a Japanese doctor, who was assisted by two male nurses. Constance and Susan had to wait several moments before he beckoned them over, the guard who had escorted them having muttered in his ear. "You strip," the doctor said, in English.

"My feet . . ."

"Strip, woman! I must look."

I'm sure you must, Constance thought. She took off her clothes, terribly aware of the guard staring at her. And the other women, too. And even more of not having bathed in a week. "The trouble is my feet . . ." she ventured.

"Sit," he commanded. There was only a table available; Constance sat on this, her legs stretched out in front of her. He fondled her toes and she winced with discomfort. "Feet not good. You no use walking," he pointed out unnecessarily. "Stand!"

So much for that, she thought, as she obeyed. The doctor walked round her; like most of his compatriots, his head only just came above her shoulder. But he did the conventional things, tapped various parts of her back across his fingers, held his stethoscope to her breasts. Constance began to get her breathing under control again, only to lose it again when he said "Bend." He indicated that she should bend forward from the waist, over the table. Jesus! she thought. But she had to obey, and felt his hands pulling her buttocks apart and then probing between. Presumably the guard was still watching. And the other women. He slapped, her,

130

lightly. "You good comfort girl," he said. "But the feet, not so good."

Constance gathered that she could straighten. "Comfort girl?" she asked.

He grinned. "You make men comfort, eh?"

Oh, my God, she thought; he is talking about an army whore! That simply couldn't be! She gazed at the doorway where Lieutenant Ishikawa stood, and instinctively reached for her clothes; for some reason, being naked in front of him was far more embarrassing than being naked in front of the rest. But her instincts told her to stand absolutely still.

The Lieutenant looked her up and down, then asked a question, in Japanese. The doctor replied at some length. Ishikawa came closer. "He say you very fit, except for feet. He say feet a problem." He grinned. "He say best to shoot you."

Constance licked her lips even as her stomach seemed to fill with air. But surely he was joking. "Just like that?" she asked.

"I tell him you go truck," Ishikawa said. Constance gave a great gasp of relief. "Then feet get better," Ishikawa pointed out.

Constance licked her lips. "Where will I go in this truck? To be a . . . a comfort girl?"

"You go camp," he said. "All white women go camp." She gave another great sigh of relief. "Now I tell you," Ishikawa went on, "Nobody name Brand among dead. Maybe dead in jungle. Maybe alive."

"Yes," Constance said. "Oh, yes."

"You no think I good to you?" the Lieutenant asked, again looking her up and down.

Constance bit her lip. "Yes," she said. "You have been very good to me."

"Then you dress," he told her. Constance was happy to obey. The doctor was now turning his attention to

131

Susan, who had more to offer, in a purely physical sense. She was submitting, as she always did, as if she were a zombie. "Now you come with me," Ishikawa said.

"I thought white women went to camps, and were not comfort girls," Constance protested.

Ishikawa grinned again. "You comfort me only, Mrs Brand. Otherwise I have you shot. Doctor has recommended this."

Sex with a Japanese officer as opposed to rape was not an ordeal Constance had really expected to have to undergo, certainly after her miraculous escape on the beach. And in a purely physical sense, she did not suppose it would count as rape – at least not as Susan had experienced it. She had merely been invited to bed, and told that if she did not comply she would be shot. As she lay naked in Ishikawa's arms she wondered how it would sound in court. She could not prove his threat. But he might be condemned simply because he was the conqueror, and she the conquered. For the time being. Because she had to believe the tide would turn, just as she had to believe that Harry had indeed survived, and would one day ride to her rescue like a knight in shining armour. But would he wish to do so, knowing she had been had by a Japanese?

The actual being had was less of an ordeal than she had feared. To begin with, it had involved the life-saving experience of a bath, and a Japanese bath at that, even if she had had to share the huge, vertical tub with her captor, and submit to his caresses. But to be clean again – even if only momentarily. As for what came after . . . like so many English women she had been brought up to believe that Orientals somehow used women in ways too disgusting to be contemplated. Constance's own sexual experience had been very limited. As she had told Susan, she had only ever known her husband, and then in strictly limited doses. Even their escape from Singapore, which she still looked upon as a belated honeymoon, had been with a husband who had begun by being severely wounded, and even at the end of their voyage had neither been inclined nor able to do much more than lie on his back. That, not being exactly the missionary position as she understood it, had been sufficiently daring. What was truly unacceptable was not so much the actual sex than that it should be happening to *her*, Constance Brand, and that she was not having hysterics.

Ishikawa wanted her sitting in his lap, facing him, while he rose into her. This in itself was less alarming that she had supposed, for he was not very well endowed, and she could not help but imagine what Harry might be like in such a posture. But it certainly left his hands able to roam with a freedom she had never previously known. It had been the most exhausting experience of her life. She dared not admit that it might have been the most sexually exhilarating as well. "You no speak of this," Ishikawa had admonished when he was finally finished with her.

She gathered from his comment that he had been transgressing Japanese military law. But in any event, there had been no one to tell, save Susan. And that hadn't been necessary. Susan had known immediately what had happened, and had appeared almost relieved. "Join the club," she had said. From that moment she had shrugged off much of her depression, and their friendship had grown.

And they had indeed had a guided tour of Burma. From Prome they had been driven north, past the burned-out oilfields of Yenangyaung – where Susan had, in turn, attempted to gain some news of her husband,

133

without success – to the ancient capital of Mandalay, hardly less burned out, but still dominated by the still unrepaired Ava Bridge south of the city, and the hardly less impressive, and relatively undamaged, Fort Dufferin, within the city itself. Everywhere there was the evidence of British defeat and disaster; in many places unburied bodies rotted beside the road, in the midst of burned-out tanks and trucks. Neither Constance nor Susan could stop themselves from making further discreet inquiries about their husbands, but they learned nothing. "Did you love George very much?" Constance asked.

Susan snorted. "I didn't love him at all. Oh, he cut a fine figure when home on leave in England. That's when we married. He swept me off my feet. For God's sake, I was only a secretary in the company, and when an executive asks you out to dinner you don't say no."

"But it turned out badly? Did he ill-treat you?"

"Good lord, no! He was just a bore. And once he'd had a go at me, he discovered that he preferred his brown popsies. I suppose he found me even more of a bore. But the fact was he had some problems."

"At least there were no children," Constance said, having missed Susan's embarrassment.

"I know. You must be so miserable about your son." Susan squeezed her hand. "You'll get back to him one of these days. And that handsome husband of yours."

Constance kept forgetting that Susan had actually met Harry. Had got to know him surprisingly well, in fact, during the retreat from Rangoon.

The railway from Mandalay leading north-east to Lashio had been repaired, and the women had been put on this for the journey to the camp, which was apparently some miles east of Lashio. By now their numbers had grown considerably, and to the already large Indian contingent were now added another dozen Englishwomen, mainly planters' wives who had not been able to escape. Like Constance and Susan, they did not know what had happened to their husbands and in several cases were still fairly hysterical about it. In addition, they, hardly less than the Indian women, took an immediate psychological dislike to Constance and Susan, the one for being an army wife in an army which had failed to do its job, and the other as being a different sort, a wealthy transient as the wife of an oil executive. Constance and Susan did not care whether they were liked or not. They had each other. Spending every moment of every day in each other's company, they insensibly began to share their every thought and every memory. At least, Constance did. She even told Susan about her remarkable courtship, about that unforgettable night in the Ritz just after Harry had been commissioned, about her pregnancy. And about the Frenchwoman, Nicole.

Susan listened with absorbed interest. And confided a good deal in return, principally about the very up-market lifestyle she had enjoyed in Yenangyaung and on her visits to either Mandalay or Rangoon, and about her house in Yenangyaung, which she had furnished to her ideal of perfection – and which was now presumably lost forever: even supposing the British ever did get back, it would be a looted shell. But Constance always felt she was holding something back, keeping a part of herself shut away. She did not resent that, but it was not in her nature to be reticent, and she found it odd in others. When things happened, they could not then be changed and it was better to bring them out, especially as they were sharing so much else.

The journey itself would have been splendid in any other circumstances, for the railway wound its way into the hills, using passes between mountain tops well over 3,000 ft. And always there was the jungle, close to either side. When the train stopped they could gawk at the monkeys and macaws that came quite close to peer at the humans, while they often saw big snakes, and could hear tigers roaring in the distance.

But every time the train stopped the women were forced to disembark and perform their necessaries under the eyes of their guards, something neither Constance nor Susan could ever get used to. And always there was the threat of physical violence, as on the day one of the Indian women cracked and attempted to run away into the forest. One of the guards brought her down with a single shot.

Despite tragedies like that, the journey in retrospect seemed a holiday when compared with the camp beyond Lashio. Lashio itself was a busy – and presumably pleasant, in normal circumstances – hill town, where elephants laboured to bring in the timber the Japanese wanted, and the Burmese were discovering that the Japanese could be just as severe masters as the British. It was quite a modern place in the process of being turned into a fortress to protect the railhead, as it was also where the Burma Road began, and was therefore of some importance, but the camp was a wasteland of barbed wire and leaking huts; the women had barely arrived when the monsoon started, and for the next six months they were seldom dry for more than a few minutes at a time. Their clothes were in rags and started to rot, and the food began to deteriorate. Fortunately, the guards were almost friendly. They were relieved at not having to take part in any fighting, and they were delighted to have the care of a hundred women, of almost every variety of race and colour. They were mostly older men than the soldiers who had attacked Constance and Susan on the beach or marched them into Taungup, and while they delighted in prying into every aspect of their victims' lives, Constance reckoned their interest was more curiosity than sexual intent. And to their great relief, the Commandant issued them with cloth to make themselves *longyis* to cover their nakedness.

But they were prisoners, for all the reasonable treatment; they were at the beck and call of little yellow men, they were beaten if they did not bow to the correct level or committed anything the Japanese considered improper behaviour, and they slowly dwindled in strength as the year drifted by. To remember the past, the great days of British power, was to go mad. Constance could not even risk allowing herself to think of Mark, or she would have collapsed in unstoppable tears. By the time the rain stopped, in December, they hardly cared.

Until this so very strange February day, when they were being offered proper food. It was not meat that Constance would have considered giving to her dog in England, but it was at least meat. Constance and Susan had never taken part in the scrum for food that usually obtained at meal times. They were anxious to preserve at least a little dignity, and there was always something left. But today, the sight of the meat stew drove them forward to take their part in the jostling and pushing, reaching out their bowls to be filled, while Matsumara, standing beside the servers, beamed at them. Then Susan was pushed from behind, and stumbled forward, cannoning into the sergeant himself. Everyone froze, except Susan, who hastily picked herself up, and cowered against Constance, trembling: she knew what happened to anyone who inadvertently touched a Japanese.

"Oh, God!" Constance whispered. Since leaving Prome they had carefully stayed out of trouble, keeping to themselves, obeying every command like puppets on a string, bowing as low as was necessary, clinging only to their essential selves amidst the continual humiliation. Even so they had not totally avoided the odd cut from a rubber wand. None of the white women had as yet been flogged. But none of the white women had as yet committed such a crime.

But Matsumara merely smiled, and his men went on dishing out the stew. "Woman is clumsy," he remarked in English.

Constance could not believe their luck. Susan was sitting beside her, eating her food; she had not been dragged off to be suspended naked between the uprights and beaten, as everyone had expected. "Something must be happening," Susan said. Then she looked up. "Oh, Lord! Here he comes."

Matsumara was walking slowly down the line of seated women. "Ladies will wash, when food is finished," he said. "Ladies should wish to be clean. Ladies will wash." He paused to smile again at Susan.

They discovered the reason for his solicitude and the good food that afternoon, when the Commandant entered the compound, accompanied by two men and two women, Europeans, wearing clean, well-cut clothes such as the prisoners could scarcely remember ever having owned. Constance and Susan hastily straightened their *longyis* and drew their fingers through their hair. One of the Red Cross representatives came up to them. "May I ask your name?" The woman addressed Constance. She had a slight accent, and was very blonde; Constance supposed she was either Swiss or Swedish.

"Constance Brand."

The woman looked down the list she carried, and made a little tick with her pencil. "Your husband is an officer in the British Army."

"Is?" Constance almost shouted. "You mean he's alive?"

"Oh, indeed! He is on the staff."

"Does he know I am here?"

"No. But I will inform him, if you wish."

"Oh, please!" Constance could have hugged her.

"And you?"

"Susan Davies. My husband was with the oil company. Do you know of him?"

"Yes. He is in a camp in South Burma."

"Oh! You mean he didn't get out?"

"No. I'm sorry. But he is alive. Now tell me," the woman said briskly, "both of you, are you well treated?"

They looked round; Matsumara was within earshot. "As well as we can expect, I suppose," Constance said, trying to look the woman straight in the eye, trying to convey some of the terror in which they lived. But the woman was writing busily.

"I have seen the food with which you are fed. Is this satisfactory?"

Constance opened her mouth, but Susan touched her arm. Matsumara had moved a step closer. "The food is satisfactory," Susan said.

"It looked very good," the woman remarked. "And you are in good health?"

"Can you not see that we are?" Constance asked, baldly. Surely the woman could see that they both were underweight?

"That is very good. Now, I am sure you have messages for your husbands. If you will give them to me I will endeavour to see that they are delivered."

"Just tell Harry that I love him, and look forward to seeing him again, soon." Constance said. The woman gave a wintry smile. And Constance looked past her, at one of the other women in the party. She could not

139

believe her eyes, felt a sensation of having been kicked in the stomach which made her physically sick. "That woman!" she said.

The Red Cross representative turned her head. "Madame Debras?"

"Madame Debras? Her name is Marion Shafter."

"No, no, Mrs Brand. She is a Swiss lady on our team."

"I tell you, she's English," Constance insisted. "And a traitor. She was a spy for the Japanese, in Singapore."

"You really are mistaken, Mrs Brand," the woman said. "And it is very unwise of you to make foolish accusations like that."

Constance stared at Marion Shafter. She had only met the woman once, when she had gone to see her, at Marion Shafter's request, in Changi gaol just before the Japanese invasion. Marion had been in gaol because Harry had denounced her as a spy, and she had wanted her revenge by denouncing him in turn – to his wife. That in the process of discovering the truth about her he had slept with her had been the last straw as far as Constance was concerned, the end of her marriage. But that was before their remarkable escape. Now, if she had forgiven Harry, she had certainly not forgiven the woman. And it was certainly her. She could not possibly be mistaken.

Marion Shafter turned from the person she had been speaking to and looked across the compound at her . . . and smiled.

When the Red Cross party had left, the women were lined up again, to be addressed by the Commandant. "I leave you, now," he said. "I go fight the British. When I see you again, the war is done, eh? Japan will have conquered."

None of them felt like arguing with that prognosis.

140

But a ripple of unease went through their ranks; Captain Hessai had been the best they could possibly have hoped for, a professional soldier who lived by the book and the rules of bushido. He was quite capable of punishing transgressors with the utmost severity, as he had demonstrated on more than one occasion in the past, but he was also absolutely fair in his punishments, and he had shown no interest in the sex of his prisoners, nor allowed his men to do so. "Probably because he's bent as a new pin," Susan had suggested.

Constance had agreed with her; she had read that homosexuality was rife in the Japanese Army – where of course it would never be tolerated in the British – but had assumed that this was pure propaganda, put out to increase the belief that homosexuals lacked any military virtues: presumably the men who had written these books had not been sufficiently well educated to have heard of Epaminondas and his Theban brothers, who in 371 B.C. had wiped even the Greek hoplites of Sparta off the face of the battlefield. But now she could only hope that Hessai's replacement would be similarly disinterested in women.

She was, in any event, still too perturbed by the reappearance of Marion Shafter, riding as high as ever, while she was stuck in this hellhole. Susan could tell she was upset. "Did you really know that woman?"

"She was in Singapore. An agent for the Japanese. She was up for trial when the city surrendered."

"I can see she wouldn't be one of your favourite people."

"You don't know the half of it! She had an affair with Harry. They'd had one before, as well. She was what one might call an old friend of his."

"Didn't he know she was on the other side?"

"Eventually. Then he turned her in. But that didn't really excuse what he did."

141

"I suppose not," Susan said thoughtfully. "But you forgave him."

"Oh . . . well, I suppose I love him."

"So you'd forgive him again?" Susan pressed.

"I don't think there is going to be an again," Constance said. "But I would just like to get at that woman's eyes before I die."

A few days later, just before Captain Hessai was due to leave, the women became aware that something was happening; the guards became extremely agitated, and there were conferences at the command house. One of the Burmese women spoke Japanese, and managed to overhear what was being said; her knowledge was hastily whispered through the camp. "The British have invaded Burma! They have crossed the Chindwin and are penetrating east!"

Constance and Susan gazed at each other in a mixture of delight and consternation . . . and disbelief, simply because they were afraid to believe it. "They are saying that this camp will be evacuated, that we are to be taken south," came the whisper.

"Do you believe that?" Constance asked.

"If the story of an invasion is true, then yes, I do," Susan said. "It is only just over two hundred miles from here to the Chindwin River."

"Oh, if it could be true!" Constance said. "And we could be left here."

The women became as restless as the guards, especially when Hessai departed before his successor had arrived. For the moment the camp was left in the charge of Sergeant Matsumara, who was the most agitated of all. "Are we going to leave, Honourable Sergeant?" one of the Englishwomen asked. Her name was Helen Eastman, and she was a confident, attractively middle-aged woman.

"Leave? Leave for where? Leave for what?"

"Well . . . that is what we heard."

"How you hear that?" Matsumara demanded.

It did not seem to occur to Helen Eastman that she might be pushing her luck. "There is a rumour . . ."

"Rumour!" Matsumara shouted. "We have no rumour here. You start this rumour? You suffer." He snapped an order at his men and before Helen could speak again she was seized and marched to the uprights.

"No!" she shouted. "You cannot do this! I am not Indian! I am English!"

That claim to better than normal treatment seemed to enrage Matsumara more. He went with his men, while the other Englishwomen insensibly moved closer together, seeking the comfort of numbers. "We must do something," Constance muttered.

"Do you want to find yourself standing where she is?" Susan whispered back.

Helen had been placed between the uprights, and her wrists, one to each secured above her head. She could stand, but she was quite helpless. Matsumara stood behind her, dug his fingers into the top of her *longyi*, and jerked downwards. The entire garnment collapsed and lay around her ankles. She wore nothing underneath, and her pale flesh gleamed in the morning sunlight. Matsumara was shouting at his men, and was handed a bamboo cane. Constance closed her eyes and he swung it, and then opened them again as Helen's scream of agony and shame rang through the camp and into the forest. There was a huge weal across the white buttocks. And Matsumara was raising the cane again.

Then one of his men said something, and he lowered the cane to face the gate, where a command car was coming to a halt, having bounced down the track from Lashio. Matsumara snapped an order, and hurried to the gate, followed by his men. No one attempted to

143

take Helen down, and she continued to hang by her wrists, all the strength gone from her feet. "We must help her." Constance stepped forward.

Susan caught her arm. "Then you'll take her place! Please, Connie. There's no sense in it."

Constance bit her lip, but allowed herself to be pulled back into the ranks. The gate swung open and the car drove into the compound. The officer in the back stepped down, and Constance caught her breath. It was Ishikawa, now wearing the insignia of a captain.

He was exchanging words with Matsumara, while his servant carried his bags into the command house. Now he advanced to stand in front of Helen and look at her. She was standing again now, panting, tears rolling down her cheeks. Ishikawa stepped past her, and surveyed the other prisoners. "This woman is being punished for breaking the rules," he announced. "You no break the rules, you no be punished. Remember this. Now, Sergeant say twelve strokes of the cane. I have doubled this. Now, twenty-four strokes. So you remember."

A ripple of horror ran through the women. Twenty-four strokes? Helen Eastman would hardly survive that. Her head came up. "Please . . .!"

"You talk," Ishikawa said, "and you have thirty-six strokes."

Constance took a deep breath, and stepped forward. "Honourable Captain." She bowed to the correct angle.

"Woman? You speak to me?" Constance straightened again, and stared at him. He stared back. Oh, my God, she thought. I am going to be caned. Then he grinned. "Mrs Brand? Ha ha! I am pleased."

"Thank you, honourable Captain." Another deep breath. "I wish to intercede for this woman."

"She friend of yours?"

"No. But she is guilty of no crime. All she did was ask a question."

"To ask question is against rules."

"I beg you for mercy. If she is caned she will get sick and die. I beg you, honourable Captain."

Ishikawa gazed at her for several seconds. Then he laughed again. "Ha ha!" He spoke to Matsumara, who looked furious, but commanded Helen to be taken down.

"I do this," Ishikawa said, "because I am your friend, Mrs Brand. You remember? You my friend, also. I send for you later."

Chapter 7

The End of a Dream

General Wavell himself conducted the investiture. It was a grand occasion, with a guard of honour and a band. A crowd of notables and their wives, bright with coloured frocks and saris, hummed and rustled, pointing out their relatives or acquaintances. The war, leeches and snakes, rain and mosquitoes, mud and filth, seemed very far away. Harry wore clean khaki, his bush hat set firmly on his head and tightly strapped beneath his chin, his boots and belts polished to a high sheen; a sword hung at his side in a leather scabbard.

"For conduct in the best traditions of the British Army, in that, although severely wounded, you fought to the last bullet on the beach at Dunkirk, with total disregard for your own life, thus enabling many men to escape the enemy." Wavell pinned the white-purple-white ribbon of the Military Cross on Harry's left breast, shook hands, stepped back, and saluted, as did Harry. Then he stepped forward again. "For conduct in the best traditions of the British Army, in that, in the recent reconnaissance in force into Burma, having completed your objective, you led your column to safety, fighting several rearguard actions with the enemy in conditions of extreme danger and difficulty." Again the Field Marshal shook hands. "Do you know," he said, "this is the first time I have ever presented a medal and bar to the same officer at the same time. Your father will be proud of you, Brand."

Harry's comrades were jubilant, none more so than Wingate himself. "This beggar Slim wants to seduce you back into the regulars," he remarked. "But I have told him I need you." He still wore the beard he had grown in the jungle months before, whereas Harry had shaved his off. "Because we'll be going back, soon enough. And this time you are going to be on my staff,"

But first, a week's leave, in Delhi. Harry took the opportunity to go down to Agra and stand in wonder before the Taj Mahal, the uttermost monument of one man's love for his wife. He had no such monument, save a son he had hardly known. He also spent some time badgering the local Red Cross to discover if there was any news of Constance, but there was none. Save the certainty that all Arakan had been overrun, in conditions of the utmost horror and brutality. Therefore, presumably, that was that. He wrote his mother with the news that while he had survived, Constance had not. "*Perhaps you may prefer not to break it to the boy, as yet,*" he wrote. In any event, Mark was only three years old; he would hardly understand, even if he could remember either his mother or his father.

It was that afternoon that he was summoned to the telephone in the mess. "I wanted to congratulate you on your success," the woman said.

"Who is this speaking, please?" The voice was vaguely familiar.

"Anne Chisholm. I don't suppose you remember me,"

"Anne . . .? Good Lord! Where are you?"

"I'm in Delhi. On leave."

"Why, so am I. There's a coincidence."

"Well," she said. "Perhaps we could have a drink together."

"Why not dinner?"

"That would be very nice."

*   *   *

147

He hardly recognised her when she entered the restaurant. She wore the uniform of an army nursing sister, she had put on weight, her auburn hair was in a tight bun, and there was no mud! "You've improved too," she remarked. "From the last time we met. Mind you, the stubble suited you."

"On the banks of the Chindwin. My dear woman, you're a treat." He held her hand, and she pulled him forward for a kiss.

"I gather yours is continuing to be an exciting war," she said. "I was at the investiture."

"I wish I'd known." He summoned gins and tonics. "And yours?"

"They keep me busy." She raised her glass. "Well, here's to victory. May it come sooner than later."

"Amen." He could not stop staring at her, as she was obviously aware, because she flushed. "I do apologise," he said.

"Don't. I'm looking at you too. It's a funny old business." She toyed with her glass. "Is there any news of your wife?"

"I'm afraid not. I have a feeling she's dead."

"You say that very casually."

"How else am I supposed to say it? With tears in my eyes?"

"I should think she'd appreciate that. Wherever she is."

"I've shed all the tears I have. Anyway . . . ours was an odd marriage."

"Ah!" she said. "So . . .?" she looked at him.

"Oh, yes, please!"

"I think I'm entitled to ask for a why."

"I find you a most attractive woman." He grinned. "I did from the start, even under all the mud. Now I would say I am entitled to ask the same thing."

"And I would make the same reply." She finished

148

her drink. "Now I think we should eat. Or we're not going to."

As Harry couldn't take her to the mess, Anne took him to her hotel. It wasn't very late, the place was crowded with people coming and going, but there were so many uniforms, male and female, nobody seemed to notice them at all. "I haven't actually seen a house detective," she said, as they climbed the stairs together.

Her bedroom was on the third floor, and the corridor was deserted. When they were in the room, she locked the door. "I suppose we should keep our voices down as this is a single room." she said, taking off her cap and releasing her hair, and thereby moving from attractive to compulsive. "Would you believe that I have never done this sort of thing before? I mean, don't get me wrong: I'm not a virgin. It's just that before . . ."

"You've always been to him." He took her in his arms and kissed her. "Don't let's talk any more."

She understood his mood, which had to be at least partly created by her questions about his wife. But she kissed him again, and moved away from him to undress, facing him. He did the same, and they gazed at each other. He supposed there was some contrast, for where he was still underweight from his exertions in Operation Longcloth, and was therefore somewhat gaunt when stripped, she was plump, but most attractively so. He took her in his arms again, to touch her breasts while her belly and pubes were pressed against him, and kissed her while hugging her as tightly as he could.

"Oof!" she gasped, freeing herself. "Are you always like this, or do you need it very badly."

"I need it – you – very badly!"

They sat together on the bed, to kiss and stroke. She

had hard nipples and supple thighs. But he . . . "Um," she commented, looking down.

"It's a problem which has nothing to do with you."

"I would say it has everything to do with me. Certainly right this minute."

"Just let's relax. And maybe it'll happen."

She rolled him on his back and straddled him. "Do you want to talk about it?"

"No."

"But it's not permanent?" She was fishing.

He reached up to hold her breasts. "There's a theory that I need to hurt my partner to get aroused."

Anne shifted herself backwards on to his thighs, out of his reach. "I'm not into that."

"I didn't think you were. Would you like me to leave?"

"No," she said. "I would like you to stay, and sleep with me. Literally. And see what happens."

She lay down beside him, and he held her close. "And if nothing does?"

"We'll still have shared something, Harry."

The last of the Chindits had been withdrawn from the jungle in April, after the six weeks dictated by Wingate as the maximum he expected his men to stand such extreme conditions. Their exploits, when released to the press, had aroused tremendous enthusiasm. Here were British and Indian troops, for so long derided as being unable to meet the Japanese in the jungle with any hope of success, carrying the fight to the enemy, and apparently triumphing.

Harry knew that the bar to his MC was as much a result of that publicity – which Wingate felt was important to the future of his brainchild – and the consequent euphoria, as to any military prowess on his part; if His Majesty's Government had awarded an MC to every subordinate commander who had led his men to safety during the retreat from Burma they would have run out of the medals in very short order. Not that he wasn't proud of both his medals and the way he had earned them. On the beach at Dunkirk he had wielded a Bren gun until he had collapsed from loss of blood. On the most recent retreat from Burma he had wielded a rifle and bayonet on more than one occasion to bring down a screaming, blood-crazed enemy. And again he had been wounded, twice, this time superficially, but none the less painfully. And he had led his men to safety. It was an experience to remember with pride for the rest of his life. And he had struck a blow for Constance.

Congratulations poured in from all sides, from his mother and his sister, and even from his father: Sir George Brand was in London, working on plans for the invasion of Europe. But Harry knew – knowledge that was admitted by only a few senior officers – that for all the cheering the first Chindit expedition had been a military failure.

Operation Longcloth had cost over a thousand casualties, more than a third of the total force, and in return had accomplished very little, A few bridges blown – easily repaired – and a few Japanese regiments disrupted to chase the marauders, seemed very little reward for such heavy losses. Even more important, the evidences of the difficulty of the country taken with the Japanese strength on the ground, convinced Wavell that there was no hope of launching a successful invasion of Burma until considerably more men and materiel could be accumulated, and this simply could not be done before the next monsoon would put an end to campaigning for several months. So the long-awaited advance had to be postponed until the end of 1943, at the earliest, and with so much of the available men and equipment being required for the projected D-Day in Europe, even that was a doubtful prospect.

Actually, both Harry and the High Command were at once right and wrong. The British indeed would have needed more men than they had available to mount a successful invasion of Burma in the spring of 1943, but Wingate's raid had disturbed the enemy far more than was immediately apparent, with the result that the Japanese plans for invading India were postponed, also by a year, and this was to prove decisive. Throughout the remainder of 1943, therefore, both sides gathered strength. As the monsoon ended, the Japanese were further distracted by a Chinese invasion of North Burma, once again led by Stilwell, more than ever disgusted at what he considered British procrastination and incompetence, and desperation to re-open the Burma Road, the end of which Lashio, in north-eastern Burma, was in Japanese hands. For although American aircraft were now regularly flying over the Hump, as they called the Himalayas, carrying supplies to the beleaguered Chinese in Chungking, they really could not take in sufficient materiel for the maintenance of any sustained campaign, and the Chinese had suffered several severe defeats.

All this time the Americans were inching steadily forwards in the Pacific, and with the Australians gaining ground in New Guinea, and by the end of the year they were poised to attack New Britain and the great naval base of Rabaul. Yet despite these distractions, such intelligence as came out of Burma left no doubt that Field Marshal Count Terauchi, supreme commander of the Japanese forces in south-east Asia, was preparing for the invasion of India that had been Japan's ambition since the summer of 1942. To do this, it was said, he had accumulated an army of 100,000 veteran troops, under the command of General Mutaguchi Renya. Stopping such a force was going to be a desperate business, and before the end of the year Wingate was told to prepare another Chindit raid, this time with the definite objective of disrupting Japanese preparations.

Code-named Operation Thursday, this was to be an altogether more ambitious project than Longcloth. Wingate, promoted to Major General, was given no fewer than six brigades, collectively (and for means of deception) known as the 3rd Indian Division, but in fact retaining the designation of the Long Range Penetration Group and the nickname of Chindits. They were going to be split up into columns, as before, but it had been realised what a waste of time and energy, and health, had been caused by the earlier necessity to march to their objectives. This time they were not only to be supplied by air, but the main body was to be transported by air as well, flown in by the American Air Force to specially selected sites, and landed by glider. A strong supporting force would cross the Chindwin and join up with them later.

This was to be no hit-and-run raid. Wingate's orders were not only to disrupt the enemy's preparations on the largest possible scale, partly by cutting the road and railway from Mandalay to Myitkyina, but also to provide diversionary assistance to Stilwell's Chinese, still battling their way south, their initial goal the communications centre of Myitkyina. To do this Wingate had developed a new concept. He intended to establish a fortress, known as the Stronghold, in the heart of the jungle, upon which the columns could fall back and concentrate when they had completed their raids, and which could be constantly replenished and reinforced by air to withstand any Japanese onslaughts. "Nothing like it has ever been done before," he told his officers. "We are simply going to drop out of the sky behind the Japanese engaged with Stilwell, and establish ourselves in an impregnable position. The enemy will have to do something about us, and that will relieve the pressure on the Chinese."

"How do we get back, sir?" someone asked.

"We don't, this time." Wingate surveyed the faces in front of him; only a very small proportion of them were, like Harry, veterans of the earlier raid. "We wait for the rest of the Army to join us."

He then went on to expand his concept in one of his remarkable Orders of the Day:

OBJECT OF THE STRONGHOLD:
The Stronghold is a *machan* (Hindustani for platform) overlooking a kid tied up to entice the Japanese tiger.

The Stronghold is an asylum for Long Range Penetration Group wounded.

The Stronghold is a magazine for stores.

The Stronghold is a defended airstrip.

The Stronghold is an administrative centre of loyal inhabitants.

The Stronghold is an orbit round which columns of the Division circulate. It is suitably placed with reference to the main objective of the Division.

The Stronghold is a base for light planes operating with columns on the main objective.

The motto of the Stronghold is NO SURRENDER.

"Major Brand?" asked the voice on the telephone.

"Yes," Harry replied, cautiously. But it didn't sound like Anne Chisholm, and he hoped it was not, at this moment in his life.

"My name is Sonia Esterhazy," the voice said. "You do not know me, but I have news of your wife."

"Constance?" he shouted. "What news?"

"Your wife is in a Japanese prison camp, in Burma, Major."

"Burma? Constance?"

"The camp is situated about twenty miles east of the town of Lashio. I visited there with my colleagues from the Red Cross a few weeks ago."

"Good God! Is she all right?"

"I would hesitate to describe anyone in prison as all right, Major. But I can tell you that she is alive and well, and that she sends you her love."

Harry found that he was sitting down. Twenty miles east of Lashio, and he was about to return to Burma. "Can I send her a message?"

"You can give a message to your local Red Cross Office, and if it is at all possible it will be got to her."

After few pleasantries the woman hung up. Harry grabbed his map case and tore it open. Lashio . . . Lashio. But Lashio was itself 50 miles north-east of Mandalay, and Mandalay lay on the Irrawaddy. There was no way any of Wingate's columns could penetrate beyond the Irrawaddy with any prospect but annihilation. But Constance was alive and well. And he was going to get her back, eventually.

The training for the second invasion of Burma was every bit as tough as before, the fall-out was again heavy, and it was March before the Chindits were ready to move, perilously close to the onset of the monsoon. However, Wingate proposed to emulate Stilwell and ignore the weather. Harry had been confirmed in his rank, and as promised given a place on Wingate's staff. Since Operation Longcloth, the two men had become good friends, and Harry welcomed his appointment; as Wingate's adjutant he would be in the very heart of things. At the same time, he was sorry to have to part company, for the time being, with his friends from the previous expedition, such as Tom Keeton and Sergeant

Lenzing. They had done a good deal of campaigning together, and knew each other's worth. "We'll be waiting for you in the Stronghold," Keeton promised him.

As a member of the staff, Harry was present when, the day before they were due to fly, a news team brought in photographs of one of the principal "drop" areas, selected because aerial reconnaisance had indicated a considerable clearing in the forest, code-named Piccadilly, but which had been obstructed with logs of wood. Ironically, from Harry's point of view, it was the nearest of the chosen sites to the Irrawaddy itself.

There was an immediate high-level conference to determine whether the site had been deliberately blocked, which would suggest that the Japanese had prior information on the coming campaign, or if it was merely a stroke of bad luck. General Slim himself flew in to hear the views of the Chindit commanders. Naturally Wingate was all for going in, even if Piccadilly was useless as a landing area. And since he was supported by Brigadier Michael Calvert, another veteran of the first expedition, and who was to have commanded the Piccadilly landing as well as another known as Broadway, permission was given to go ahead. As it turned out, the Piccadilly landing area had not been blocked by the Japanese, but, totally coincidentally, by Burmese loggers. "Stop, start, stop, start, just like the last time," Wingate growled. "But now we're off."

There were inevitable mistakes and confusions, and one or two tragic errors, such as when gliders were put down in the midst of Japanese forces. But the Japanese were again taken completely by surprise. They had never actually worked out what was behind the first Chindit raid, or how many men had been involved. And once the United States Engineers, commanded by Lieutenant

Brockett, got to work with their bulldozers to create proper airstrips, the operation grew in intensity. Dakotas flew non-stop to and fro ferrying a total of 9,000 men and well over 1,000 mules. By 11 March the drops had been completed and Wingate could issue an Order of the Day telling his men that: "This is a moment to live in history!"

Once Operation Thursday was launched, Divisional Headquarters were moved forward to Imphal, a delightful spot in the Naga Hills near the Burmese border. Here Wingate had the operation more under his hand, as it were, and it was as well that he did, for after the initial success of getting the Chindits in, things did not go altogether according to plan. Calvert's men, deep in enemy territory, were meeting severe resistance; reports came in of old-fashioned bayonet charges and hand-to-hand fighting, even with swords. More serious were the problems encountered by the support column sent across the Chindwin on foot, commanded by Brigadier Bernard Fergusson, who, like Calvert and Harry, was a veteran of Op Longcloth. This powerful force, some 4,000 men, had as its target an area north of the railhead at Indaw, where the Stronghold was to be set up in accordance with Wingate's requirements: closely wooded and broken country, an area which could be cleared and levelled for use by the Dakotas, neighbouring friendly villages and an inexhaustible and uncontaminatable source of water. The chosen area was code-named Aberdeen, and it lay on high ground some distance to the east of the Chindwin valley.

The march got into trouble from the start. The country was horrendously difficult, and the weather already remarkably bad. In this sense, the British decision not to go into Burma in force until after the monsoon was justified. Progress, therefore, was slow. Wireless communications were also poor, and headquarters did

157

not always know the exact whereabouts of the various columns. Meanwhile news began to come in that the Japanese had been alerted and were reinforcing Indaw itself – known as Rail Indaw to differentiate it from another town called Indaw, and known as Oil-Indaw – which they could quite easily do by rail. This would put them in the heart of the Chindits' operations, rather than vice versa.

Being on the staff as opposed to in the field could be intensely frustrating, as Harry now discovered. Instead of being out there with a column and a definite objective, able to radio back to HQ for instructions, he found himself the recipient of such requests, often contradictory and backed up with insufficient information for him to give the General any coherent summary of what was happening. Wingate knew that Indaw had to be captured, and quickly, or the Japanese might bring sufficient force to bear to destroy the invaders before the Stronghold could be set up. He therefore ordered Fergusson, as soon as Aberdeen was secure, to advance on the railhead.

Then came more confusion. Fergusson assumed, with good reason, that Rail-Indaw had priority, and that he would be supported by all the Chindits in the area; this specifically meant 14 Brigade, commanded by Brigadier Ian Brodie, situated on Fergusson's left. But Wingate had already ordered Brodie to move south-west against the Japanese lines of communication – Indaw lay south-east. With messages racing back and forth, orders and counter-orders blistering the air, and the weather steadily deteriorating as rain teemed down accompanied by recurring thunderstorms, Wingate realised that his entire operation was in danger of foundering in one enormous snafu. "I'm going to have to go in myself and sort things out," he announced. Actually, like all his staff, he was itching to see action.

He selected those officers who were to go with him. To Harry's chagrin he was not among them. "You help Tulloch mind the shop, Harry," Wingate said. Brigadier Derek Tullock was his Chief of Staff. "Expect me back in about forty-eight hours."

Harry went outside and found the RAF weather officer, Flight Lieutenant Bonnor, and Lieutenant Hodges, the United States Air Force pilot who flew the Mitchell B-25 loaned to Wingate for his personal use. "When are you off?" Bonnor asked.

"I'm not off," Harry said bitterly. "I'm staying."

"Well, you could be the lucky one. It's eight oktas – total cloud cover – up there. You going to tell the old man about it, Lieutenant?"

Hodges surveyed the sky. "Reckon I'd better. Looks like I might not be able to find where he wants to set down." He went inside, and Bonnor and Harry took shelter beneath the porch of the headquarters building. Hodges returned ten minutes later. "He says go. These storms are local. I guess that's it. See you guys." He trudged away into the rain to find his machine and crew.

Wingate came out a moment later, followed by his staff. They were well wrapped up, and well armed, too. "I'll call you when we're down," the General told Harry. "Shouldn't be more than two or three hours." Harry saluted, and the little party disappeared into the rain.

Bonnor and Harry heard the Mitchell's engines roar into life, and watched the twin-engined machine taxi down to the end of the runway, then turn and take off. Within seconds of leaving the ground it had vanished into the low cloud, but they continued to hear it for several seconds before the sound died. Then it was just a matter of waiting for the General's call. Three hours passed without a summons. Harry went along to Communications, where he found Bonnor prowling up and down behind the operators. "Should've got down by now," the met man grumbled.

It was not until dusk that they received the message: the Mitchell had crashed on the side of a hill, and all on board were presumed dead.

Wingate's death meant the end of the Chindit operation, both in plan and in spirit. After some consideration, Slim chose as his successor Brigadier Lentaigne. Calvert might have been a preferable choice, as he understood Wingate's ideas better than the more orthodox Lentaigne, but Calvert did not suffer fools gladly, and the Chindits' new orders were to forget Thursday and link up with Stilwell's Chinese, who were still battling their way towards Myitkyina, determined to prove that it was possible to campaign successfully in the monsoon season. The Chindits were placed under the command of Stilwell, who had no concept of what Wingate had been trying to achieve. He regarded the Chindits as being an undisciplined mob, and even resented being given them. Thus he immediately turned them into ordinary line infantry, and a few months later the remnants were withdrawn for rest and recuperation in India, unhappy and exhausted.

All of this might have happened anyway, whether Wingate had lived or died, because only two days after Operation Thursday had commenced, on 7 March 1944, the Japanese invasion of India – Operation *U-Go* – began. This had been expected, in view of the large numbers of men known to have been accumulated in Burma, but not when the monsoon was about to commence, nor had British Intelligence properly estimated the strength of the Japanese concentration. Additionally, of course, part of the objective of Thursday had been to disrupt Japanese plans; this had not happened. Now, as before, the British-Indian Army was bedevilled by the speed and ferocity of the Japanese onslaught, which repeated all the familiar infiltration and terror tactics that had been so successful in Malaya.

More than any of Wingate's personal staff, Harry had been devastated by the General's death; no matter how unlikely the prospect of personal success, he had seen the expedition, with its approach so close to the Irrawaddy, as being a step towards the possible release of Constance. Now he seemed to be left looking at a brick wall: Lentaigne had his own people and his own ideas. Harry therefore wired Slim, and asked if there was still a place for him with the regulars. The reply came back promptly: *Report Richards at Kohima.*

This was rather disappointing. At that time Harry had no more idea than anyone else that the long-expected Japanese invasion had actually started. Kohima was nothing more than a frontier post some distance north of Imphal itself, and thus his new appointment sounded like a spell of garrison duty, the very last thing he wanted. He knew Colonel Hugh Richards, who had been in command of one of the early Chindit columns, and had been hastily pulled out when it had been discovered that he was 50, ten years older than the British Army allowed any officer to be when serving in the field. Harry had a high respect for the man's toughness of both mind and body, but in the circumstances it seemed obvious when Richards had been sent to command the Kohima garrison on 22 March it was because Slim did not anticipate any severe fighting in that area.

Harry arrived in Kohima on 31 March, having taken the train to Dimapur and been driven south-east from there. The road followed the border between India and Burma, and as it was the only good surface for miles it was of vital importance for the reinforcement and replenishment of the frontier positions south of the railhead at Dimapur, which was the main supply centre. Thus, when Harry's driver pointed out Kohima, Harry immediately realised that this little hill village might not be such a dead end after all: it could be of enormous strategic importance. It was an obvious natural stronghold, and whoever held it would control the supply road.

Richards was delighted to receive another Chindit officer as his Chief of Staff. The two men drank tea on the verandah of the Deputy-Commissioner's house – long abandoned by that individual – situated on a spur to the north of the village, high above the road which looped right round the little hill. Beyond and to every side, despite Kohima being several thousand feet above sea level, was very thick jungle indeed.

"I'll take you on a tour of inspection tomorrow morning," Richards said. "But I can tell you that we really have no more than garrison troops here: a battalion of the 1st Assam Regiment, a Nepalese State battalion, which frankly I don't rate very highly, and some platoons of the 3rd Assam Rifles. In all some 2,500 men, but only 1,500 are combatants. They're good chaps, but their name says it all as regards weapons: rifles and a few machine-guns. And of all of those, a good third are currently in hospital with various ailments." He brooded for a few moments. "We actually had a battalion of the West Yorks here last week, but they were ordered off again, to Dimapur."

"So what do you think of the situation?" Harry asked.

"From the reports I've been receiving, it seems clear that the Japs' main effort is going to be directed at Imphal, well south of us. This makes sense; if they can take Imphal, the plain to the west is all theirs. You could say, next stop Calcutta. However, they must know that Slim is expecting them and is prepared to defend Imphal to the last man. And it's possible that Mutaguchi may make it his business to cut Imphal off from Dimapur, and prevent men and materiel getting through to reinforce the garrison. If he decides to do that, then the obvious place for him to cut the road is right here,"

"I spotted that coming in," Harry agreed. "Put a few thousand well-supplied Japs on this hilltop and they could be a bloody nuisance."

They walked over the position the next day. From the south, the ground undulated gently upwards, while the road clung to the shallow valley, which accounted for the loop. South of the road was Detail Hill, immediately north of it was FSD Hill. At the bottom of the steeper slope up to the administration centre was a third potential strongpoint, marked as Kuki Piquet. Above this, and behind the Commissioner's bungalow and some other houses once occupied by British planters, was Garrison Hill, which was the dominating feature of the entire position. The whole hill was thickly wooded. "If I could lay my hands on some barbed wire I'd feel a lot better," Richards confessed. "But apparently there isn't any in Dimapur. So we must do the best with what we have. Garrison Hill provides us with a sort of keep if we are attacked in overwhelming force." He grinned. "We must hope it won't come to that."

But next day a message arrived from GHQ: *Elements identified in Japanese force moving north of Imphal make it possible entire Japanese 31st Division under Lt. Gen. Sato advancing in your direction. Estimated strength 15,000 men. Please advise dispositions.* Richards passed the paper to Harry without a word. "Holy Jesus Christ!" Harry commented.

Richards was already writing on his pad: *Require explicit orders and reinforcements.* The reply came back briskly: *Position must be held until relieved. No substantial troops available between Kohima and India save 161 Brigade under Brig. Warren. Am moving this back to you now. Good luck. Slim.*

"Well, that's good news at any rate" Richards remarked. "You and I will have to take a back seat when Warren gets here, Harry. I imagine he'll have some ideas of his own. But meanwhile we'll put ourselves in the best defensive posture we can." They placed the men themselves, and checked their weapons. They had no artillery, but they were at least armed with Bren guns, sighted to fire .303 rounds to a range of 2,000 yards, with a theoretical firing rate of 500 r.p.m. As the magazine only held 30 rounds, this remained theoretical. The Bren was a most efficient killing weapon, as Harry well knew, having used it with the Chindits, but he also realised that because of the jungle, the coming engagement would largely be close combat, and was inclined to put more faith in the proven rifle and bayonet.

The huge trees, thickly packed, and the tangled undergrowth which stretched away to the south, limited visibility to 50 yards. The Japanese, moving through the jungle, would have an unlimited view of the British position, and the opportunity to employ their favourite tactic of advancing almost up to their enemy before starting action. But 161 Brigade was coming to their aid. The odds – one brigade and Richards's motley command against a veteran Japanese division – would still be great, but it could only be a matter of at most 48 hours before their position became a really strong one.

* * *

164

The following day some Naga tribesmen arrived with the information that Japanese units were not very far away. "We need the earliest possible accurate information on the enemy's whereabouts and strength," Richards told his officers. "I want a reconnaissance to the south." Harry immediately volunteered; since Wingate's death he had been desperate to regain physical contact with the enemy. But Richards vetoed that. "You're on the staff," he pointed out.

A company of the Assam Rifles was sent out, with instructions to move cautiously south through the jungle, establish contact with the enemy, and then fall back with all speed; the Japanese were still thought to be several days away. When the patrol had left, the garrison waited, gazing anxiously up the road towards Dimapur, from which direction the brigade was expected.

That same afternoon they heard shots, and Richards put every man on the alert. It was dusk when the remnants of the reconnaissance company staggered in. "Japs," said their English lieutenant, Caldwell. "In considerable force."

"At less than a day's march?" Richards was astounded.

"All around, sir. Every bloody place." He had lost several men, and several more were wounded.

That meant the Japanese were advancing twice as fast as anyone had thought possible.

"Where the hell is that brigade?" Richards growled.

That night, shells began to fall in and around the village. "Those are 75s," Harry said.

"Against machine-guns," Richards said grimly.

For the moment the firing was inaccurate, but close enough to frighten inexperienced troops. Next morning Harry was greeted by a furious lieutenant colonel. "The beggars have run off!"

"What? Who have run off?"

"My Nepalese State Battalion. Can you believe it? I'm down to officers and NCOs." These at least reported to Richards.

"Poor devils," the CO commented. "They'll be cut to pieces in the bush. Never mind. Brigade will be here today." That very morning the 4th Battalion of the Royal West Kent Regiment arrived, some 500 men, together with the 20th Indian Mountain Battery. Richards and Harry saluted as the regulars marched in. "Now we have an army," Richards said. "With more to come."

But the West Kents' lieutenant colonel, Laverty, was not optimistic. "We had to fight our way in here," he told them. "The Japs are round to the north as well." But some India Sappers and Miners, with troops of the Rajputs and Punjabis had also got through.

Harry immediately got on the wireless to Brigade HQ. Brigadier Warren was aware of the situation, but could do nothing about it. "My orders have been changed. I am now instructed to remain here and prevent any incursion to the north of your position." he said. "Whatever happens, the enemy must not be allowed to reach the supply dumps at Dimapur. You must do the best with what you have. We shall maintain our position as close to you as possible, and if there is any sign of the enemy pulling back we shall come down to your relief. We will, in any event, give you all the artillery support we can, and you will be supplied as necessary by air. Report your situation hourly."

Richards stood on the verandah of the Commissioner's house, hands on hips. He was the senior officer present, and therefore retained his command, but instead of a fresh brigade and his own people, he now had just over 3,000 men, of whom only about half were actually fit for duty. "Right," he told them. "General Sato, who commands the Japanese 31st Division, will have about

15,000 effectives. I want you to remember this. We need to take about ten of his for every one of ours."

Harry was reminded of the orders for the defence of Singapore. The difference was that Richards meant what he said. As they had planned, Harry evacuated his staff from the Deputy Commissioner's bungalow and set up a command position on Garrison Hill, with an artillery emplacement in front of it. He then walked round the perimeter. The defenders had now been pulled back across the road, thus leaving a brief open space which the Japanese would have to cross to get at them; the Brens had been carefully sighted and enfiladed as far as possible for maximum fire power. Above the road, the bungalows provided some cover, but up the hill, between the bungalows and Garrison Hill, was a considerable open space occupied by, of all things, a tennis court with a little pavilion. "If it were a bit larger, we could develop it as an airstrip," Richards comemented. "As it is . . ." he gave orders for shelter trenches to be dug on either side of the court, and then with Harry worked out a fire plan for here as well.

"If they get this far, they'll be just about home and dry," Harry commented.

"Like hell they will," Richards said. "Home base is the top of that hill . . . with the last of our men dead. That includes you and me, Harry."

Chapter Eight

Kohima

Then it was simply a matter of waiting, as dusk fell
eerily. The artillery bombardment continued into the
night, but in a desultory fashion. The Japanese were
still unsure of the exact position and strength of the
garrison. It was uncanny to gaze at the wall of trees and
know that out there, perhaps only a few hundred yards
away, were 15,000 fanatical and totally merciless enemy
soldiers. That evening Harry was down in the Deputy
Commissioner's bungalow chatting with Captain Lawrie,
in command of that section of the defence, when they
heard the first call. "Hey, Johnnie, let me in. Let me in,
man, the Japs are right behind me."

"Douse that lamp!" Lawrie snapped, while a ripple
went through the men who hurriedly took their positions
at the windows.

Like Harry, the West Kents were jungle veterans, and
were not going to be taken in by any tricks. But the
nearest bungalow to the road was held by a company
of the Assam Rifles, and Harry hurried over there to
find Caldwell in a state of some agitation.

"It could be one of our chaps who went missing from
the patrol," he muttered. "Just finding his way back."

"It isn't," Harry told him. Caldwell gritted his teeth.
Even in the darkness the sweat could be seen gleaming
on his face, and his men were equally jumpy.

The calls continued well into the night, but the British
officers had their men well in hand and there were no
replies. The artillery fire also stopped, and the night

was hideously quiet save for the buzzing of cicadas and, incongruously, the occasional roar of a distant tiger, no doubt irritated by the presence of so many men. It was utterly dark, because although the night sky was clear the stars were invisible behind the branch and leaf canopy which overhung the houses.

Soon after midnight, when Harry was just considering returning back up the hill, hopefully for a few hours' sleep, a shot rang out. It was impossible to tell from where it had come or where the bullet went, but instantly several of the Indian troops returned fire. "Cease fire!" Harry snapped.

"But they're shooting at us!" Caldwell gasped.

"No, they're not. They're just shooting, hoping for a reply like that. Now they have you pin-pointed." He decided to stay with the frightened men, and used the field telephone to talk to Richards, and ask if some reinforcements could be sent down.

"Can't be done," the Colonel replied tersely. "They must hold with what they have. We have no idea where the main Jap onslaught will come, and I must keep my reserve companies of the West Kents to plug any gaps. But you have my permission to remain where you are and give Caldwell a hand."

"Thanks!" Harry said, a trifle sarcastically. He looked at his watch. It was past three. There had been several other isolated shots, but these had not been answered. The Japanese would literally be attacking in the dark if they came now. He reckoned, and hoped, that they would probe for a while longer.

When the attack came he was as surprised as everyone else. One moment the darkened bungalow was silent save for the odd cough or scrape of a boot on the floor, and the next it was a mass of screaming, shooting men, behind whom the inevitable bugles blasted the morning.

The Japanese had approached the perimeter in great

strength, and crossed the road, totally unseen by the defenders. "Fire!" Caldwell bellowed, and his men obeyed. But after only one volley the enemy were in their midst, thrusting with their bayonets and swinging their rifle butts. In the darkness it was next to impossible to tell friend from foe, and the once attractive little house became a pit of hell.

Harry fired his revolver at one yellow face, side-stepped a bayonet thrust, swung his left arm to catch the man a blow on the side of the head and tumble him over, and bumped into Caldwell just as the lieutenant fell, a bayonet in his chest. There was no time to discover whether he was dead or only wounded. Harry was being forced back by the weight of bodies, snarling, shrieking, wailing; he was surrounded by steel, and gagging on cordite fumes. And the Indian riflemen were already fleeing.

His revolver clicked on an empty chamber and he could do nothing more. He had been pushed into the kitchen by the melee. Desperately he hurled himself at the dilapidated glassless window and went straight through in a welter of splintering strips of wood, landing on his hands and knees. He regained his feet and ran for the trees, about 20 yards away. Something exploded in his face and he fell, more from exhaustion than from being hit. "Don't shoot," he gasped. "It's Harry Brand."

A moment later he had been pulled to safety by a sergeant of the West Kents, and panted for breath while the regulars fired volley after volley to accompany the chatter of their Brens.

The Japanese onslaught had also driven the West Kents from the Deputy Commissioner's bungalow, although there the retreat had been more orderly. The enemy now paused to consolidate and regroup, but the respite was only brief. With full daylight they surged on again, regardless of the casualties inflicted by the Bren guns and other small-arms fire, and the West Kents and Indians were forced back by sheer weight of numbers.

Harry had by then returned up the hill to report on the situation to Richards, who immediately ordered a counter-attack. This was successfully carried out, and fighting desperately the Japanese were tumbled back out of the bungalows. They were even occupying the iron cookhouse ovens as individual strongpoints, but these were easily dealt with by an enterprising NCO, who merely walked the length of the kitchen dropping a grenade into each oven in turn. The re-established perimeter could not be held, however, as the houses were now in flames and uninhabitable, so the British and Indians withdrew, while the Japanese lapped round to their positions and came up the hill to the tennis court. "They can't come any closer than that," Richards said. "From now on we die where we stand." It was 9 April.

The next week became an unending nightmare of noise and terror and sudden death. The Japanese attacked again and again, sometimes during the day, sometimes at night. They forced their way right up to the trenches, and the defenders were compelled to withdraw yet again, but only across the tennis court. The Japanese then occupied the trenches on the south side, so that the opposing forces faced each other at a distance of hardly 20 yards, utterly exhausted, yet both as filled with fight as ever. The defence was now assisted by the deadly accuracy of the Indian Mountain Battery, firing at close range and often delivering its barrage only a few feet in front of the British and Indian position. As promised, and having established local air superiority – a great and most welcome change from a year before –

171

the RAF regularly came over to drop supplies for the garrison, but with the perimeter now so shrunk it was inevitable that a lot of these should fall into Japanese hands. Thursday 13 April was the most disastrous day of the siege, which had already then been going on for five days: an entire drop drifted down the hillside into the Japanese positions. On this day too, the enemy artillery finally got the range of the Advanced Dressing Station, and began shelling it. There were well over a thousand men inside, and the slaughter was immense. The day became known as the 'Black 13th'.

The command post was shelled often enough, but the Japanese were not exactly sure where it was, and although from time to time some of their more fanatical men burst right through the British defensive line and charged up the hill, they were always killed by revolver fire from Richards and Harry and the wireless operators. Moving the wounded was impossible once the hospital had been hit; they lay where they fell, given what field dressing and analgesics were available.

Kohima turned into a vast cesspool, in which decaying flesh and human excreta vied as the most pungent and repulsive odours, in which men fought, with fists and feet as much as with rifle and bayonet, and moaned, and shrieked in agony, and prayed, and died.

It was a world which had entirely lost touch with reality. One became used to being filthy and unshaven, to killing again and again, to the stench and the sounds of men dying. Coherent thought was almost impossible; one lived by instinct and training. It was not possible to remember when last one had slept for more than a minute or so, had eaten a square meal, or drunk a glass of clean water. Yet obviously one was getting some rest, one was eating and drinking, or one would not have had the strength to fight.

Equally was it not possible to control such thoughts as were coherent, if disjointed. These ranged from the serious, such as Harry's wondering whether, if the defenders of Singapore had fought with this much guts and determination, the entire course of the war might not have been altered; to the sublime, such as almost hoping for death, for the relief it would bring from the filth and the pain – there was not a man of the garrison who had not been wounded at least once – and most of all from the total exhaustion.

To the erotic. Memories of Constance during that first affair, so brief and yet so splendid, when the entire world had seemed their oyster, to the even greater pleasure of holding Nicole d'Aubert naked in his arms, to the total mental collapse of holding her dead in his arms, what had been left of her, to wondering where Constance was now, what was happening to her, and if, as seemed inevitable she had been captured by the Japanese, there would be any pieces of her left for them to pick up? As if it mattered? Because the most overwhelming thought of all was that he *was* going to die, because they were all going to die, because the Japanese strength was simply too overwhelming to be resisted.

But Kohima held. Farther south Imphal was also holding, and the Japanese were sustaining enormous casualties. At last the firing died down, and the next attack did not come; the command post picked up a message from Brigade: the Japanese were retreating, and a relief column was on its way. Next morning, binoculars were turned to the north, and at last the convoy, spearheaded by tanks, could be seen moving along the road. The Japanese had been defeated at their attempted invasion of India.

173

WHEN YOU GO HOME
TELL THEM OF US AND SAY
FOR THEIR TOMORROW
WE GAVE OUR TODAY.

[Inscription on the memorial at Kohima.]

Although only vaguely aware of it at the time, Harry had actually been wounded in four places during the battle. None had seemed life-threatening, or had even interfered with his mobility, but two of them were beginning to fester by the time the relief arrived, and he was shot off to hospital in Dimapur. "My God!" commented the senior surgeon. "You could well lose that arm, Major."

"You have got to be joking," Harry told him. "I have a lot to do with that arm."

They managed to drain the wound, and then sewed up the 4 in-long gash, almost certainly caused by a Japanese bayonet, although he could not remember the exact incident. But he was clearly going to be out of action for several weeks. "Not that it matters," Slim said, visiting him. "The monsoon is here, and there's not going to be a lot happening for a few months,"

"And then, sir?"

Slim gave one of his infectious grins. "Then I would say it'll be our turn, don't you think? Don't worry, Harry. There'll be a place for you. When you're fit again."

Getting fit again meant a convalescent hospital in Delhi. Harry was supposed to be in bed for the next fortnight at least, but he managed to get a message to the Red Cross, and just about the time he was feeling totally well again, physically, and beginning to think of getting out of hospital, Sonia Esterhazy came to see him. "Well, Major Brand," she said. "Doing your best to get yourself killed, I see."

"It's an occupational hazard," he pointed out. "But I don't suppose you understand that."

"We Swiss like to think we are a little more intelligent than to fight wars. I'm afraid there is no news of your wife. All Burma has been closed to our representatives while this stupid offensive has been carried out."

"But now it's over . . .?"

"I doubt the Japanese look at the situation quite the same way as you do, Major. I should think the ban will continue while they either prepare for another offensive, or for an assault from the British."

"Don't you think there is a chance the camp may have been evacuated, moved somewhere farther away from the fighting zone?"

"We have no information on that. I hope you are well soon, Major."

He watched her walk away from him down the ward, a woman of vast superiority. Well, fuck her, he thought, and realised suddenly that he desperately felt like fucking someone. Supposing he could? "When last I was in Delhi," he told the nurse, "there was a nurse in this hospital named Anne Chisholm. She wouldn't still be around, would she?"

The nurse raised her eyebrows. "You wouldn't be referring to Staff Sister Chisholm? She is still 'around' as you put it, Major Brand."

"Well, would you tell her I'd like to see her?"

The nurse looked more surprised yet, at his audacity. But the next morning Anne appeared, very spruce in her white uniform and with her hair in its tight bun, accompanying the surgeon on his rounds. "Are you a sight for sore eyes!" Harry remarked.

175

"I can't say the same for you," she riposted. "Fortunately, my eyes aren't sore."

"I didn't know you two knew each other," the surgeon commented.

"Oh, we are old friends!" Anne assured him. "Major Brand got me out of Burma, a couple of years ago."

"Is that so?" He checked the various charts, and then inspected Harry himself; the wound had been on the inside of the right bicep, the entire arm having been torn open from just above the elbow to very nearly the armpit. The stitches had come out a couple of days previously. "I'm afraid you are going to carry that scar for life, Major."

"It's not a place that shows very often," Harry said.

"That's true. Well, I think you can desert us, now. But I am putting you down for another fortnight's convalescent leave." Harry looked at the window; it was raining. "You could try going up to Simla," the doctor suggested.

"That might be fun. If I had company," Harry said, gazing at Anne.

"Yes. Well, that's something you'll have to sort out for yourself," the surgeon said. "Good luck. Coming, Sister?"

"I think Major Brand wants to have a chat," Anne said, with utter composure. The doctor departed without comment.

"I suppose you think it would be a total waste of your time," Harry suggested.

"Wouldn't it?"

"Was the last time that frustrating?"

"Actually, no. You're an interesting subject."

"Who badly needs additional investigation! Actually, I'm feeling as randy as hell. I really thought it was the end. I guess we all did."

She considered him. "You don't suppose you may have greater responsibilities?"

"I know I do, Anne. But I'm not going to be able to honour those responsibilities for a long time, if ever. And I certainly am not going to be able to honour them as only half a man. Think of yourself as a sex therapist."

"I've often considered going into that branch," she admitted. "When does your leave start?"

"Right now, I would say."

"Too soon for me. I could make it the day after tomorrow. Friday. Just for the weekend."

"Then the day after tomorrow it shall be. But in the meantime, what about dinner tonight?"

She shook her head. "I think you should save yourself. And see about booking us an hotel room and train tickets. Anyway, I already have a date, tonight."

She had a quality of self-possession Constance had always lacked, save for that magic fortnight on the boat escaping from Singapore. Constance needed to be in total control properly to express herself, and the possibilities of that in this world were slim, for a woman, except in exceptional circumstances. On the escape, not only had he been wounded and dependent upon her for everything, but she had known how to sail small boats, and he hadn't. So, did that not obtain with Anne? She hadn't been half so sure of herself when she had been a rain- and mud-soaked refugee in the Burmese jungle. But in a hospital now . . .

Should he feel guilt? But he had been through this so often before. More than either of the women, *he* needed to be in control, and no man could be in control in his circumstances. He had been in total control when he and Constance had first got together. Which was undoubtedly why she had fallen for him. Women like Constance might

177

like to be on top, but if they could not, then they wanted to submit, utterly. He wondered if Anne was like that?

But that control had been before Dunkirk and his wounds, and Nicole. Since then it had been absent. And Constance, dear, sweet Constance, who had been unable to cope with the sudden, dramatic change in the man she had married, was now also absent. Living in hell. That was what he should feel guilty about. But there was nothing he could do about it, until the war was over. And to think about it would be to go mad. Equally, there was no guarantee they would both still be alive then, and would both be the same people. He had a feeling he would not be the same person. And if, from her point of view, he had undergone a complete character change once already, what would she make of yet another Jekyll and Hyde act? As for Constance herself . . .

Anne was on the platform five minutes before the train was due to depart, wearing a frock instead of her uniform, with her auburn hair loose beneath her picture hat and floating in the breeze. She looked totally unmilitary, and with her high heels might have stepped straight out of the pages of *The Tatler*. "You look good enough to eat," he told her.

A porter dealt with their bags – they had only one each – and they sat opposite each other as the train pulled away and into the hills. "What am I?" she asked. "Or – who am I?"

"Mrs Harry Brand. I thought that was best. I bought you this. Hope it fits." He held out the thin gold wedding-band.

She pulled off her glove and tried it. "Tight. I hope I can get it off again. What is your real name?"

"Harry Brand."

"Weren't you christened Henry?"

"As a matter of fact, no. I have an odd family."

"I've heard something of it. You go back in the Army for years and years and years."

"Blenheim. Actually, before Blenheim."

"I'm surprised that a race of soldiers managed to keep going, as a race, I mean."

"A surprising number of them managed to die in their beds."

"But still, all of them trotted off to Sandhurst or whatever the moment they left school!"

"Not all of them. Believe it or not, I wanted to be a doctor." He grinned. "You could've wound up working for me."

"I always was lucky! So, family pressure . . ."

"Nothing as conventional as that. I merely flunked out. I could't take the smell of blood."

"And you survived both Dunkirk and Kohima? With Singapore and Rangoon on the way? This weakness of yours must have been a while ago. Will you go back to medicine when this is over?"

"I don't think so. I'm stuck with this, now."

"And the family expects it! I'm glad I don't have to meet any of them."

"I would say that is highly unlikely. Unless . . . forget it."

"I really cannot contemplate stepping into another woman's shoes while she is still alive and kicking. Hopefully." She pulled a face. "But isn't that what I'm doing, even if temporarily? Talk about hypocrites!"

Harry had never been to Simla before, was immediately struck by the beauty of the place, and the climate. They had even left the rain behind. "It is an attractive spot, isn't it?" Anne asked. "One can understand why the

179

British, and the Mogols before them, made it their summer centre. Now the Burmese government-in-exile is situated here."

"You certainly wouldn't know there was a war on," he commented. "I didn't realise you had been here before."

"I've lived in India since I was a child."

"Ah! So you came up here with your parents."

"I didn't say that," she pointed out.

At least no one at the hotel seemed to recognise her.

It was dusk before they checked in and were shown to their room. "I think a cold shower is recommended before dinner," Anne said. As before, they undressed facing each other. He had forgotten how voluptuous she was. He took her in his arms for a long, deep kiss, and she put her hand down to hold him. "Do you think we're going to make it, this time?" she asked, leading him into the shower-stall.

"I hope so!"

"So do I. In fact, I am prepared to break the rule of a lifetime, if that's what's called for."

They held each other while the water bounced off their skins. "You serious?" he asked.

"It's a medical matter," she reminded him. "Therapy. You do me, first." He soaped her shoulders and breasts, then moved down to her pubes and buttocks and between her legs. "But maybe," she said, starting on him, "it won't be necessary." They dried each other, and she looked at her watch. "Half an hour to grub. Let's try some therapy. I have a theory about these things. You lie there and let me get on with it. When last did you get off?"

"God knows."

"Exactly. And then there's your hang-up. I would say there's just too much in there. What you need is sex on

180

a regular basis. In any event, you're not going to tell me that after so long you won't be ready and able in a matter of minutes after the first time. All I'm going to do is release the pressure. And play with my favourite toy."

"Brother, you needed that!" she said, hurrying to the bathroom to wipe her hands. "Actually, I think you need another shower."

He obeyed. Right that minute she was in command, and he was happy that it should be so. "You know something," she said as she dressed. "I'm relieved that lot didn't end up inside me. I didn't come up here to get pregnant! You don't have a problem with that as well, do you?"

"I have a son."

"Congratulations. Let's eat!"

"One whisky before dinner," Anne said. "Two glasses of wine with dinner. No brandy or port."

"Is this out of a book, or from experience?" Harry asked.

"It's common sense. A little alcohol is a very useful stimulant, as well as a relaxant of whatever inhibitions may be roaming around in there. But alcohol is also a sexual deterrant, physiologically if not psychologically. Intake has to be balanced very carefully, having regard to the size and capacity of the subject."

"I've never been a subject before."

"Don't kid yourself. We're all of us subjects, of some one or something, all of the time. Most of the time we don't even know it. You're lucky. You do." She also selected the menu for dinner. "No indigestion," she insisted.

"I'm not sure I actually feel replete," he remarked, as they sipped their coffees in the lounge.

"You can have a big breakfast. Right now you have to concentrate on me."

"So tell me about yourself. Warts and all. Have you always been a nurse?"

"Oh, yes."

"In India?"

"Nowhere else."

"And that was?"

"Since I was eighteen. Which, in case you didn't know, was fifteen years ago." She gazed at him, eyebrows arched.

"I didn't know, but I sort of guessed."

"And you are thirty. I know, because I looked up your vital statistics. Does that bother you?"

"No. But you weren't always an army nurse?"

"Oh, no! But having a white skin, and the right connections, and, I would like to think, being reasonably intelligent, I progressed rapidly, and became a sister at an obscenely early age. Perhaps it was a guilty conscience, but I volunteered when Stevens advertised for help at his rather remote clinic in the Naga Hills. That was in the summer of 1941. It was only for a year, according to the contract. The rest you know. After you had got me back here I was inducted into the Army. Seemed the natural thing to do. A woman can want her revenge as much as a man, you know."

"How come you never married?"

Anne shrugged. "Never had the time, I suppose."

"But?"

"Oh, indeed, but! Or I wouldn't be here now, would I? Thirty-three is a bit late to start losing your virginity, especially when you are not sure it's going to happen."

"Touché! Did you sleep with Stevens?"

"It's not polite to ask questions like that." She gave his hand another of her intimate squeezes. "It'll happen. Take my word for it. Shall we go up?"

182

*   *   *

"Tell me about your wife," she said, when they reached the bedroom. "Her name is Constance, and . . .?"

"She is tall, and slim, and very beautiful."

"And you have a sex problem?"

"It's a long story."

"Which you have to tell me, if I am going to help you. Undress."

He obeyed. "Actually, I can be brief. We had an affair. We were friends, and then one thing led to another, and we wound up in bed."

"And thus married? Are you asking me to believe that beneath that horny exterior you are actually a gentleman?" He was naked. "Just get on the bed and lie there," she told him.

"As a matter of fact, I did ask her to marry me," he said. "But she turned me down."

"Sensible girl." Anne started to undress herself, slowly and sensually, and although he knew what she looked like he found it entrancing. "So what changed her mind?"

"She found out she was pregnant."

"Real Maida Vale stuff." She hung her dress in the wardrobe, added her slip, stepped out of her shoes, faced him wearing only her knickers and stockings and suspender belt. "But that shouldn't have caused you to go dud. Or did you hate her because of what she'd done?"

"Constance isn't the sort of woman one hates. But . . ." he told her about Nicole, and Dunkirk. While he spoke she took off her brassiere, but remained standing at the foot of the bed, idly playing with her nipples. Only it wasn't idle, he knew; it was part of her ideas on therapy, and it was beginning to work.

"Tough," she said, when he told her of Nicole's death. "At last I can begin to understand your problem. So then you started to beat Constance up," she suggested.

183

"I told you, I never beat her up. Because . . ."

"She's not the sort of woman one beats up, either."

"The idea . . . well, there was a woman during the escape from Burma."

Anne raised her eyebrows. "I thought I was the woman during the escape from Burma."

"There was one before you."

"And you had the time to fight a war as well? I can see why you have the MC and bar. When next you get together with your beautiful wife, I suspect you are not going to need any therapy."

"Save that . . ." he sat up.

"Um," she agreed. "She'll have spent a couple of years in the hands of the Japanese. She'll be the one needing the therapy. Are you up to it?"

"I don't know. May I be perfectly frank?"

"In our situation, I can't see there is much point in being anything else."

"I don't know if I am going to *want* to, well . . ."

"One used wife." She came towards him. "You're not exactly unused yourself. Or are you one of those all-male men who say 'I can do what I like, but my wife, never!'"

"Would I be that unusual, if I were?"

"Not at all. Which is what is wrong with the world, from a woman's point of view. Or is it really because it's the idea that she has been used by little yellow men that bugs you?"

He bit his lip.

"That's a problem you are going to have to work out for yourself," she said. "It doesn't come under the heading of sexual therapy. It comes under the heading of manners and mores, guts and humanity, marriage and motherhood. And of course, love. Now, see what I've done with all this serious chat?"

"Yes," he agreed. "Looks like another quiet night."

"I didn't come up here to have a quiet night," she pointed out. "And I agree with what you said on the train, when you were trying to justify us being here at all. Your first step has got to be to get rid of all physical problems before you can hope to cope with your mental ones. So, I'll make a little bet with you. Ten rupees you can't get my knickers off if I don't want you to."

He frowned at her. The garment was about 6 in from his nose. "You have to be kidding!"

"Try me." He threw both arms round her thighs to bring her against him and dig his fingers into the elastic waistband. But before he could pull it down she had fallen forward, taking him with her, and at the same time rolling, so that she wound up on top of him. His hands had instinctively come up to defend himself, as she had given a very good impression of being about to hit him or scratch him, and she caught his wrists. He had never supposed she was a weak woman, but she was a good deal stronger than he had supposed. She grinned at him, her breath rushing into his face, which was in any event clouded with her hair. "I'm not going to hurt you," she said.

"*You* hurt *me*?" He exerted all his strength, and rolled her across the bed, so that he was on top. He freed his hands as he did so, but when he again reached for her thighs she was back at him, and he had to defend himself again. They lay against each other, wrestling, and she got one of her legs between his, smiling all the time. He pushed her knee down, and again grabbed at the silk.

This time there was no resistance; her kicking feet assisted him to get rid of the garment, and only then spreading her legs to allow his entry. "Well," she said when she got her breath back. "I think I may get a diploma to hang up."

He kissed her. "You are a dream."

Anne pushed him on to his back, rose on her elbow,

studied him for several seconds. "You won that bet," she said. "So let's have another bet, one I guarantee you're going to lose. I bet you a hundred pounds that your Constance is alive and well and just waiting to get back into your arms. And if you don't take her, then you lose double."

The arrival of new inmates always provoked a flurry of interest in the prison camp; the women went to the fence to see who was coming. They moved slowly, like people just awakened from a long sleep. In fact, most of them were half asleep all the time, their bodies worn down by emaciation and exhaustion; meals such as they had had just before the visit of the Red Cross were hardly even memories now. Even their *longyis* were in rags; their feet were bare and a mess of festering sores, as were their heads.

Several of them had died during the two and a half years they had been in this camp. Unless they were rescued soon, several more were going to die. But rescue seemed impossible. They had no news from the outside world, save of Japanese victories. They could only use what mental energy they still possessed to attempt to work things out for themselves. The fact that their rations had been halved might have been Japanese callousness; the fact that the guards' rations had also been cut indicated that all was not going quite so well as their captors pretended. But there was no suggestion that the British were making any serious effort to return to Burma. The rumour that had so nearly caused Helen Eastman to be flogged to death had apparently been nothing more than a rumour.

Constance often tried to get some information out of Ishikawa. She was in a privileged position. As the Commandant's mistress she was better fed, and better dressed, and generally in better health, than any of her companions. She knew she was hated by them for her advantages, as if she had had any choice in receiving those advantages, but she did use her superior strength and alertness to attempt to help the others as best she could.

And Susan remained a friend, especially as Constance from time to time managed to secrete items of food from Ishikawa's table, to be taken back to their hut and shared. Susan never asked any questions about what it was like, to belong to a man of another race who was also an enemy of her own people. Which was just as well, because Constance would not have known what to answer.

There was no acceptable answer. She could take refuge in the simple fact that she had had no choice. Ishikawa had always been gentle with her, but she had seen sufficient evidence that he could be harsh to those he regarded as his inferiors or his enemies, and when the two were combined, he could be positively cruel. Of course, she ranked as both an inferior and an enemy, but he was prepared to make an exception of her. What was unanswerable was that she went to him without a moment's hesitation, and with a good deal of anticipation. Again she could take refuge in the thought that by doing so she not only avoided ill-treatment, was allowed to bathe – indeed, he insisted upon it – and received enough additional rations to maintain her health at an acceptable level.

But the fact was that she also anticipated the sex. It had not been so in the beginning. The first time he had sent for her, as he had promised to do, she had been terrified, had taken refuge in the memory that he had had her in Prome, and it hadn't been all that bad. But the idea that she might be forced to endure him on a regular, permanent basis had been at once nauseating and frightening. She had stood before him, shivering and ashamed. She was Constance Lloyd. She came of a wealthy, successful family and she had married into another. That her marriage had turned out a disaster was irrelevant in that context. She was an Englishwoman, tall, strong and handsome, and proud. She stood several inches above this little runt who would make her his. And she was utterly in his power.

She had been surprised to discover that he actually valued her as a human being. In fact, he took enormous pride on being in possession of her. He took endless photographs of her, using a huge and very old-fashioned camera and tripod. Some of the photos were of her wearing her *longyi*, and with her hair carefully dressed; these, she gathered, were for his family. She did not suppose she could object to her likeness being admitted into the Ishikawa family home, even if she hadn't been his prisoner. But he also took what could best be described as art shots of her, naked and in the most provocative poses he could think of, and she had a terrible suspicion that these were not merely intended for his private album, but would be displayed to his fellow officers whenever he regained the comfort of a mess.

Those were masculine frailties, which she might have encountered in an Englishman. More remarkable was his desire to please her. This might take the form of little presents, and endless compliments, both of which were entirely acceptable. What was distressing was his determination that she should get the same amount of pleasure out of sex as he did. This was a concept wholly to be rejected, in the abstract. But it was not one that *could* be resisted, in practice. She would have to be totally lacking in sensation not to feel herself submitting to the caress of a man's hands, seeking out every sensual place in her body – most of which she had not previously known to exist. Certainly places where Harry had never sought to explore. Nor had Harry ever taken her sitting in his lap, or on her hands and knees. The first time Ishikawa had demanded that position of her she had nearly fainted with the fear that she was going to be sodomised. Instead it had been the most sensually satisfying experience she had ever known, as he had been able to hold her breasts while entering her, and had left her gasping with satiation long after he had climaxed.

Constance Lloyd, brought to the ultimate orgasm by an enemy of her race and her nation. Save that she was Constance Brand now. She kept forgetting that. Or was she? Could she, any longer, be Harry's wife, without confessing to him what had happened to her? And having done that, even less, could she? But Harry was a distant, dream-like memory. He had, apparently, been alive when the Red Cross had visited the camp, a year ago now. As the war continued, and the Japanese continued to be still winning, could he still be alive?

But as with the general situation, there was always the chance that any new arrivals might have news, and so she crowded against the fence with the other women, eager to see who had come to join them in their misery. And like the other women, to experience an almost painful pang of consternation as the prisoners disembarked from the truck. "Men!" someone whispered.

"Men!" The word ran along the line of women. Many of them instinctively tried to straighten their tattered clothing, to draw their fingers through their hair. Others just clung to the barbed wire and stared.

"Men," Susan muttered. "My God! Some of them are white!"

"And some are soldiers," Helen Eastman whispered.

Soldiers, Constance thought, staring at the khaki-clad figures being herded past them towards the new square of barbed wire that had been erected some distance away. Oh, my God! That simply could not be possible. She strained her eyes. But Harry was not among them; she would have recognised that huge figure anywhere. On the other hand . . . she caught her breath. One of the prisoners was John Wishart.

Part Three

The Martial Brood

'O goodly usage of those antique times,
In which the sword was servant unto right;
When not for malice and contentious crimes,
But all for praise, and proof of manly might,
The martial brood accustomed to fight:
Then honour was the meed of victory
And yet the vanquished had no despite.'

Edmund Spenser

Chapter Nine

The Road Back

"Lady not press so hard against the wire," Sergeant Matsumara said. Anyone else would have received his rubber truncheon across the buttocks. But Constance was the Commandant's lady. Yet every muscle in her body instinctively tensed as she turned. She had so wanted to attempt to signal John. But he had looked so exhausted, so beaten. Could a man like John Wishart ever be beaten? Matsumara was grinning at her. "Lady press too hard against the wire. Lady will mark skin, and maybe Captain no longer like Lady."

The implication was, maybe then Captain will give lady to me. The friendliness of the early days was quite gone now. It was gone now as regards all the women, which was the surest indication they had that the war was not going well for the Japanese. But it was particularly gone as regards her, because she had rescued Helen Eastman from the punishment he had decreed and was so enjoying carrying out, and even more because she had risen above his orbit – as long as she was the Captain's lady.

She joined Susan. "Did you see him." she asked.

"See who?"

"Dr Wishart. From Taungup."

"No. I didn't look very hard. Were there other men from Taungup?"

"I don't know. I didn't recognise any. But Wishart was the only one I knew at all."

"Of course. You were staying in his house."

Constance flushed. "It wasn't what you think. He was looking after me, that's all."

"So don't worry about what I think, because it doesn't matter. Do you think you'll be able to have a word with him? Maybe he knows what's happening out there."

"I thought of that. I'll surely try." She found it odd that Susan had not suggested that her own husband might be in the newly arrived group of prisoners, or that they might know what had happened to him. She reckoned Susan had written George Davies off in her mind. But she was desperate to make contact with the new arrivals, and not just to find out what was happening, out there, she knew. Just to hear John's voice, maybe touch him . . .

Neither of those things was going to be easy. The new camp had been erected half-a-mile away and this was for the men. At such a distance it was not even possible to recognise any of them. "Captain no want ladies having babies, eh," Matsumara remarked, standing at her shoulder.

"That would be a nuisance," she agreed. "Can you tell me why those men have been sent here?"

"No," he said. "You want know this, you ask Captain. He say you go him, now."

Constance raised her eyebrows. It was mid-morning, and Ishikawa had never before sent for her during the day; he was a stickler for form, even if he knew that everyone in the camp was aware that he did send for her, at night. She made sure her *longyi* was secure, and walked slowly across the compound, feeling the hostility in the gazes around her. She almost feared being rescued – because surely one day they would all be rescued – more than having to remain here forever; these women would probably tear her to pieces.

The gate was opened for her, and she crossed the outer compound and went up the three steps to the command hut; the sentry grinned and saluted. The door was open, and she entered the outer office. Usually when she came in here it was deserted, but today there were three men, one banging a typewriter, the other two busy with clerical work. They too grinned at her. The door to the inner office was also open, as was the door beyond, which led to the commandant's living quarters. Ishikawa sat behind his desk; he had watched her through the open doorways from the moment she came up the steps. "You know some of those men?" he inquired. "The new prisoners?"

Constance caught her breath. It was difficult to tell his mood. But she did know that he was a jealous man. "No," she said.

"Some of them are from Taungup. You were in Taungup."

"Only for a few days."

"But you know some of those men. Maybe just one."

"No," she said again. "I . . . I thought I might know someone. But I didn't."

"You lie to me?"

"No. No, I would not lie to you." She hated the flush she could feel gathering in her cheeks. She had never been able to lie.

"I make you say truth, you know," he pointed out, and opened a drawer in his desk. "You know this?" Constance drew a deep breath. He was holding a length of wire. "I put this between legs, and draw tight, and I cut you in two," he said. "When I move to and fro . . ." he demonstrated. "You bleed. You all cut up. You no longer have sex, eh? But only you know this. And me." He smiled. "And next man who wants you."

Constance was trying to get her breathing under control. "Then I would be no use to you either," she said, and wondered if she might have made a mistake.

His smile faded and he glared at her. "You think I not do this? Take off *longyi*." Constance glanced at the doorway. "Leave door," he said. "Maybe they need hold you." He was really going to do it. But he couldn't. She couldn't. Her entire body seemed to have congealed along with her brain. But the *longyi* had fallen to the floor. Ishikawa got up and came round the desk. "Spread legs," he commanded.

Constance moved her feet apart, She stared at the opposite wall, knowing that in a few seconds she would be screaming her heart out. They would hear her all over the camp. And they would smile; she would have got her come-uppance at last. She wondered if Susan would smile?

She felt his hands between her legs, then the touch of the wire. Oh, God, she thought. Oh, God! Oh, God! Oh God! She could feel her muscles tensing . . . and listened as a howling, screaming sound filled the morning. She was hardly aware that Ishikawa was no longer touching her, or even standing beside her; he had run outside, with his men, to stare at the aircraft which had swooped low over the camp. Cheering and waving, the women were gathered in the centre of the compound as the Hurricane gave a victory roll before zooming way again.

Several of the guards fired their rifles, but the plane was moving too quickly to be hit. To the west there were more planes. These were bombers, and the smoke columns rising above Lashio indicated that it had been their target. The Royal Air Force, over Central Burma? That was not a sight she had ever expected to see.

Ishikawa was jumping up and down in rage, but more at the behaviour of the prisoners than at the appearance of the planes in a sky that was suddenly empty of Japanese aircraft. "Whip them!" he bellowed. "Whip them all!" He pointed at Constance. "Whip her too."

*   *   *

"Welcome back, Harry." Slim held out his hand and Harry grasped the offered fingers.

"I gather congratulations are in order, sir."

Slim grinned. "Lieutenant General Sir William Slim. Never thought that day would come. But the Viceroy knighted Christison, Scoones and Stopford at the same time, you know. I'm not likely to get a swelled head. It's good to have you back. You're in time for the finish."

"Will it happen, sir?"

"It's about to. Everything is now moving in our favour. As you may have heard, the powers-that-be have at last realised we are here. So we have a new Supreme Commander, Lord Louis Mountbatten. He's not old enough for the post, and he hasn't the experience; he's been a destroyer captain most of the War. But he's a glamour boy, he's a member of the Royal Family, and he's been sent here to give this show a high profile; that means we should at last get what we need to finish the job. In fact, we are already getting it. We have obtained total air superiority over Burma, and our intelligence, as well as the aircraft observations, indicate that Mutaguchi's army has just about been destroyed. Mainly malaria and poor logistics, but we managed to kill a few. As did you, at Kohima. Now, again, as you may have heard, we have a new Army Commander, General Sir Oliver Leese. He's come to us, reluctantly, I can tell you, from Eighth Army and all its triumphs in the desert and Sicily and now Italy."

Harry could not help asking, "Shouldn't you have got the overall command, sir?"

Slim grinned. "I'm too junior for an enlarged theatre, Harry. But I still have Four and Thirty-Three Corps. All I've been relieved of is responsibility for Arakan. That suits me fine. My brief is the recapture of Upper Burma. So Fourteenth Army has been given the go ahead. And this time we mean to do the job. I should tell you that there has also been a change in Chinese arrangements. Stilwell has got the push back to the US; he was rude once too often to Chiang Kai-Shek, I reckon. Pity. I liked Vinegar Joe; he was a fighting soldier. Anyway, he has been replaced by Dan Sultan in the field, Wedemayer at Chungking. Not everybody's choice. But still, they're committed to pushing south and re-opening the Burma Road. Which has to help us. Now down to personalities. I don't suppose you've bothered to look at a gazette recently, but you are promoted half-colonel."

"Thank you, sir. But . . . that's a bit quick, isn't it?"

"You deserve it."

"Then again, thank you, sir. My command?"

Slim shook his head. "No regiment. Something more important." He grinned at the expression on Harry's face. "It's not on the staff, either, except in a manner of speaking. Intelligence. I am not at all happy with the intelligence I've been getting. When it comes to Ultra, we're still poor relations to Europe. But then, we've always been poor relations to Europe. Our other sources haven't been reliable either. Over the past year I have gained a strong impression that the Japanese know one hell of a lot more about what we are doing than we do of what they are doing. So you can say that there are a hell of a lot more Indians unhappy with our presence here in India than there are Burmese unhappy with the Japs in Burma, but the fact is there. I must have intelligence if I am going to get back into Burma.

"For instance, these reports that Mutaguchi's command has disintegrated. I've accepted those without question, because it's given me the necessary arguments to persuade Mountbatten that we can go back in with a chance of success. Now I have to be sure that Mutaguchi *is* on the run. You know the jungle, and you know the people. And you have experience of the Japanese. I want you to hand pick a company, fifty to a hundred men, two officers. You have carte blanche where you get them from; you know who are best in the jungle. But they have to be volunteers. You will accompany our spearhead, but once we are across the Chindwin in strength you will proceed wherever possible in advance of our main body. Your objective is information. However, you will remain in close contact with our main body, so that you may interrogate such prisoners as they take. Can you handle that?"

"Yes, sir."

"The Yanks have Merrill's Marauders, and we had the Chindits. Now we're going to have Brand's Scouts. Right?"

"Yes, *sir!*"

"Just remember, at all times, that your brief is information before engagement. Now get to it; we move out in a week. Is there any news of your wife?"

"Not for over a year now, sir. I'm assuming she's still in the camp east of Lashio, if it's still there. But the Japanese haven't allowed any Red Cross people in since before their offensive started."

Slim nodded. "The camp is still there; the RAF carried out a bombing raid on Lashio a week ago, and one of their escorting fighters reccied the prison camp. But Brand . . . you do understand that your wife, and the other prisoners, are liable to be moved as soon as the Japanese realise we mean business this time?"

"Yes, sir," Harry said. "We'll just have to get a move on."

The first person he contacted was Tom Keeton, who was delighted to volunteer for the intelligence unit. Through Keeton he was able to recruit Gurkhas, including his old friend Lenzing, now a sergeant major. His other officer was Clive Mearns, who had also served with the Chindits,

199

although in a different column to Harry's. Then there were 20 British troops, of whom 10 were radio experts; these were under the command of Sergeant Robbins. "Do we go in in disguise?" Keeton asked.

"Definitely not. We're a combat unit. However, the fact that we're in uniform is unlikely to do us much good if we're captured. So caution is the word we need to remember."

He gave them time off to collect their gear and say goodbye to their units. He himself went in search of Anne. She was back on duty, and therefore in the nurse's quarters, but he carried her off to an hotel for the night. "This has a faint whiff of farewell about it," she remarked.

"Could be," he agreed.

"You're not going home?"

"I have some unfinished business here, remember?"

"And about time," she smiled, kissing him. "I've been reading the news from Europe. They're virtually camped on the Rhine, waiting for the spring. And here we are, still behind the Chindwin, with the monsoon just over."

"So, as you say, I may be gone for a while, fairly soon."

"And after you come back?"

"I'm going looking for my wife, Anne. You know she's in Burma?"

"I know she was in Burma, yes."

"Latest information is that she still is." He grinned. "Don't you want to win your bet?"

"Did anyone ever tell you that you're a bastard?"

"So I'm a bastard. You're very important to me, Anne. You got me back into being a human being."

"But I've served my time, is that it?"

"Funny. I thought you of all people would under-stand."

She ruffled his hair. "I do understand. That doesn't

make it any the easier. I've fallen in love with you, you great oaf."

"Then I am a bastard."

"Not really. Just a man. You'll find your wife, Harry. And she'll find you. That's a cast-iron prophecy. Now, are we going to have sex, or not?"

It was about a month after the arrival of the men that Helen Eastman was taken ill. All the women in the camp suffered from dysentery more or less continuously; lack of good food and any proper sanitation accounted for that. And Helen Eastman was not a young woman. She had kept going only because of her indomitable spirit. When she was too weak to use the latrine trench she was clearly very sick; she had always been a stickler for niceties.

The women carried out a well-rehearsed drill. Cases of serious illness had to be reported to the Commandant. Then, some time afterwards, an army doctor would come out from Lashio and examine the victim. Sometimes, very occasionally, there would be a dose of medicine. More often there was a kick in the ribs and a command to get up and bow on pain of a caning. And sometimes the patient would be removed on a stretcher. Most of the women presumed Helen would be taken to hospital in Lashio and given proper treatment; Constance suspected that the sick were merely taken outside the camp and buried, possibly while still alive – none of them ever came back. But she kept that opinion to herself.

Helen's condition was reported to Sergeant Matsumara and thence to Captain Ishikawa, and the next day the Captain himself entered the camp. He was, as always nowadays, surrounded by several armed soldiers. Since he had lost his temper on the day the RAF pilot had buzzed the camp the antagonism between command

201

and captives had become so thick it could have been cut with a knife; the women could not forget the pain or the humiliation of being caned, one after the other.

By now, Helen's condition was much worse, and two other women who had slept near her were also affected, They had no control over their bowels, they were too weak to move, and they cried out for water all the time.

The atmosphere in Helen's hut was so foetid it was nigh unbearable. The Captain stood in the door of the hut, trying to hold his breath as he listened to the description of the symptoms, then he hurried for the gate, which was promptly closed and double-locked.

It was Constance who summoned the courage to go to the fence and protest. "Mrs Eastman needs help, Sergeant Matsumara," she said. "You must send for the doctor."

"You must help her," Matsumara said. "The doctor is too busy to come. Anyway, he cannot help you now. You must help yourselves."

"But what do you mean? Has she got the plague or something?"

"The plague," Matsumara said. "Yes, the plague. Mrs Eastman has cholera."

When Constance told them, the women stared at each other in appalled silence for several seconds. Then some screamed. Others just slumped to the ground in horror. That evening their food and the buckets of water were placed just inside the gate; no guard entered the camp.

"Connie," Susan said. "You have got to do something."

"Me?" Constance asked. "Why me?"

"Because you're the only one who can. You're the strongest one here. Ishikawa may have thrown you out, but you were still once his woman. He must have some spark of feeling left for you. If you don't do something, we're going to die. All of us. Don't you want to see Harry again?"

Constance knew she was just being bloody-minded. For too long she had kept to herself, sharing little even with Susan. It had been no wish of hers to become Ishikawa's mistress; to refuse him would have been impossible. And through him she had tried to mitigate the lot of the other prisoners as far as possible. Yet they considered her a collaborator. Someone had even talked about cutting off her hair. They had not dared attempt that; emaciated as she was, she was bigger and stronger than any two of them put together. But she knew that they all still hated her, would almost certainly denounce her as a collaborator when the war ended – supposing the British actually won. And the woman most likely to do the denouncing was Helen Eastman, self-appointed leader of the European contingent. Who was now mortally ill, and in her dying was threatening all of them.

Keeping to herself would not stop cholera running rampant in the crowded camp, and already the stench of approaching death was worse than the usual smell of the latrines. But she had no idea what to do about it. On the other hand . . . She went to the fence. "Sergeant Matsumara," she called. He came towards her, but remained several feet away. "Is there cholera in the men's camp?" she asked.

"Not yet, Lady."

"Well, listen, I think there may be a doctor in that camp." She still dared not give herself away. "They have come from Taungup, some of them. There was a doctor in Taungup. He may be in that camp."

"You think doctor come to you?" Matsumara asked. "To catch cholera? You crazy, Lady."

"I think he will come," Constance said. "You tell him,

203

Constance Brand is here, and he will come." She forced a smile. "You surely don't suppose he will get any of us pregnant, when we have cholera?"

"How he to help you?" Matsumara asked. "He has no medicine."

"I know," Constance said. "But he will know what we can do. You said we must help ourselves. He will help us to help ourselves. Otherwise we will all die." She wasn't sure that was a good point to make; the Japanese might be quite happy to see them all die of disease rather than maltreatment. On the other hand, as they did seem keen on keeping in with the International Red Cross, up to a point, they would obviously not want to have to explain how an entire camp of women had died of cholera; at the very least that would mean a loss of face.

In any event, Matsumara went off muttering to himself. Constance did not know if he reported her request to Ishikawa or acted on his own initiative, but that evening the gate swung in to admit John Wishart, and then was very sharply closed again.

The women stared at the apparition. Wishart wore a pair of trousers and a tattered shirt. He was barefoot, his beard was shaggy and long and now entirely white, as was his hair. But he was the first white man any of them had seen close to in more than two years. "You have cholera?" he asked.

"John?" Constance asked.

He gazed at her in consternation for some seconds. "Constance Brand," he muttered.

They both took a step forward, then stopped, within touching distance. "Can you help us?" she asked.

He continued to stare at her for several seconds, and she knew he must be thinking of all that she had suffered over the past three years. Then he said, "I will do what I can." He clapped his hands. "Listen to me, ladies." They gathered round him in a huge circle; Matsumara and the guards watched them from beyond the fence. "I'm appointing Mrs Brand my assistant," he told them, and grinned at them. "My staff nurse, right? But you are all going to be nurses, or at least medical assistants. Now, the first thing you must do is take all the women who have cholera from the huts and place them against the far fence."

"You mean we have to touch them?" someone asked.

"I'm afraid you must. Those women who have not yet contracted the disease but are too weak to assist must also form a group, against the other fence. They must be segregated. Now, everyone who is not ill and can move must get to work. I want all the huts emptied of every content, except for those where the disease is known to be present. Mrs Davies, you take five women and gather all the dried leaves and branches that you can find. You are going to make a bonfire. Mrs Brand, you seem to get on pretty well with that sergeant."

"In a manner of speaking."

"Well, I want you to obtain the loan of the largest cooking pot he has, and a box of matches."

Constance went to the fence, where Matsumara continued to watch with interest, and told him what the doctor needed. "He making fire?" Matsumara asked. "Maybe you all burn." But he sent one of his men for the cooking pot, and gave her a box of his own matches.

As soon as she returned, Wishart, who had himself been helping with the removal of the infected women, set fire to the stack of leaves and branches, This immediately ignited the diseased hut, which went up in a gush of flame and smoke, so much so that even Ishikawa came out of the command house to look at it – presumably, when the disease had been stamped out, Constance thought, he would punish them for destruction of government property.

Wishart left some of the women to keep an eye on the burning hut, armed with blankets to beat out the flames if they showed any sign of spreading. The others he set to digging a pit in the earth, and in this he built another fire. Over this he suspended the cooking pot, and emptied all the water containers into it. "No one is to drink any water unless it has been boiled," he told them.

Wishart had correctly gone about limiting the possible spread of the disease and taking the essential hygienic steps to protect the still-healthy women before doing anything else. Now he had to do what he could for the sick and dying. "Will you help me?" he asked Constance.

"If you'll tell me what to do."

He looked at Susan, who gulped. "The very idea makes me want to vomit."

He ignored her, knelt beside Helen Eastman. But she had started to eat her own tongue. There was nothing Wishart could do save prise her jaws apart with pieces of stick, lodge them between her teeth, and bind her wrists so that she could not tear them out in her agony. Then he looked at Constance. "Is she a friend of yours?"

"Not really. But I hate to see her this way. Is there nothing . . ."

"If you still have a God, pray to Him that she dies quickly."

Helen died an hour later. She was the first. "Shall I call the guards to bury her?" Constance asked.

"They won't touch her," Wishart said.

"Well, then, we'll have to do it. Where do you recommend?"

"Nowhere."

Constance's jaw sagged. "You can't mean just leave her there?"

"The body must be burned," Wishart told her. "All her clothes and effects must be burnt. Give me a hand." Between them they carried the emaciated body, head and arms drooping, to the still burning hut. "Do you wish to pray?" Wishart asked.

"Afterwards," Constance said. She knew she would not have the resolution to go through with it if she hesitated. They threw the body onto the fire, watched with gaping eyes and mouths by the other women.

Helen Eastman's body took a long time to be consumed, because they had no petrol, and soon it was joined by others. Cholera is a disease in which the internal organs literally rot while the victim is still alive. Constance had supposed that her experiences over the past three years had gone a long way towards off-setting the gentility of her upbringing, but nothing, in Singapore or Burma, or in the dreadful intimacy of this camp or the embraces of Ishikawa, had prepared her for anything like this, as the sick had to be tended and cleaned, their voracious thirst for water satisfied as much as possible, while the fire had to be kept going and the water boiled. While always, hanging in the air, there was the stench of excreta and death. She discovered an enormous admiration for John Wishart. She had admired him almost from the moment of their first meeting, but then he had been on his home ground, so to speak, in his own house with his faithful servants about him, his medicines and his radio, his books and his self-possession. Since then she did not know how much he had endured; it could hardly be less than her own experiences, even if the middle-class Anglo-Saxon in her revolted from the idea that he could also have been raped. She could tell from the marks on his body that he had been beaten often enough, and from the body itself that he had been existing on survival rations for some considerable time. The manner in which his hair and beard had turned white revealed that the mistreatment had entered his mind and soul. Yet now, faced with a challenge which could well be deadly, he never flinched, nor did he ever collapse from exhaustion. His energy and determination inspired her own, although there were occasions when she could hardly drag one limb in front of the other.

They hardly spoke, save about work to be done or the situation of one of the victims. When they slept, although it was often together, and they were always aware of each other's presence, something Constance, at least, always found very reassuring, they never touched. They were mutually aware of how filthy they were, that it was days since they had cleaned their teeth or brushed their hair; Constance's, indeed, was now a tangled black mat reaching past her thighs. One of the minor miracles of her experiences was that her hair had not turned as white as his. But then there came the morning she awoke with a start, realising that she had overslept, that the sun was high in the sky, and that Wishart was gone. She sat up, scooping hair from her face, looking left and right, and saw him walking towards her across the compound. "What's happened?" she asked.

He squatted beside her. "There were no new cases last night."

"But . . . does that mean . . .?"

"The epidemic is over. Which isn't to say it can't come back. You simply have to keep on boiling your water. I imagine even Matsumara understands that now. He'll let you gather materials for your fires. Or if he won't, Ishikawa will. He seems quite a sensible chap."

Constance bit her lip. He simply did not know. Wishart was grinning at her. "Do you realise that in three weeks time it'll be Christmas?"

"No," she said. "I have no idea of the date."

"Well, now you do. I'll be thinking of you."

"But . . . where are you going?"

"I'm afraid, much as I would like to, I no longer have any reason to be in this camp. I must report that this particular epidemic has run its course, and I think it would be best for all of us if I took the initiative about returning to the men's camp instead of waiting to be herded off."

"Oh," she said. "It's been so nice having you here."

"It's been good seeing you again, Constance, even if I can't say it's been fun." He stood up. "Stay healthy."

She caught his hand. "Do we have any hope, John?"

"One must always hope," he told her. "The Japs are definitely losing, now."

"Are you sure? How do you know?"

"Three reasons. One is the rumour we heard on our way here, that Mutaguchi's army tried to invade India and really came a cropper. The second is that the Japanese air force has been shot out of the sky, at least over Burma."

"Yes," she muttered. "We saw that."

"And the third, and probably most convincing of all, is that I'm here. I mean, all the men. Our camp was in Arakan. The British have been trying to get a foothold back in Arakan every dry season since 1942; that's the path back to Rangoon. Well, their earlier efforts didn't bother the Japs none. But suddenly a couple of months ago, they decided to move us. My guess is that their intelligence have found out that the Brits intend a big offensive this year."

"Gosh!" she said. "That would be tremendous."

"Do you have any news of your husband?"

She flushed. "Not for two years."

"Well, who knows, he may come storming up here like the Seventh Cavalry. Wouldn't that be great?"

"Oh, yes!"

They gazed at each other. "Trouble is," he said. "If the Brits get too close to Lashio, we'll certainly be moved."

"I don't think I could stand that. John . . . if we were to be moved, wouldn't there be a chance?"

"You do understand what would happen to you if you tried to escape and were caught? They'd tie you to a tree for bayonet practice, and from what I've seen they can take a long time killing you."

She licked her lips. "So? They're taking a long time killing me right here. But they're doing it."

He regarded her for several seconds. "If they decided to evacuate us," he said at last, "it would be because they have been beaten again. Their Burma army would be disintegrating. Conditions would be grim, for them and for us. But in those circumstances, there would also almost certainly be some breakdown in discipline. This might be very unfortunate for us. But it might just be that chance, too. You're quite sure you'd be prepared to risk it?"

"Yes," she said fiercely.

Another long consideration. "What about Mrs Davies?"

"That's up to her."

"But you mustn't discuss it with her. When the time comes, should it come, she will have to make up her mind then."

Constance nodded. "How will I know when the time has come?"

"Keep your eye on me. If I ever beckon you, come to me, regardless. Will you do that?"

"If I can."

"I'll only beckon you if it's practical. Well . . . you know, I suddenly feel that we might do it."

"Hope," Constance said. "What would we be without it?"

Chapter Ten

The Plan

On the morning of 3 December 1944, the British-Indian Army crossed the Chindwin. In accordance with his orders, Harry and his intelligence company had crossed two days earlier, and penetrated some distance into the bush. This was country he had traversed both coming out in 1942, and with the Chindits in 1943; he knew it as well as any British officer, except perhaps Keeton. Yet even he was surprised by the total absence of any Japanese forces. "Japanese gone," explained the head man in the first village they came to.

"Do you believe him, Sergeant Major?" Harry asked Lenzing, who was, as usual, interpreting.

"Well, sir," Lenzing replied. "There are none about."

Harry sent the required coded message back to Major General Rees, commanding 19 Indian Division, who was following him, and then pushed on. His business was to find out what the Japanese were up to.

It was the third day before Harry's Gurkha scouts returned to say that there were Japanese a few miles away. "Only a small force, Colonel," Lenzing said; he had commanded the patrol. "Maybe twenty men. They are eating their midday meal."

"Those we must have," Harry said. "And we want at least six of them alive. Tom, you take thirty men and sweep to the right. Clive, you do the same to the left. Sergeant Major, you'll lead me and the remainder straight at them. I want everyone in position in one hour." They checked their watches, "I will fire the first shot," Harry told them.

But after they had crept through the bush and the sergeant major indicated that he should peer through the tree-screen, Harry was taken aback to discover that their target was actually a Burmese village, and that the Japanese soldiers were in the midst of at least an equal number of civilians. Lenzing, of course, identified all Burmese as potential enemies, or at best collaborators. Now he waited for his colonel, for whom he had the highest respect, to give the signal for the attack.

There was at least sufficient time to think; Harry had to wait until he was sure Keeton and Mearns were in position. But he didn't see that he had any choice as to what the decision was going to be; his business was information, if possible without endangering the lives of his men. His experience of the Japanese left him in no doubt that to walk out to them, even with 30 men at his back, and with more coming in from either side, and call upon them to surrender, would involve a shoot-out in which some of his own people would be killed – and the civilians would be at risk. To go in shooting meant that the civilians would still be at risk, but his men stood a better chance of survival.

He looked at his watch. "Ten minutes, Sergeant Major," he said. "Remind your men that it is the Japanese we are after. They are not to kill any Burmese unless they are fired upon."

Lenzing grinned, and loosened his kukri.

Harry studied his watch, and listened to the sound of ringing. He raised his head to peer at the Japanese again, and the saffron-clad monk who was moving around them, tinkling his little bell. "By God!" he remarked.

"It is the same man, sir," Lenzing agreed,

"Who is now a pal of the Japs. He we must have also, Sergeant Major. Alive."

"Yes, sir."

Harry watched the second-hand ticking round its last minute, drew a deep breath and ran forward, firing his rifle as he did so. The Gurkhas cheered and came behind him, while Keeton and Mearns led their men forward at the same time. The Japanese were taken entirely by surprise. They leapt to their feet and reached for their weapons, but more than half of them had fallen in the first volley. The Burmese screamed and threw themselves to the ground or into the dubious shelter of their houses.

The battle was over within a minute, as the Gurkhas, with fixed bayonets reached their enemies. There were screams and shouts and oaths, blood spurted, and then suddenly there was hardly a sound at all, save for the gasping breaths of the victors and the moans of the wounded and dying. "Casualties?" Harry demanded.

"Three wounded," Keeton told him. "None seriously. In exchange for twelve Japanese dead, and nine wounded. We have four prisoners, and five got away."

"And the Burmese?"

"I'm afraid they suffered three dead and four wounded."

"Shit! Very well, Tom. Prepare a burial detail and have it done. Have Cowley see to the wounded." He stood above the Japanese prisoners, who squatted in a row, their wrists bound behind their backs. "Anyone speak English?" There was no response. "Sergeant Major Lenzing!" There was no response to that, either. "Where is the Sergeant Major," Harry asked Sergeant Narine.

"He went into the bush following the priest, sir."

"Damn!" Harry muttered. He had told Lenzing he wanted Ba Pau alive, but not at the expense of Lenzing dead, or even wounded.

But a few minutes later Lenzing returned, marching

the priest at the end of his bayonet. Ba Pau had lost his bell. "Does he remember me?" Harry asked.

Lenzing grinned. "Oh, yes, Colonel. He remembers you. And me."

"Well, tell him I want information. Ask him why there are no substantial Japanese forces in this area, and where they are actually concentrated."

Lenzing spoke to Ba Pau, who retorted vehemently and angrily. "He says he is a man of God, who knows nothing of Japanese troop movements, Colonel. He says it is a violation of the laws of heaven for him to be treated like this."

Harry considered. The Burmese civilians were still weeping and wailing over their dead, but they were also keeping an eye on the proceedings. It would not do the British cause any good further to antagonise them by ill-treating a monk. On the other hand, he was only going to get information out of the Japanese by ill-treating them. He had not come to a decision when there was an agonised scream. He spun round, instinctively drawing his revolver, and watched Sergeant Cowley slumping across the body of the man whose wound he had been dressing, stabbed in the side by the wounded man's bayonet.

Harry ran forward, but Cowley's assistant, Private Gooding, had already shot the Japanese at close range. "Jesus!" Mearns said.

"They just don't know how to give up." Keeton knelt beside Cowley, but the sergeant was dead. "I reckon we should shoot the whole bloody lot of them."

"Just take away everything that could possibly be used as a weapon," Harry told them, knowing he was very close to a mutiny. To have suffered not a single serious casualty in the fight, and now to lose a man like Cowley to an assassin, even if it had been the sergeant's own carelessness in not making sure the wounded man

215

was unarmed. He turned back to Ba Pau, who was on his knees, gabbling. "What the devil is the matter with him?"

Lenzing gave one of his disarming grins. "I have told him, now we shoot everybody, Colonel."

"And he believes you?"

"Oh, yes, Colonel! It is what the Japanese would do."

"So ask him where General Kawabe's main force is."

Lenzing asked and listened. "He says, Colonel, first, that General Kawabe has been sacked. It is General Kimura now."

"Right. Then give me General Kimura's dispositions. How many divisions has he got?"

Lenzing translated. "The General has ten divisions, sir."

Harry calculated. Ten divisions, if they were at full strength and with the requisite number of back-up and communications troops, sounded like well over 200,000 men! And Mutaguchi's army was supposed to have been destroyed! "Where are these divisions situated?"

"Ba Pau says there are three in the north, facing the Chinese, three in the south, covering Arakan, and four north of Mandalay."

"He says there are four divisions covering Mandalay? And all we have seen is a single patrol?"

"Ba Pau says that General Kimura has determined to hold Mandalay above anywhere else, because of its rail and road communications. Thus his main force is concentrated around Shwebo, north of the city. He does not intend to commit it piecemeal here in the jungle. With the weather now dry and the plain hard, he intends to counter-attack out of Shwebo, with all of his armour, the moment Fourteenth Army debouches onto the plain; he estimates that Fourteenth Army will then be at the

216

end of its line of communications, while he will have Mandalay and ample logistical support immediately in his rear. Farther south, Japanese units will stand on the defensive until the battle in the north has been fought. General Kimura does not believe General Slim can move sufficient force to advance on Rangoon until Mandalay has been taken, because there are no roads suitable for heavy vehicles west of the Irrawaddy, and if he is prevented from taking Mandalay, the British advance will be held up, at least until the monsoon, which will give General Kimura the time to build up his forces."

"All very logical," Harry commented, remembering the difficulty of getting the remains of the Army out of Burma in 1942 – after most of their heavy weapons had been abandoned. "Right. And thank you, Sergeant Major."

"What am I to do with this fellow, sir?"

"I think we will have to treat him as a prisoner of war. We can't turn him loose to hurry back to Shwebo and tell Kimura we know of his dispositions."

Lenzing informed Ba Pau that he was a prisoner, and the monk, regaining his nerve as he realised he was not to be shot, protested strongly. "He says this is not legal, Colonel," Lenzing said.

"Tell him the choice is up to him," Harry said. "Either he is a prisoner, illegally, at least until our people have taken Mandalay, or he can be shot, even more illegally, in which case what happens at Mandalay won't interest him."

Harry called through to 19th Division and gave them the gist of what he had learned. Almost immediately the command came back for him to report to headquarters. "You'll have to hang on here, Tom," he told Keeton. "I shouldn't be very long. Don't forget to keep a sharp lookout, and fall back in good time should any sizeable Japanese force approach you. I'm afraid you'll have to keep the prisoners here for the time being."

Keeton nodded. "And the Burmese?"

Harry grinned. "Make friends with them."

'Pete' Rees was a small man with a somewhat sad face. His had been an uneven war, which, as regards field command, had begun in North Africa, where he had fallen foul of General Gott over the dispositions made for the defence of Tobruk. The result was that he had been shunted to India, as had another ex-North African commander, Messervy, where, both being of the attacking class of general – as opposed to the slow but sure methods of Gott's successor, Montgomery – they found Slim and Leese far more congenial; Leese had, of course, also served in North Africa under Montgomery, and men like Rees and Messervy were exactly what Slim was looking for, in view of the sort of campaign he knew lay ahead – while Leese was not about to harness his brilliant subordinate. "Is this information reliable?" the General inquired.

"I believe so, sir," Harry said.

Rees nodded. "I've contacted Army HQ, and the old man wants a meeting. We're to fly down this afternoon."

Slim's HQ was in fact close behind 19th Division, and Harry found himself in the midst of a group that included every high-ranking officer in IV and XXXIII Corps. "Good work, Brand!" Slim said. "Now I wish you to repeat, word for word, what this Buddhist monk told you."

Harry obliged, reading from his notebook. "Well, gentlemen, there you have it," Slim said when he had finished. "I am going to assume that the information

218

Colonel Brand has secured is accurate; it always has been in the past. So . . ." he gestured at one of his staff officers, who immediately unrolled a huge map of Burma on the table, while Slim beckoned the officers to gather round.

"Brand estimates that Kimura commands a quarter of a million men," Slim said. "Of which, according to Brand, the vast majority are waiting north of Mandalay for a climactic battle. This is somewhat more than we have previously been led to expect, and Kimura apparently reckons that we are obliged to fight on his terms because of our transport difficulties. And, of course, he is absolutely right, as things stand at the moment. However, it seems to me that, knowing his dispositions, we might just be able to do a little counter-planning of our own. The important thing is not to let him realise that we do know what he is about.

"Now, Fifteen Corps is already advancing into Arakan, its objective Akyab. That is not of course any longer under my direct command, and I don't propose to interfere with it; Brand's information suggests that they will meet with negligible opposition. Once they have Akyab, they will prepare an amphibious assault on Rangoon. Kimura will no doubt rub his hands with glee; he has enough down there to hold them. However, he will also be pleased because the main thrust of our army will appear to be entirely as he wishes it to be: out of the jungle and on to the plain, first stop Shwebo. Pete, your Division will spearhead this advance. You will be supplied by air. My headquarters will be right behind you, and you will transmit back to that headquarters at least once a day, occasionally using clear as if concerned with the situation. We want to be quite sure the Japanese know what we are about. Understood?"

"Yes, sir," Rees said, a trifle uncertainly; around him there was some shuffling of feet.

"However," Slim went on, "you must also bear in mind that there will actually not be a lot behind you. Including me." More shuffling of feet. "Second Division will advance on your right, but I propose to move Thirty-Three Corps, and the two remaining divisions of Four Corps, *south* of Mandalay. Now there can be no doubt that Kimura will anticipate an enveloping movement of some sort, but he appears to be certain that we cannot attempt such a manoeuvre in time to beat the monsoon. This is where we must outfox him." He turned to Major General Hasted, the chief engineer officer of 14th Army. "I need a motor road from here to Pakokku, Bill. That's just over a hundred miles. Of pretty rough country," he added.

Hasted stroked his chin as he surveyed the map. "Six weeks," he said.

"You can lay a road, capable of taking all the tanks and mechanised transport we are going to need, over a distance of a hundred-plus miles of mountain and jungle, at two and a half miles a day?"

Hasted nodded. "Are we allowed to inquire how you mean to do this?" someone asked.

"Bitress," Hasted said, briefly.

"Say again?"

"Bitress," the engineer repeated. "It's the wire-mesh stuff the Americans have been using to create instant airstrips. It comes in rolls. Obviously the surface needs some preparation, and we will have to fell the trees in our way, but once you have the surface, it just unfolds. If it can take B-29s, it can take our trucks and tanks."

There was a moment's silence. Then Slim said. "Then go to it. Forty-two days. Our objective will be Pakokku, a hundred miles below the city, where there is a practicable ford over the Irrawaddy. I shall accompany the main body, with my actual headquarters staff, and force that river crossing, while hopefully convincing Kimura that

I am still up here with Thirty-Three Corps. Now, gentlemen, once we are across the river, Thirty-Three Corps will swing north and attack Mandalay from the south. Again, Kimura will have made some provision for such an eventuality. However, the remaining two divisions of Four Corps will not turn north, but continue to the east, their objective Meiktila. Once we have Meiktila, far more than Mandalay, we will have cut Burma in two, and more important, we will have cut all the practicable rail and road routes out of Burma.

"So you see, we shall do exactly what Kimura wishes, attack Mandalay before doing anything else, but in a somewhat different fashion to how he expects it, and the end result will, hopefully, be that he is entirely cut off from Siam and any reinforcements."

The officers burst into spontaneous applause. The plan was so utterly simple, as are all good plans in warfare. "Now, it will be obvious," Slim went on, when the room was again quiet, "that the essence of this operation is speed. Once Kimura understands what we are doing, he will redisposition his forces. Therefore he must not know what we are doing until the main body is already across the river. Now, gentlemen, I can tell you that Sultan and his Chinese are about to resume their advance in the north. This will not only commit Kimura's three northern divisions to stopping them, but will be a further indication that we intend an orthodox frontal attack from the north and west. But there is another reason for speed: the monsoon. We have got to be in Mandalay by the end of March, or our chances of getting down to Rangoon before the monsoon and, thus, this year, are going to be jeopardised. Thank you, gentlemen. Your exact orders of march will be given you by the Chief-of-Staff. Pete, stay a moment. And you, Harry."

The general and the colonel waited as the other officers filed from the room. "I want you to understand just how

221

difficult a job I have given your Division to do," Slim said. "You must advance, leaving the enemy in no doubt that you are the spearhead of the army. But you don't have an army. Your advance must be rapid enough to force Kimura to keep his main body concentrated north of the city. It must *not* be so fast that you run into overwhelming enemy forces and get yourself cut up."

Rees nodded.

"Remember," Slim said, "you are not the force designated to take Mandalay" – he gave one of his grins – "Much as you would like to do so. Your business is to link up with Sultan's Chinese and maintain the pressure in the north."

"I understand, sir."

"Once that link-up is accomplished, you may move south as fast as the enemy permits, again without taking undue risks. Sultan's army will manoeuvre on your left, its primary objective the railhead at Lashio. It follows therefore that for you more than for the rest of us, intelligence will be at a premium. I am therefore giving you Brand's Scouts. Now, Harry, the same thing applies to you as to General Rees. You must probe as far as you can, and keep Kimura busy. But you must not let yourself be overrun at any stage. Understood?"

"Yes, sir."

"Very good. Then let's move it." He held out his hand to each of them in turn. "I'll meet you in Fort Dufferin. In eight weeks' time."

Rees and Harry were back at the Sittaung bridgehead by dawn. "Where are your people?" the General asked.

"In a village about twelve miles inland," Harry said.

"Right. Pick them up and move ahead. I'll be there tomorrow. With the Division."

Harry raised his eyebrows, and Rees smiled. "Speed

is the essence, eh, Harry? The only caveat is not to get chopped up. But we're going to take advantage of the Japanese plan as far as we can, and advance as fast as we can, until we make contact. I'm relying on you to inform us about that. As Bill Slim said, my aim in life is to to join up with NCAC. Once we have done that. Kimura can do what he likes. You with me?"

"Yes, *sir*."

Sergeant Narine was waiting, and Rees had also released a supply team to accompany them; they would bring the Japanese prisoners out. "Is there going to be a battle, sir?" the sergeant asked

"One of these days, Sergeant."

"Am I glad to see you!" Keeton said.

"Problems?"

"All the villagers have run off."

"To the Japanese?"

"I imagine so."

"Well, they can't tell them anything they don't already know: that Four Corps is advancing towards them. What about the prisoners?"

"One more of them has died." He grinned. "Quite naturally."

"Well, they are to be sent back with these chaps. And Ba Pau?"

"I'm afraid he's run off as well."

Harry reorganised his men, saw that everyone was fully replenished with food and ammunition, bade farewell to the supply captain, and resumed his advance. Immediately behind him was 19th Division; it lacked both artillery and motor transport, as there had not been sufficient boats to ferry these across the Chindwin,

223

but this was perhaps a blessing in disguise; the heavily forested country of the Zibyu Hills was far easier to traverse on foot and with mules than with vehicles, and as promised the RAF kept them fully supplied with Chindit-like drops.

And still there were no Japanese to be seen, not even a patrol now. It was 16 December before Sergeant Major Lenzing reported that there was an enemy force in front of them, straddling the railway line at Indaw. "How many?" Harry asked.

"Divisional strength, at least, Colonel."

"Shit," Harry commented. "They're not supposed to be there." He sent the requisite message back to Division, then moved his entire company forward, carefully. They arrived at a vantage point overlooking the town and the line, which was a hive of activity. Divisional strength at the very least, Harry agreed, and equipped with tanks and artillery as well. Could this mean that Ba Pau had fed him incorrect information? That would mean that Slim's entire plan was at risk. Save that this large concentration was too far north to affect the crossing at Pakokku, or the advance on Meiktila.

On the other hand, it was far too strong a force for 19th Division to brush aside. He frowned, and levelled his glasses. He had been so sure Ba Pau was telling the truth . . . He refocussed on an officer who was directing traffic immediately beneath him. The officer wore a coal-scuttle type helmet, khaki uniform, gaiters, and had a holstered pistol hanging from his belt. And his face, if now sun-browned, was clearly that of a white man.

Confirmation rested on the little Stars and Stripes adorning his helmet. "Holy shitting smoke!" Harry said, handing the glasses to Keeton. "We've linked up!"

From that moment the advance gathered speed. The

American-led Chinese were just as eager to be in at the finish, but Rees disengaged himself from too close association with them. "I want to be first to Shwebo," he told Harry.

The advance continued without cessation over Christmas and into the New Year. Now they were meeting more resistance, but this continued to be of the patrol variety, and was easily brushed aside. So fast was the forward movement that Harry's intelligence company was now absorbed into Rees's headquarters staff, its principal duty the interrogation of prisoners. And on 7 January they were in the suburbs of Shwebo. "You've been here before," Rees reminded Harry.

"Going the wrong way," Harry agreed. "It is very good to be returning."

Then they were ordered not to advance farther, but to swing to the south to secure the railway line which ran from Shwebo to Sagaing. The actual occupation of the town was to be left to 2nd Division, following closely behind. There was some swearing at this, but Rees took it philosophically. "The fact is," he told his senior officers, "now that we're actually winning the war, people are starting to look ahead. Prestige, and the regaining of it. So, we are a British-Indian Division and 2nd Division is all British. The powers-that-be obviously wish Shwebo to be taken by an entirely British force, just to remind the Burmese who controlled them before the war, and who intend to control them after it. However, please keep this to yourselves."

"I don't think they are going to control Burma after the war," Harry confided when he and the General were alone. "Not unless they intend to maintain an entire army here to do it."

"I couldn't agree with you more, Harry," Rees said. "Let us thank God we are simple soldiers who do not have to worry about things like prestige and the problems

225

of peace. Our business is to get across the river. Let's do that thing."

Harry was privately disappointed that they were being shunted south towards Mandalay; he had dreamed – an impossible dream, he knew – of leading his scouts into Lashio itself. Now that would no doubt be accomplished by the Americans. He could only wait and pray. Once both Mandalay and Lashio were in Allied hands, it would be a whole different ball game.

There were actually very few Japanese left in Shwebo, and these proved no problem to 2nd Division, although the few that remained were as fanatically determined as ever to fight to the end; one unlucky tank commander, confronting and assuming the surrender of an unarmed Japanese officer, found himself attacked and his throat torn out – by the enemy's teeth! When the occupation of the town was completed, there were only ten Japanese prisoners.

Meanwhile 19th Division moved south, to a position some 40 miles north of Mandalay, where Rees had been informed there was a ford. While he did this, he sent Harry and his scouts farther south to observe the situation at Sagaing, and the condition of the Ava Bridge. Again there was only scattered Japanese resistance on this side of the river, and the next day they were looking at what was familiarly known as Tit Mountain. Sagaing is dominated by a huge pagoda entirely surrounded by statues of the Buddha in alcoves around its base. Dominating the pagoda in turn is a great dome with at the top what appears to be an exact replica of a human nipple. The nickname was obvious, from a British point of view, nor was it the least fanciful, as legend has it that when a couple of centuries ago the dome was commissioned, the architect asked the then queen what shape she wished, whereupon she removed her upper garments and asked the lucky fellow how he proposed to improve upon nature!

Apart from Tit Mountain, however, the reconnaissance proved of no value: the Ava Bridge was exactly as Harry had last seen it three years before, its red girders twisted, its two central spans destroyed; in all that time, the Japanese had not got around to repairing it.

By the time Harry rejoined the Division, Rees had made his crossing of the river, at Kyaukmyaung. He had even got tanks across, as well as his infantry, but had promptly been counter-attacked by everything the Japanese could throw at them. For a couple of days the situation was critical, as not all the Division had as yet made it across, and some found it hard going, having to use small boats on a fast-running river in the darkness to escape Japanese fire. Harry took his men across on the night of 11 January, getting soaked to the skin in the process, but linking up with the infantry forces surrounding the perimeter.

"The fact is, Brand," said the General, "although they're fighting like mad, they really don't have anything with which to stop us. Next stop Mandalay." And then Lashio, Harry thought.

"Listen," Susan said, nudging Constance awake. Constance sat up with a jerk. It was just before dawn, the most horrible part of the day, because the entire day lay ahead of them, a day of eating inedible food, of using the latrine trench cheek to cheek, of endeavouring to keep out of trouble, of being afraid. One was always afraid.

"Can't you hear it?" Susan asked.

"Thunder," Constance said. But it was early for the monsoon.

227

"That is gunfire," Susan declared. "I heard it at Prome."

Constance frowned, and concentrated. Perhaps it was gunfire. She stood up. It was coming from the north. Other women had heard it too, and were stirring, sitting up and jabbering at each other. Instinctively, Constance and Susan turned to the gate, which was swinging open, to admit Ishikawa and Matsumara, well backed up by guards, as always. "Out!" the Captain shouted. "Outside. You leave this place, now."

The women looked at each other, then stooped to collect the various artifacts they had fashioned for themselves over the years. Instantly Matsumara was striding among them, rubber truncheon flailing to and fro. "You hurry, eh?" he bawled. "You no take anything, eh?"

They stumbled to the gate, rubbing their arms and backsides, wherever the hose had landed. Constance looked across at the men's camp; there too the inmates were being marshalled. This was what Wishart had prophesied would happen, when the Allies got too close. He had said, look for me, and come to me, when I call. But now was surely not the time. Yet they were being moved out. Together? It had to be, together.

Trucks were arriving, engines growling, exhausts adding to the morning mist. "In!" Matsumara bawled. "You get in."

Constance saw Ishikawa getting into a car to be driven away. She wondered what he felt, to know his side was being defeated. To know that he might have to answer for his crimes. She had every intention that he should.

The women clambered into the canvas-enclosed trucks, more and more of them into each. Constance reckoned each truck was designed to hold about 20 people, and there were 50 in each. Not that it mattered, either hygienically or personally; they all knew each other too well by now, had shared too much, to be bothered about being pressed against one another. Constance's only fear was that one or two of the weaker women might drop dead.

Being taller than most of the others, she could see out of the back, at least until the flap was lowered to plunge them into gloom. "Where do you think we're going?" Susan asked, huddled against her.

"The only road leads into Lashio," Constance said. She was praying the men were following.

They were. After an hour's uncomfortable journey the truck finally stopped and the flap was thrown up, she could see the men disembarking some distance away. But she didn't have the time to locate Wishart, as they were made to get down, to find themselves in the middle of total chaos. Lashio was like a disturbed antheap, with soldiers running to and fro, officers barking orders, women screaming or just weeping as they sat beside the road, children wailing, some, having lost their mothers, wandering about with a dazed expression on their faces, dogs barking, chickens clucking, goats braying . . . and over all, the sound of the guns, much closer now. "Jesus!" Susan muttered. "What's going to happen to us?"

Matsumara answered that one. "Hurry, hurry!" he bawled, and they realised they were outside the railway station, and that there was a train waiting to leave, with some proper carriages up front behind the engine, but the women were being herded towards the cattle cars in the rear, where they were driven into the noisome interior by the truncheons and whips of their guards.

Once again a vast huddle, made worse now by the fact that they had been given nothing to eat and no time to use the latrine trench before they left the camp. Most of them just let go where they stood, others shouted their complaints, adding to the cacophony. But the train was moving, out into the jungle track they remembered so well from three years before. "If we're on the train," Susan said. "We must be going to Mandalay."

Constance supposed she was right. She was more interested in what they had seen in Lashio. It had reminded her of Rangoon, on her brief visit there. That meant the Japanese had to be preparing to pull out. That meant some enemy must be very close. But who? Coming from the north, it could only be Stilwell's Chinese. Oh, if they could overrun the train!

The journey turned into an experience in hell. The day grew very hot as the sun rose, and there was neither food nor water. Nor did the train ever stop. The interior of the cattle car became a cesspool, with many women too weak to stand any longer, collapsed in their own filth. "We're going to die," Susan muttered. "If we don't have water soon, we're going to die."

Constance suspected that a good number of them were already dead. Her mouth was so dry her tongue seemed to have stuck to the roof of her mouth. But I am not going to die, she vowed to herself. Not after having survived so much, and not with help so near at hand. She put her arms round Susan and hugged her. "We are not going to die," she said fiercely.

Susan was weeping. "Listen," she said. "There is something I must tell you before we die."

"We are not going to die," Constance repeated. "So save it!"

The train passed through several towns without stopping. Constance was able to identify only one of them, a place called Maymyo, a delightful spot of wide streets and handsome buildings, which she remembered from the journey up. It was late afternoon when the train finally stopped. There was a lot of shouting outside the cattle car, but to Constance's disappointment the noise of heavy gunfire had ceased, although there was a good deal of indiscriminate small-arms firing going on. She pressed herself against the door.

"Help!" she shouted. "We need help. We need water, or we will die. Matsumara! Ishikawa!" She didn't care if they flogged her for breaking the rules. She had to have water.

The door was opened so suddenly and so violently that she fell out, followed by most of the women who had pressed beside her. Another station yard. But when she looked up she saw huge walls rising above her head: Fort Dufferin! Mandalay! And Matsumara.

"Water!" she begged.

Matsumara gave orders, and buckets of water were brought round, as well as buckets of rice. Now was not the time for dignity. Each woman gulped as much of the precious liquid as she could manage, dug her fingers into the rice and crammed it into her mouth. Constance saw that the Japanese had turned a hose on the interior of the cattle car, and ran forward to be immersed in the water before a sharp cut from Matsumara's wand drove her back. She lay on the ground and watched four dead bodies being dragged out. She sat up and looked back along the track. The men had also been disembarked. But where was Wishart? Surely he was with them! But she did not even know if he might have died back at the camp.

She looked up at the walls again, and then behind her at the tumbling river. There was less obvious panic in Mandalay than there had been in Lashio, but then the bombers came, flying low, meeting with almost no resistance. There were huge explosions, and great clouds of smoke. Constance scrambled to her feet and was herded, with the rest of the women, into the shadow of the walls of the fortress. Susan came to her. "They're British," she said. "We're going to be blown to bits, by the British!"

Constance hugged her, which always seemed to reassure her. She kept watching the men, seeking some sign. But they too had been herded against the wall by their guards.

The planes departed, and the city seemed to reawaken to a huge hum. There was no evidence of any casualties in the station yard, apart from the bodies dragged from the cattle car. Ishikawa appeared, waving his stick, shouting in Japanese. Constance knew enough of the language by now to understand that they were being marshalled. The guards moved up and down, arranging them in ranks of four, then they were marched forward and out of the yard, for some minutes still under the walls of the fortress, then into the residential area of the city.

Here they were surrounded by people, and for the first time in three years Constance felt ashamed. She was wearing hardly more than a bath towel, her hair was a tangled mess, she was filthy and she was being stared at. But these people were at least as frightened as they were curious, and parts of the city were on fire. They knew who was responsible, too, and who was coming. Some of them threw stones at the white women, and were driven away by the guards. At least the men were still following.

They came to a square where there were several trucks, in a row, parked but with their engines running. Around them there was a considerable number of soldiers, holding back the crowds of civilians who were clamouring for places. Ishikawa's men joined in the clamour, pushing their way forward, and the prisoners lost cohesion, their ranks breaking up in several gaggles of screaming people. Strong arms went round Constance, and she looked up at the white beard and hair. "John!" she gasped. "Oh, John! Can we get out?"

"I don't think we can, here," he said. "But we're being moved on."

To confirm his words, Matsumara was shouting at them. "Up, up! Get in trucks! Up, up!"

"Don't leave me," Constance begged.

Wishart hesitated a moment, then lifted her up and thrust her into the nearest truck, pausing only to do the same for Susan before scrambling up behind them. Other women were climbing in, and they found themselves being thrust to the very front of the truck, pressed there by the crowd. Constance didn't know whether or not Matsumara saw Wishart getting into the women's truck but he was clearly in too much of a hurry to be away to start emptying them back out again.

Taller than the others, Constance and Wishart, pressed by the crowd, had Susan sandwiched between them but were able to look out the back at the rest of the prisoners being loaded, and at the mob of people still trying to find places, but now being forced aside by the soldiers to allow eight women to come through. They were young, looked Chinese, and were quite well dressed. "Comfort girls from the military brothel," Wishart said. "Koreans, mostly. The Japanese always have comfort girls in their various headquarters."

Constance shuddered. She could have been one of those. But would she have been any worse off? The girls looked healthy and well-fed, and responded to the soldiers' commands as complete equals. But to be one of them she would have had to sleep with about a dozen Japanese soldiers a day, every day, for three years!

She gave another shudder, and Wishart held her closer yet. Then she seemed to freeze, for the soldiers were opening another passageway through the crowd to allow several obviously high-ranking officials to reach the trucks. With them was a blonde woman – Marion Shafter!

Chapter Eleven

The Vanquished

Once across the bridgehead with all his force, Rees ordered a general move south. "Are we supposed to do this, sir?" Harry inquired, remembering Slim's orders that 19th Division were to occupy the Japanese north of the city while XXXIII Corps came up from the south to deliver the knockout blow.

Rees clearly remembered the orders as well, and grinned. "I would say we're keeping them occupied, Harry."

But the Japanese resistance was strengthening, and five tanks of 7th Light Cavalry were damaged in frontal assaults upon positions reinforced with anti-tank guns. These were only pinpricks, but then the road, which 19th Division was following, entered a defile, and the advancing British/Indians were checked by a hail of fire from artillery, mortars and emplaced tanks; clearly the position had been carefully chosen to halt the advance. The troops were ordered to take cover while Rees conferred with his officers, studying the map.

"It will be too costly to rush it," Rees said. "So we turn its flank. Here."

He pointed to the area between the road and the river, where there were several cart tracks. "Risky," someone muttered.

"So is war," Rees pointed out.

"What I meant, sir, was that there are still Japanese positions on the west bank. They will be able to enfilade our advance."

"Then we'll clear those out as well."

He called up massive air support and sent 98 Brigade back across the river against the enemy on the west bank. The Japanese, most of whose companies were by now hardly stronger than platoons, fought with their usual desperation, but nothing was going to stop Rees. While the west bank was being cleared he continued forcing his way south, day after day, over-ruling his tank commanders when they complained that their tanks were being improperly used and their men exhausted. When they arrived at a deep-sided chaung which appeared to prohibit tanks from crossing at all, the General commanded that trucks be driven into the defile to fall on their sides, so providing an impromptu bridge for the tanks to proceed.

By now the Japanese had abandoned their roadblock and were in full retreat into Mandalay itself. Rees continued to insist upon a continuous advance. He clearly intended to take the city himself, unless he encountered major Japanese resistance. "But we can do more than that, gentlemen," he told his staff. "NCAC are having trouble advancing on Lashio, which is being strongly defended. Now . . ." he prodded the map. "On the railway line between Mandalay and Lashio is this town Maymyo. If we nab that, the defenders at Lashio are out on a limb which is being sawn off behind them. So, Sixty-Two Brigade, do that thing."

"Permission to accompany the Brigade, sir," Harry said. "They will need someone to interrogate prisoners."

Rees looked at Brigadier Morris. "Brand will be welcome," Morris said. "As long as he remembers that our objective is to take Maymyo."

*   *   *

Harry was content. He was well aware that it was nearly a hundred miles from Maymyo to Lashio, but at least he was moving in the right direction. Maymyo was only 30 miles away, and Morris opted to ignore both road and railway and move directly across country, his intention being to take the defenders by surprise. Almost immediately they were climbing out of the steamy valley of the Irrawaddy into relatively cool foothills. The going was hard, but there was no opposition. "You ever been to Maymyo, Harry?" the Brigadier asked

"No, sir."

"Apparently it is named after a British Officer, a Colonel May, who got hold of it during the war of 1886. It was also the summer headquarters of the British administration here in Burma, before the war. A sort of Burmese Simla. Should be worth a visit."

For the next day they climbed up and down hills and in and out of valleys, the jungle-hardened troops finding few obstacles in either the flora or fauna they encountered, and that night their guides assured them that Maymyo was just over the next hill. Morris promptly made his dispositions, sent Harry and his scouts forward to reconnoitre the situation, and detached one of the battalions in a sweep to the south-east, not to cut the railroad, but to cross it and prevent the Japanese from withdrawing into the jungle. "What do you reckon?" Keeton asked, as Harry led his men forward; they were down to just under 50 now, but he had not attempted to recruit; his 50 were worth five times that number of inexperienced troops, and as far as he was concerned the word inexperienced covered even the so-called veterans of 14th Army.

"Piece of cake," Harry assured him.

"I was thinking of Mrs Brand."

"There is no way she'll be in Maymyo, Tom. Much

236

as I would like to think that. I'm just hoping she'll still be in Lashio."

Although he knew the chances of that were remote, with the Chinese/Americans probing down from the north. On the other hand, where could they possibly send the prisoners from Lashio? The map indicated nothing but jungle for hundreds of miles before one came near civilisation again. It would be a death march. But the Japanese were quite fond of death marches, he recalled, his blood running cold. And all this was supposing that the camp hadn't been moved months, if not years, ago.

His map also told him that Maymyo was at an altitude of over 3,000 feet; it was certainly delightfully cool as they made their way down the slopes to the head of the shallow valley which overlooked the town.

"Some place," Harry remarked, studying the broad, spacious avenues and attractive houses. "One can see that the British spent a lot of time here." But his main business was to discover the Japanese defences. These were fairly easy to establish, but as he had hoped and anticipated, most of the trenches and gun emplacements faced north and north-west; they had been relying on Lashio protecting the north-east, and on the fact that there were no Allied forces south of the town; indeed there was nothing south of the town at all save bush-covered mountains.

There was also a good deal of bustle in the town, with convoys of trucks getting ready to move out, taking the open road that did lead south, and according to Harry's map that very soon degenerated into a track before disappearing altogether. He had no intention of breaking radio silence to alert the Japanese of his presence. "Sergeant Major Lenzing," he said. "Choose four men who will take a message back to Brigade."

"What are you going to tell them?" Keeton asked.

237

"I am going to recommend that we drop finesse and just rush the place. Coming in as we are from the south-west they are certainly not expecting us, and they don't have too much to offer on this side."

It was a great temptation to do some rushing on his own, but commonsense told Harry that would only be risking his men's lives; Brigade was just a march behind. Meanwhile he watched the Japanese convoy making its way along the road south of the town and then disappearing into the trees. As to whether it might be a good idea to sweep to the south himself, his duty was to wait for the arrival of Brigade HQ and give them his observations; in any event, the truck column seemed to be mostly civilian personnel, so far as he could judge, nor was it likely to get very far, considering the country into which it was heading.

Brigade arrived that afternoon, still apparently without the Japanese being aware of the impending blow. Maymyo had settled down into considerable quietude after the departure of the evacuees, but the attention of the garrison was still occupied by what might be happening to the north-east. Indeed, as the attackers watched, a train arrived from Mandalay, but disembarked no troops. It was apparently unaware that one of Morris's battalions had already crossed the line and was south of the town. "You propose an immediate assault?" the Brigadier inquired.

"I do, sir." Harry was aware of the implicit question being asked. "I am pretty sure there are no prisoners in the town."

"Right. I gave Colonel Foster three hours." Morris looked at his watch. "Half-an-hour to go. To your posts, gentlemen," he told his officers. "Your people need not be involved, Harry," he said.

"We want to be involved," Harry told him.

"Very good. I imagine their headquarters building will suit you best. I have not called for air support, as I do not think it necessary, and we do not want to destroy the town. At four o'clock, we go in."

Harry saluted and rejoined his men, passing on the Brigadier's instructions. The Gurkhas no less than the British were anticipatory. They had engaged in a dozen serious skirmishes since the scouts had been created, but this would be their first full-scale battle, and although they knew they represented overwhelming force, they also very well knew the Japanese capacity for fanatical defence. But for Harry, Maymyo was just a step on the road to Lashio. And, hopefully, Constance.

"Five minutes to," he told Keeton. "Pass the word." Behind them, in the trees on the hillside, he was aware of a gigantic rustle. It seemed impossible that the Japanese should not be aware of it. But there was no evidence of any alarm in the town.

"Four o'clock!" Harry rose to his feet and waved his men forward. They advanced down the slope and through the trees, Harry and Keeton to the fore. They had actually reached the outskirts of the town before anyone noticed them. Then a shot was fired, and instantly the afternoon erupted into flame and noise. Women and children screamed, indicating that not all the civilians had been evacuated in the truck convoy. Bullets sang through the afternoon. Harry led his men at a run along the street, firing at any Japanese who showed himself.

But the Japanese had been attacked in the rear, and were slow to respond. Harry and his scouts had reached the town centre before they encountered any resistance. Then there was a roadblock, and several machine-guns. "Take cover!" Harry bellowed, and went to ground himself on a street corner. He peered round the building behind which he was sheltering. Like so many of the streets in Maymyo, in front of him was a broad, tree-lined avenue. But two blocks up the avenue there was a square, and on the far side of this was a larger-than-usual building, from which there flew the Rising Sun ensign. That was his target. But not with 40 men. "Tell Brigade we need support, town centre," he told Robbins.

The radio chattered. "Ten minutes, sir."

The noise was tremendous, all around them, screams and shouts overlaid with the chatter of rifle and automatic fire. The Japanese holding the block continued to spray the avenue with bullets, and trees burst open as the lead tore through them, while glass shattered and bullets crunched into stonework. But as promised, in ten minutes there arrived four mules drawing a mountain-gun. "The block, or the building?" inquired the captain in command.

"You take the block, and we'll take the building," Harry told him.

The gun was unlimbered and set up. The Japanese were well aware of what was happening. and kept up a stream of fire, but the actual work was done in the shelter of the building, which was now empty. Then the gun was wheeled round to face the enemy. Bullets clanged off the protective shield, while the captain laid off his range with careful precision. "Fire!"

The first shell hit the open space between the block and the Japanese headquarters. An adjustment was snapped, and the second shot struck immediately in front of the Japanese position, which was momentarily lost to sight behind a cloud of dust and exploding asphalt. "One more, Colonel," the Captain remarked, and another adjustment was made.

The third shell burst immediately over the block,

sending men and materiel cascading in every direction. Harry waved his arm and his men surged forward, bayoneting the few Japanese who had survived the direct hit, and then charging across the square for the headquarters building, only to be brought to a halt, seeking shelter amidst the various flower beds and ornamental shrubs that decorated the square, as a hail of fire swept them from the windows. Harry looked over his shoulder, and the Artillery captain gave him a thumbs-up sign. Harry would have liked to be able to remind him that he wanted as much of the building as possible intact, but the gunner knew his job, and the next charge was neatly aimed at the top of the front steps and the doorway above. There was another huge explosion of shattered concrete, wood and dust, and Harry was able to advance his men another 30 yards, before the firing resumed, but only from the upstairs windows.

Harry looked back again, and this time himself signalled, thumbs down. The gunner understood, and held his fire. Harry drew a deep breath, waved his arm, then stood up and ran at the steps. The firing was not as intense as before, the Japanese being aware that there might be another shell in their midst at any moment, and Harry gained the steps and the shattered doorway in a long burst, rifle and bayonet thrust forward. "Ground floor first," he snapped at Keeton, who was, as always, at his elbow.

The Gurkhas used grenades to clear out the downstairs offices, obliterating the men who had survived the shell blast. Then they drew breath, while Harry surveyed them and the situation. He had 33 men left, including Keeton, Mearns and Lenzing, and Robbins. But the battle was won, as he could tell from the victorious cheers echoing from the streets around him. "Make to Brigade: Am securing GHQ," Harry told Robbins. "Let's go."

He led the run up the stairs. Faces, and rifles, appeared in doorways, and he threw two grenades in rapid succession. Bullets slammed into walls and ceilings as his men opened fire behind him. He emptied his own magazine then used the bayonet as a pike to send the nearest Japanese reeling back against the wall, blood pouring from his chest. The bayonet was embedded, so Harry abandoned it, drew his revolver, and shot a second man just emerging from another doorway.

He stepped into the room, as Keeton came through another door from the rear. Between them they faced a Japanese officer, a colonel, Harry deduced from his insignia, flawlessly dressed but bareheaded, and armed with sword and revolver. Both Harry and Keeton levelled their weapons. "Make a move and you're dead," Keeton said, somewhat melodramatically.

The colonel hesitated, then gave a short bow; clearly he understood English. Carefully he extracted his revolver from its holster, reversed it, and held it out. Keeton took it. Then the colonel, still obviously assuming that Keeton was the senior of the British officers, as he was the one who had spoken and neither he nor Harry wore any very obvious insignia, equally carefully drew his sword. He kissed the haft, then held out the sword on both hands, the blade horizontal to the floor. Keeton glanced at Harry, who nodded, quite happy for his second in command to accept the surrender.

Keeton stepped forward, but, moving with startling speed, the Japanese colonel switched his hands from the blade to the haft, at the same time whirling the sword around his head with tremendous force. Keeton shot him through the chest, but could not prevent the sword from slashing into his neck with such force that he was decapitated, his horrified expression coagulating as his head shot across the room and struck the wall.

Harry was firing as well, and the Japanese officer was

dead before he struck the floor. Harry stood above the two corpses, watching the blood spurting and trailing away from Keeton's severed neck, feeling quite sick. Lenzing ran into the room and dropped to his knees beside his captain; he had served even more closely with Keeton over the past three years than had Harry. Then the sergeant major levelled his rifle and shot the already dead Japanese colonel again.

As usual, only a handful of prisoners were taken, but one of them was a badly wounded lieutenant. "Has he been searched for weapons?" Harry asked the medical attendant.

"He's clean, sir," the corporal said. "Well, in a manner of speaking."

Harry beckoned Lenzing, and they knelt one on each side of the wounded man. Lenzing quickly established that he spoke Burmese. He was also quite willing to talk. "He says the prisoner-of-war camp outside Lashio was closed over a week ago, Colonel," Lenzing said.

"Then where are the prisoners?" Harry demanded, not daring to anticipate.

"They were taken by train down to Mandalay."

"Shit!" Harry growled, and hurried off to Brigade HQ to radio Division. "There may be European prisoners of war in city."

A reply came promptly. "There are no prisoners in city. Japanese prisoners taken say European and Indian POWs evacuated by truck for Meiktila."

"Straight into the arms of Four Corps," Morris said.

"If they got there," Harry pointed out. "The Japanese must know about Four Corps by now."

"Then where?" They studied the map. "Assuming that the Japanese by now know we are attacking Meiktila, and have therefore cut Burma in two," Morris

243

said, "the only way out for non-combatants is Loilem and Siam."

"That means crossing the Karen Hills," Harry muttered. "There aren't any roads."

"Presumably there are tracks. But I agree, they'll probably wind up walking. It's a pretty grim picture."

"With your permission, sir," Harry said.

Morris considered for a few moments. Then he said. "I think it would be to the advantage of our forces, Colonel Brand, if you were to endeavour to find out on what scale the enemy is withdrawing to the east. I am therefore ordering you to undertake a reconnaissance into the Karen Hills, as far as the Salween River. You will keep in daily radio contact with Nineteenth Division Headquarters. I will inform General Rees of your orders." He held out his hand. "Good hunting, Harry."

The trucks were still in sight of Mandalay when the bombers again came over, screaming low above the tree tops as they blasted Fort Dufferin. They were not interested in the truck convoy, already half hidden by the trees, but the vehicles stopped until the commanders were sure they were not going to be attacked. Inside Constance's truck was already a seething cesspool. But she was more interested in the knowledge that Marion Shafter was in this convoy with them. Of one thing she was determined: if she was going to die, then Marion was going to die with her. But for the moment she was sustained by John Wishart's arms, to which Susan was also clinging; in all the chaos in Mandalay and the changing of trucks, they had become separated from the other Englishwomen, and those in this truck with them were all Indian. They were all again suffering from thirst, despite the alleviation of the water given them in Mandalay.

Then the trucks started rolling again, and continued to drive for some three hours, while it grew hotter and hotter. To either side the land was cultivated and looked quite civilised, with pagoda temples rising above the villages they passed through, every one containing very agitated Burmese, who were well aware that perhaps the climactic battle of their war was taking place only a few miles away. The prisoners were not interested in the scenery. Most of them could hardly stand any longer, yet stand they did; to lie down was to risk being trampled to death. So they held each other up, in a sea of sweat. But at last the convoy halted again, the tailgates were opened, and the guards were shouting, "Out, out!"

The prisoners fell out, looking only for fresh air and some rest for their agonised muscles, but immediately they were kicked back to their feet and herded into a huge circle, surrounded by guards, and given food and drink, although it was hard to tell the difference between the thin soup and the muddy water. "We mustn't be separated," Constance told John.

"Not if I can help it."

He was trying to see beyond the guards, studying the officers who were also lunching, with considerably more comfort, up by the forward trucks, and discovering that the convoy had been split up. What had happened to the others he did not know, but there were only four trucks left in this group, out of which had been discharged some 40 prisoners, men and women, all Indian except for himself and the two Englishwomen. There were, he estimated, some four dozen soldiers still with them, as well as the officers and four civilians, three men and the yellow-haired woman. The comfort girls were on their own to one side, chattering animatedly to each other, in contrast to the prisoners, who for the most part sat in dispirited silence. "Who's the blonde, do you think?" John asked Constance.

"She is a bitch named Marion Shafter," Constance told him.

"You mean you know her?"

"Let's say she knew my husband."

John considered this. "Now she seems to know one or two Japanese officers."

"She should. She works for them."

"Complicated." But he wouldn't probe further.

"When, do you think?" Constance asked.

He gave a quick glance at Susan, and then a quick shake of his head. "Too many guns right now."

"I heard one of the guards saying there will be a train waiting for us in Meiktila. Once they put us on a train . . ."

"Patience is the name of this game, Connie."

Constance knew he was right, but the thought of Marion Shafter, wearing crisp clean clothes and lunching on sushi and saki while she was clad in hardly more than a rag and was eating slops, made her blood boil. All the nearly four years of pent-up frustration that had been her marriage, to which could now be added the three years of total humiliation she had suffered as a prisoner of war, had come together in an all-consuming fury, directed simply at that one woman, even more than at Ishikawa. Had there not been an Ishikawa, there would have been someone else, and her sufferings might have been even greater. There was only one Marion Shafter. But for the time being, as John Wishart had insisted, patience. Her only fear was that they would be separated. But when the call came to return to their trucks, again no one seemed to care that a man had inserted himself into the midst of the women.

Once again they bumped and clattered along the road, until they stopped with surprising suddenness, and surprisingly soon after their lunch break, as well. The women immediately set up a clamour, which made it difficult to grasp anything that was being said outside the truck. But there was a good deal of shouting. "Something's up," John said.

The trucks began to shunt to and fro; turning to go back the way they had come. As their truck manoeuvred, John and Constance were able to look south along the road, and see a roadblock, bristling with machine-guns. Obviously that was what had stopped them. But it was a Japanese roadblock. "A roadblock, between Mandalay and Meiktila," John muttered. "That can only mean the Brits have got Meiktila, or are about to get to it."

"Then what happens to us?"

"I would say we're going back to Mandalay. Glory be. Maybe we won't have to make a run for it after all, Connie."

She just couldn't believe they would be that lucky, and they weren't. They had driven back north for an hour, and just about regained their lunch site, when they were stopped again. More clamour from the women, more shouts from outside the truck. Then more shunting, before they turned off a side road, leading east. This was by no means as good a surface as the Mandalay-Meiktila road, and the bouncing became very uncomfortable; the women shouted and screamed their anguish, but no one paid any attention.

When at last the trucks stopped, two hours after taking the turn-off, having driven for most of the time in low gear, the prisoners as usual were happy to fall out and onto the ground. This time there was no immediate summons to their feet. They had in fact stopped in a very small village containing hardly more than a dozen huts. The road was so narrow that there was no means of getting off it, and the trucks were parked in a long line. Japanese troops were spreading out to either side to prevent any attempt at escape by any of the prisoners, while the Burmese women and children also gathered round to stare at them; Constance wondered if they had ever seen British or Indian women before.

John was more interested in looking about them. It was rapidly growing dark, the sun already nestling behind high ground far to the west. Beyond the forest he could see the valley of the Irrawaddy. "We must have climbed something like five hundred feet," he said. "Due east."

"Is that good, or bad?"

"It means we're making for Thailand," he said. "Siam. But there are no roads, so far as I know, except for the one out of Meiktila."

"Oh, shit!" Constance commented.

They were fed, and allowed to bivouac. It was such an enormous relief to be free of the noisome interior of the truck Constance would have enjoyed the evening anyway, but actually, this high up, it was extremely pleasant, and free of bugs. Constance, Susan and John naturally stayed together. No one seemed to mind. The Japanese were clearly more interested in getting to safety than in maintaining their old rigid discipline over their prisoners. Not that they intended to allow any of them to escape; that was obvious from the considerable number of guards that were mounted, right round the village.

Constance was content to wait for Wishart to call the tune; she knew he was evaluating every situation, while at the same time he was determined not to risk getting them shot or bayoneted. "We're not going to have to walk to Siam?" Susan asked, anxiously.

"It looks likely," Wishart said.

Susan lay on her back with her hands beneath her head, staring at the stars.

"Did you ever hear anything about your wife?"

248

Constance asked. They had never had the time to talk, during the cholera epidemic.

"Yes. She got to Calcutta. I think she's gone home to the States."

"At least you know she's safe."

Their arms were lying next to each other, and now his fingers closed over hers. It had to be a gesture of affection, nothing more, she knew; they were both so filthy and so debilitated anything more than that was out of the question. "Are we going to make it, John?" she asked.

"We're sure as hell going to try, Connie! I just wanted you to know that if we don't . . . well, I have never met a woman who compared with you for guts." He grinned in the darkness. "As well as looks." She let her hand lie in his as they fell asleep.

They were aroused before dawn, fed, and packed back into the trucks. The villagers were also awakened by the bustle, and gathered round to stare at them. Now the road was even worse, and the convoy could only proceed in low gear, up and down. Peering through the canvas whenever it was possible, Constance could see only jungle to either side. "If only we knew just how many guards there are," John whispered. "And how many prisoners. Because some time soon they are going to have to abandon the vehicles."

This happened at the noonday break. As usual the prisoners were by then so exhausted they were only capable of falling out of the trucks and lying on the ground. But now they were shouted at by their guards, for they were in a clearing, and there was just room for the trucks to turn round. The guards wanted the prisoners out of the way. One of the women who was too exhausted to move was bayoneted where she lay.

249

Another was left lying, panting, behind the truck, which promptly ran over her as it reversed. "Jesus," Susan muttered. "They're going to kill us all."

John put his arm round her and hugged her. But he was also watching, and listening. There had been four trucks. The first one had contained the several Japanese civilians who had accompanied them, as well as Marian Shafter. And ten soldiers. The second had contained the comfort girls, who were now standing around disconsolately, their finery looking distinctly tarnished. With them had been another ten soldiers. The third truck had contained the male prisoners, 18 of them. There had been two soldiers with the driver in the cab. The fourth truck had contained the white women and John Wishart, and again two soldiers with the driver in the cab. And the fifth truck had contained 20 soldiers, their job to prevent any attempt at escape. But once the trucks had been turned, it became apparent that this rearguard was being sent back with the vehicles. So were the soldiers in the cabs. "That leaves twenty-four," Wishart said. "Plus three officers and four civilians. I wonder if they're armed."

"And there are fewer than forty of us, unarmed," Constance said.

"Even supposing these people would follow you," Susan muttered.

"So, we'll just have to wait until the odds are reduced," Wishart said. "You girls game for a stroll through the bush?"

Susan and Constance looked at each other. "We've done it before," Constance said.

"Here they come," Susan whispered.

"Up, up," Matsumara was shouting. They scrambled to their feet. Ishikawa was marching down the track, four armed men at his heels. Also with them, Constance realised, was Marion Shafter, looking as trim as ever in her britches and boots, her white shirt and her topee. She was even smoking a cigarette, from a long Bakelite holder.

Wishart seemed able to feel Constance's emotions. "Easy," he warned.

"If we go, or even if we don't go," she said. "We are taking her with us." He made no reply, because the official party had reached them.

"Now we go Siam," Ishikawa declared. "We walk Siam, eh? Anyone who do not walk, we shoot. You understand?"

His gaze swept the women, and came to rest upon Constance. "You walk good, now, eh, Mrs Brand?"

Constance bowed. "I walk good now, honourable Captain."

"This lady know you," Ishikawa remarked.

Constance straightened, and gazed at Marion Shafter. "We have met, honourable Captain," she said. "Is honourable lady going to walk to Siam with us?"

"She is an insolent bitch," Marion Shafter said. "I wonder you do not have her flogged."

Constance stared at her. But Ishikawa merely grinned. "When we get Siam."

The comfort girls were not at all pleased to be told they were required to walk through the jungle. They set up one of their great clamours, and Ishikawa had to shout at them for silence. "You know," Wishart said. "Those aren't Japanese. They're Burmese or Koreans or Chinese, recruited as whores. I don't think they have any great love for the Japs. Could be useful."

"Now remember," Ishikawa bellowed, addressing both the men and the women. "You stop walking, you die. We go now."

The trucks had disappeared down the track. Most of the soldiers took their places to either side or behind their captives; the male prisoners were each loaded with a pack of supplies; Wishart, as clearly being the eldest, being spared this additional burden. Then they set off, the officers and civilians leading the way, together with the guide they had picked up in the village. This guide, Constance observed, was a Buddhist monk, who carried a little bell, which he rang from time to time. He had shown no great interest in the prisoners before, but to her surprise, and alarm, he soon fell back from the lead position to walk beside the women. And made a remark. He was addressing Constance, but she had no idea what he was saying, although, to her amazement, she recognised the word Brand. "Says he knows your husband," Wishart interpreted.

"Harry? But . . . how? Where?"

Wishart asked Ba Pau various questions, which were readily enough answered. "Says he has guided your husband in the jungle. Also says Colonel Brand is with British Army attacking Mandalay."

"Harry a colonel? Glory be! But . . . how does he know that, when he is here?"

Wishart asked some more questions, and Ba Pau rang his bell several times. "Says he was minding his own business when your husband put him under arrest. Apparently he managed to escape, and decided to get home just as fast as he can, but has been overtaken by events. Brace yourself, Connie: he wants to know if he helps you, will you intercede with your husband for him? Apparently he has just realised that the Japanese have lost this war, and is making plans."

"Well, of course I would do what I can," Constance said. "Can he really help us?"

"That we shall have to find out."

At that moment Matsumara arrived to chase the monk back up to the front of the column. But Constance found that for all her physical discomfort, and the fact that her feet were already beginning to ache, she was happy. Harry, a colonel. And making his way steadily towards her.

Chapter Twelve

The Victors

Harry took his surviving 33 scouts, refusing the extra help offered by Morris. Clive Mearns was now his second in command, Sergeant Major Lenzing third. Harry was well aware that the three of them were seeking more than the prisoners, vital as those were, at least to him. They were also seeking revenge for Keeton's murder, and that could not be achieved while subject to Army regulations and restraints, and therefore outside observers – the scouts were whole-heartedly behind them. It was not a matter they had discussed. But none of them had any doubts what they were about. Sergeant Robbins was of course included, as signaller. Harry also took six well-laden mules, as they would be out of touch with any replenishment for several weeks.

Before leaving Mandalay, now a smoking ruins in the hands of the British and Indians, although Slim had managed to fly in and hold an impromptu victory parade, Harry was given access to various reports filed by RAF reconnaissance pilots. Several groups of refugees had departed such places as Lashio, now again in Chinese-American hands, and Maymyo, and Mandalay itself, during the last fortnight, as the invasion had reached a climax. Constance could have been in any one of them. But they all had one thing in common: they had set off for Meiktila, discovered that it was in British hands, and veered off into the jungle, in several different convoys. It was simply a matter of following them.

And keeping out of trouble.

The roads and tracks leading east, which rapidly all became tracks, were in many places blocked by death-to-the-last-man Japanese detachments. But the main Japanese forces were engaged in a ferocious attempt to recapture Meiktila and open communication with the south. Harry was quite happy to lead his men across country well north of the battle, even if it was some of the toughest jungle they had yet encountered, made more difficult by the pre-monsoon rains, which began the day they left. The land rose steeply away from the valley of the Irrawaddy; in places the mules had to be hauled up the steep escarpments. Then it would fall away again into the next shallow valley before recommencing its climb. The jungle was very thick, and in places progress could only be made by hacking at the undergrowth with their kukris, while as the ground turned to mud they slipped as often as they went forward.

As they moved higher they escaped the attention of the myriad insects that had swarmed in the valley, but they were not short of company, which ranged from birds sitting on the branches above them and then flapping their wings to fly away from these strange intruders, through monkeys that chattered constantly about them – also in the branches, quite unaware that had Harry not forbidden shooting just in case there were any Japanese in the vicinity, they would have wound up in the pot in very short order – to the inevitable snakes. Most of these were of the small and very poisonous variety, such as kraits, and although the party was equipped with boots and puttees stout enough to withstand most fangs, the mules were a constant worry, as was bivouacing for the night, which had to be preceded by a very thorough search of the selected area.

Harry was navigating by compass, his idea being to get behind any of the various Japanese detachments, and then seek information. And on the third day one

255

of his scouts reported that there was a village not two miles away. Harry carefully scrutinised village, track and surrounding jungle through his binoculars. But there were no Japanese to be seen, although he had no doubt that there soon would be, as several of the villagers ran off at the appearance of the Gurkhas.

The headman, however, was perfectly willing to co-operate with Sergeant Major Lenzing's questions. "He says there were British and Indian prisoners here, Colonel," Lenzing translated. "Men and women. Maybe 40. They went there . . ." he pointed at the eastward leading track, which was certainly rutted, despite the steady drizzle.

"How long ago?"

"Maybe two days."

Harry pulled his nose. Two days, and they had trucks. All would depend on how far the track remained usable.

"But," Lenzing went on, "he says the trucks came back, yesterday. Without the prisoners." Lenzing's face was grim. They had to accept the likelihood that it might have been an execution party.

"Then they are really only two days ahead of us, and on foot," Harry said, refusing to consider that possibility. But he had to be sure they were following the right group. "Ask him if he can describe any of the prisoners. Ask him if any of the white women was unusually tall." Constance, he had no doubt, if not that unusual in London, would stand out like a beacon in the midst of any Japanese or Burmese.

"He says one woman, yes, was very tall, Colonel," Lenzing translated. "And two were very fair, with yellow hair."

Harry, his heart leaping about his chest at the thought that after three years he was within 48 hours

256

of Constance, frowned. But the other women? Could one of them be Susan?

"But one of the women with yellow hair was not a prisoner," Lenzing said.

Harry couldn't make head or tail of that. He had Robbins call in on their allotted frequency, giving only the map reference of where they were, and then the map reference of where he was heading; Robbins also added the code word for an aerial reconnaissance, if possible. Then after a quick meal and the purchase of some fresh food from the Burmese, they were on their way again.

"How far do you think we've come?" Constance asked, as they ate their midday meal. It had started to rain, and this was actually a relief, although it meant that they were squatting in mud and that their soup was even more watery than usual.

"From where the trucks dropped us yesterday? Maybe ten miles," Wishart replied.

"And how far to civilisation, the way we're going?"

"If, as I imagine, we're making for Loilem, maybe another fifty miles."

"Jesus!" she muttered, and looked at the other women, all of whom were already exhausted. "What's at Loilem?"

"A road, and there used to be an airstrip. I imagine the Japs have got it operational."

"So if they get us there, we're done."

"If they get us there, in time, by their calculations," he told her. "Loilem is on the road out of Meiktila. If the Brits have Meiktila, they might just be pushing along that road."

"We can't chance that, John. We can't even keep on like this. None of us are going to be left alive after walking fifty miles through this jungle."

Wishart eyed the guards who paraded up and down to

257

each side of the prisoners. There were only six of them on duty at a time, but they were all armed with rifles and bayonets, and their 18 comrades were only a shout away. His trouble was that his only accomplices in the proposed escape were Constance, Susan, and, hopefully, Ba Pau. He had not dared communicate his plans to any of the Indian prisoners for fear of an over-reaction which would betray them. Thus he had no idea of how many of them would follow him into action – if any.

But he knew that Constance was telling the absolute truth; that afternoon when they were summoned to resume their march, two of the Indian women refused. Their feet were in a terrible state from blisters, and they were generally too weak to move. Matsumara raged at them and beat them with his stick, and they still would not move. Ishikawa was summoned. He looked decidedly agitated, and after haranguing the woman for several minutes, abruptly turned and marched away. "Out!" Matsumara bawled. "Move out. Haste. Move out."

The women were left lying on the ground.

"Now there's an idea," Constance said. "Worth a beating, don't you think, to be left behind?"

"No," Wishart said. For two of the soldiers had also remained behind, and when they rejoined them an hour later their gaiters were stained with blood.

Ba Pau walked with them for a spell that afternoon, ringing his little bell and muttering as if in prayer. "What's he saying?" Constance asked.

"It's not good. Seems we're running low on food. He has heard the officers say it might be better to kill all the prisoners."

"But they can't do that!" Susan protested. "We *are* prisoners. The Red Cross know about us."

"If Ishikawa stumbles into Loilem and says we all

died of disease, or even that we all escaped into the jungle, the Red Cross are going to have a hard time proving otherwise."

"Then what are we going to do?" Constance asked. "Does Ba Pau have any ideas?"

"Not really. But he's afraid they may include him in the killing, once they get close enough to Loilem not to need him any more."

Constance felt sick. She couldn't believe that she had endured so much merely to be shot in the head and left dead on a jungle trail; within 24 hours the ants would have reduced her to an unrecognisable skeleton. A ripple ran through the column.

"Aircraft!" Wishart snapped.

The guards were running up and down the line of prisoners.

"Lie down," Matsumara was shouting. "Everybody down!"

They obeyed him without hesitation; it was such a pleasure to be lying down instead of stumbling onwards. Constance looked along the column; everyone was lying down that she could see: the forward party was lost to sight round a bend in the trail. She wondered if even Marion Shafter was getting mud on her spotless clothing?

Because of the rain, they did not see the plane until it was right over them. Then it burst through the clouds at not more than 100ft above the trees, before soaring away again. But they had seen the RAF wing markings. "Do you think they saw us?" Constance whispered to Wishart.

"Not very likely. But it's interesting that they knew where to look."

"You mean there could be someone actually searching for us?"

"It's possible." The rain was falling more heavily

259

now, but they could still hear the aircraft engines, as the plane circled, and no one moved. "You game?" Wishart whispered.

Constance's head jerked. But she saw what he meant. The party had insensibly become separated by the bend in the track. Thus the male prisoners, the officers, and the main part of the guards were actually out of sight although only a few yards away. Lying down not 6ft away, and between them and Ba Pau, was one of the guards. She looked to her right. Another guard lay just beyond Susan. "Both," she said.

He hesitated, not wishing to expose her to the risk, then realising that the risk was going to be just as great no matter how they went about it. He nodded. "We're going to go for it," Constance told Susan.

Susan gulped. But she could tell they might never have an opportunity like this again, while the Japanese were entirely concerned with the marauding aircraft. "On a count of three," Constance told them. "Three . . . two . . . now!"

She and Susan acted together, both rolling over towards the nearest guard. Constance then reached her feet. Susan remained lying down, but she was now against the soldier. He ignored her, looked up at Constance in alarm, rolled over in turn, and tried to bring up his rifle, but Susan had seized it and was hanging on for dear life, while Constance stamped on the man's groin with all her force. Nothing had ever given her such satisfaction.

The man screamed, and Constance stamped again. Even as she did so she heard the sound of a shot and then several more. But she hadn't been hit and she didn't really care whether she was hit or not. She continued to stamp on the man's groin and belly. He brought up his knees, and released the rifle to try to roll away from her and reach his own feet. Constance kicked at his face and missed. His hands grasped her ankle, and she fell heavily on his far side. He grinned, half in anger and half in pain, as he rose on his knees, reaching for her throat, and then fell forward, across her. Constance had not identified the shot amidst the others, the screams and shrieks which were bouncing off the raindrops, but she saw Susan holding the rifle she had just fired into the soldier's back.

Then she could take in what was happening. Wishart had despatched the other guard, seized his rifle, and shot the Japanese on the far side of the track. The main part of the shooting had come from the guards beyond the bend, who had come hurrying back through the rain, firing indiscriminately: several of the women had been hit. Wishart was shouting at them, telling them to run into the trees.

"Come on!" Constance screamed at him, at the same time retreating into the trees herself. Susan came with her, carrying the rifle. Of one thing Constance was determined: they were not going to be recaptured alive.

They threw themselves into the shelter of the trees, and were joined a moment later by both Wishart and Ba Pau. Ba Pau had also equipped himself with a rifle, and Constance reminded herself that Buddhist monks possessed few of the pacifist instincts of their Christian counterparts. They looked back up at the track. Some of the Indian women had followed their example and their exhortations and run into the forest; the rest had remained lying down, although now the Japanese were stamping among them, shooting anyone who moved. "We have to help those poor people," Wishart said. "I hadn't meant them to be slaughtered."

But at that moment there was a fresh eruption of noise and shooting from round the bend in the track: the male prisoners had at last also reacted. "I think we should get out of here," Susan muttered.

"We cannot abandon those people," Wishart repeated, taking careful aim and firing. One of the Japanese soldiers uttered a shriek and fell. The rest dropped to their knees and returned fire, for some moments, until they had emptied their magazines. The bullets wanged and ricochetted among the trees, but the four fugitives kept their heads down and were not hurt. Then Ba Pau and Wishart both fired again. At least one more of the soldiers was hit, and the rest hastily retreated out of sight.

Wishart was shouting at the women again, and those who could joined them in the trees. Seven of their number lay inert on the ground. There was still a good deal of shooting from round the bend. "We have to get up there. We need the food," Constance said.

Wishart nodded, and told the women who had gathered round them to stay where they were, and that they would come back to them, depending on the outcome of the battle farther on. "Wait a moment," he told Constance, gave her his rifle, and ran out of the trees and on to the track. She held her breath as he dashed to and fro, to return with two more rifles, so that they had one each and one spare, and more important, four bandoliers of ammunition. "Now we have some odds to play with," he told them. But the firing beyond the trees had stopped; now there were only cries and groans.

Again Wishart admonished the Indian women to keep still and out of sight, then he crawled forward, parallel to the track. Four Japanese soldiers appeared on the track, moving cautiously, rifles thrust forward. Constance glanced at Wishart, but he shook his head, continued crawling through the undergrowth. Four Japanese soldiers were dead. Four more were now behind them. That still left 16, enormous odds – not to mention the two officers and the three civilians . . . and Marion Shafter. She did not suppose the comfort girls were going to take sides.

They crossed the angle of the bend, and encountered five of the Indian men prisoners; they had three rifles between them. "What happened, Corporal Chowdhury?" Wishart asked.

The men were all soldiers. The corporal grinned. "They were distracted. You did that, Doctor?"

"With my friends," Wishart said. "What about the others?"

"Some are dead," said a second man. "Others ran the other way." Unfortunately, in running away, the Indians had discarded the sacks of food they had been carrying.

Constance peered through the undergrowth. The Japanese soldiers had taken up a defensive posture, while their superiors argued. She could make out Marion Shafter, her breeches and shirt sadly stained with mud and rain, arguing as hard as any of them; she had lost her hat, and her yellow hair was plastered to her scalp. The comfort girls remained on the ground, regardless of the mud; they had no intention of joining in any shoot-out. Close by lay the backpacks discarded by the fleeing prisoners. Those were their real objective. And Marion!

"We kill those people?" one of the Indians asked.

"If we can. But it's still better than two to one against us. Our advantage is that they don't know where we are, or how many. Listen. We are going to flank them. You stay here, but do not fire until we do. Ba Pau, you come with me."

"And us," Constance said. Whatever was about to happen, she did not intend to let Wishart out of her sight, and she knew Susan felt the same way.

They crawled away, listening to the chatter of voices. Some of the Japanese clearly felt that the prisoners had just run off, and the best course was to abandon them and get to Loilem as fast as possible; without the prisoners to feed there would be ample food. But equally, others were arguing that some attempt should be made to find the fugitives; equally clearly they seemed unaware that their erstwhile captives might now be armed and prepared to fight back.

Wishart led them through the undergrowth until, as he had planned, they were actually in front of the Japanese. "No exposure," he told them. "This is cold-blooded murder, but that's how they want it."

"I want Marion Shafter alive," Constance said. "And Ishikawa."

"I want Matsumara," Susan said.

Wishart nodded and levelled his rifle. The others followed his example, and the four shots rang out virtually simultaneously. One of the Japanese officers spun round and hit the ground. One of the civilians dropped like a stone. The other two bullets appeared to miss, although the remainder of the Japanese, and Marion, dived into the mud. The comfort girls screamed and ran into the bush.

The soldiers turned to face this new threat, and were distracted by the shooting of the Indian POWs behind them. Two of them fell, and the rest retreated off the track and into the trees. But Wishart and his companions were firing again and again, and three more of the Japanese were hit.

Then the track was empty, except for the people lying down, and the morning was silent, save for the screams of the birds scattering away, and the steady patter of the rain. Wishart passed out cartridges. "We go in, now?" Ba Pau inquired.

"No way. Those characters don't understand the word surrender."

"I have an idea Ishikawa might," Constance said. "Now that he's cut off from his men and exposed. And I know Marion Shafter would. She's a great believer in survival."

264

"Matsumara is the one I want," Susan muttered. "But I don't see him."

Wishart considered the situation. They had to have the food, and he could understand Constance and Susan's desire to be avenged for all they had suffered, but he really didn't want to inflict any more casualties on his own people, and there were at least a dozen Japanese soldiers, still armed and unhurt, in the jungle on the far side of the track. "They're moving," Constance said.

As some five minutes had passed without a shot being fired, the Japanese trapped on the road were starting to wriggle towards the safety of the trees. Constance levelled her rifle and fired, just above their heads. The movement immediately stopped, but in return there came a hail of fire from the trees on the far side. Constance buried her head in the ground as the bullets crackled through the trees immediately above her, but now there came more firing from their right, where the Indians were joining in the action. Then there were some deeper explosions. The Japanese were hurling grenades at the Indians, as the others were too far away and there would be a risk of hitting their own people on the track. "Shit!" Wishart muttered.

Both sides were pinned down, and now, under the cover of the grenades, the Japanese on the road slid away into the trees.

"Fuck it!" Constance snapped.

"We go now," Ba Pau suggested.

"I want that woman," Constance insisted.

"We need that food," Wishart said, more logically. "But, you know, so do the Japs."

The sacks of food lay in the track in the rain, the key to whatever happened next. "The Japanese probably have iron rations in their haversacks," Susan grumbled. "They can last longer than us."

"They still need to make a move," Wishart assured her. "They have to get to Loilem. We don't have to go anywhere."

"You reckon?" Susan asked.

"We go, eh?" Ba Pau inquired.

"Not without the food."

"I get food, in jungle," Ba Pau said.

"You serious?"

"This my home," Ba Pau said, apparently including both Burma and Siam in his claim.

"You can supply food for thirty people?" Wishart asked. He reckoned there were about that number of ex-prisoners of war scattered about this particular area, and he wasn't meaning to abandon any of them.

Ba Pau apparently was prepared to do just that. "I can feed us four," he said.

"Then do that," Wishart told him.

"You come."

"No, we stay. You go find food and come back here."

Ba Pau hesitated, then muttered under his breath and crawled away. "Think he'll come back?" Susan asked.

"If he seriously wants to save his skin," Wishart said. "You okay?" he asked Constance.

She lay on her stomach, half resting on her rifle, gazing across the track at the trees. She was soaked through, and very tired, but not yet very hungry as they had been fed immediately before making the break. And oddly, she was happy. After so many years she was her own mistress, even if not yet totally triumphant. But if she did not yet know if she was going to live or die, she now felt sure she would take Marion Shafter with her. What a final ambition! she thought. But it was the only one she had left. To think of being reunited with either Harry or Mark, or both of them, was one of those heady dreams that had served to keep her alive until this moment. It was not something to be considered now. So she turned her head and smiled at Wishart.

"I'm okay"

He looked into her eyes. "You are quite a woman, Constance Brand," he said.

"And you're quite a man, John Wishart."

"You know, Connie . . ." his hand touched hers.

She shook her head. "After, John. If there is an after."

The day drifted by. Now that the firing had stopped, the bird and animal life began to return with raucous cries and chirps. The rain even stopped, and the forest steamed. And the sacks of food lay untouched. "I wish Ba Pau would come back," Susan grumbled.

The two women were alone, as Wishart had returned to the Indians to make sure they were all following the same plan. This was simply to attempt to gain the food under cover of darkness, now only a few hours away. "I don't think he means to come back," Constance said. "I wish John would come back."

Susan rolled on her back, regardless of the fact that her yellow hair became even more stained with mud. "I am dreaming of a hot bath in the Savoy Hotel," she said. "George and I had the first two nights of our honeymoon there, before leaving for Burma. They have tubs in the Savoy big enough to take four people. Certainly two."

"I know," Constance said. "I honeymooned at the Savoy too."

"Did you?" Susan rose on her elbow. "With Harry?"

"We only had the one night, before Harry had to go back to France."

"And when he came back he was so badly wounded you couldn't . . . gosh!"

"Actually, we had got together before," Constance said. "At the Ritz."

"You only move in the best circles, right?" Susan asked. "I didn't know you could get together in the Ritz, if you weren't married."

"Well, of course, we pretended we were married."

"You've had an awfully romantic life," Susan remarked.

"Do you really think so? It didn't seem at all romantic while it was happening. And then . . . well, it doesn't matter."

Susan reached out and squeezed her hand. "It does matter. It must! You have so much to go back to."

Constance squeezed her hand in turn. She had been so bound up for so long in the quest for survival, in hatred and the desire for revenge that she hadn't reflected on people like Susan, who had nothing to go back to, save the humdrum existence she had known before her oil tycoon had swept her off her feet . . . supposing that that humdrum existence was still there at all. "It's odd how things turn out," Susan said. "Connie, I want you to know that no matter what happens, if it hadn't been for you I wouldn't have survived these last three years."

"Snap!" Constance said. "But we're both going to survive, Sue. For ever and ever and ever."

Wishart returned half an hour later. "I've spoken with the Indians," he said. "They're getting pretty hungry,"

"Join the club," Susan muttered.

"They're going to move in as soon as it is dark. So are we."

"And the Japanese?"

"If we get into a melee, the odds are on our side, if the women come too. And I reckon they will."

They waited, while the evening drew in, assisted by the low cloud and the drizzle, which returned towards dusk.

"Fucking Ba Pau," Susan said. "I bet he's back home in Siam by now."

"Stuff Ba Pau," Constance told her. She was getting very hungry as well. "When do we move?"

"See that taller-than-usual tree over there?" Wishart pointed. "I told the Indians to act as soon as they can't see its crown against the sky."

Constance licked her lips. She wondered what Marion Shafter was thinking, crouching in the mud and the wet on the far side of the track. What was *her* agenda? But that Marion Shafter, whose adventurous career had taken her from Ethiopia to Malaysia and now Burma – and that only covered what Constance knew about her – would have an agenda for survival, could not be doubted. Well, Constance thought, we shall see about that.

"Listen," Susan whispered.

There was a rustle of noise from the jungle in front of them. "They're coming first," Wishart muttered. "Right! This is it. Now, you two sit tight. That's an order!"

"Bugger off," Constance said, and rose to her knees as she saw shadowy movement in front of her. She levelled her rifle and fired into the shadows, then ran forward, firing again and again.

Susan and Wishart were at her shoulders, also firing, while from their right the Indians also charged. The Indians were infantrymen, and accustomed to the bayonet. But so were the Japanese. Constance had never imagined life and death could be quite so desperate, as she was surrounded by shadowy figures, firing again and again, being knocked off her feet to go rolling against a tree, hastily cramming bullets into her magazine. A figure loomed above her behind a bayonet gleaming in the dark, and she remembered the beach in Arakan, the knowledge that she was about to die. But this time she could take her assailant with her. Back pressed against the tree trunk, she fired upwards and he disappeared. Then she was on her feet again. But the skirmish was already over. The Indian women had indeed joined in the assault on their captors, and they had secured some weapons from the other dead Japanese. The evening became bestial as they avenged themselves.

But Constance had some avenging of her own to do, and pushed her way through the murderous throng to reach the far side of the track. Wishart held her arm. "You can't risk it."

"They're in there, John."

"We'll find them when it's light. To go after them in the dark would be suicide."

"And if they get away?"

"They're not going to get very far without food," he assured her.

Wishart, Susan and Constance withdrew a little way up the track, away from the Indians. There they were visited by Corporal Chowdhury. "We have gained a great victory," the corporal said.

"Yes, we have," Wishart agreed.

"What do you think we should do now, sahib? The women are preparing food."

Constance shuddered, as she imagined what else those cooking hands had just been handling. "When they have eaten, they wish to return to India," Chowdhury went on. "Do you think that is possible?

"I would say so. They just have to go back the way we came. But it's likely to be a long walk."

270

"We will be going home, sahib. That makes all the difference."

The Indian women had made a fire, and already pleasant smells were arising from the cooking pot, partly overlaying the other smells that lingered from the battle. But they all had had to eat too often in the presence of death to be put off by that. Wishart counted the corpses. "Sixteen, and three of ours," he said. "That means a good dozen got away. As well as the comfort girls."

"When do we go after them?" Constance asked.

"As I said, when it's light. But they're very long odds. I don't know if the Indians will come with us. They just want to go home. That leaves you, Susan and me."

"You mean, you think we should go with the Indians?" Constance asked.

"One must be practical, Connie," he said.

"The thought of those bastards getting away makes me sick."

"Connie!" He held her hands. "Listen to me. The war is over for them. They have nowhere to hide. You have to let justice belong to those whose business it is. Your business is to pick up the threads of your life, to attempt to forget all of this, to think of getting back to your husband and your son."

"My trouble is, John, I'm not at all sure that I am still the wife and mother that either of them remember. Am I still the woman that you remember carrying into your bungalow in Taungup?"

"Yes," he said. "You're tougher, and harder, and you've proved you can survive. But you're still the same woman."

"I hope you're right. I had never been raped, then. And I had never seriously thought of killing anybody." She half-smiled. "Not even Marion Shafter, then. That came later."

271

He squeezed her hands. As he did so, a shot rang out. He spun round and crashed to the ground.

"Listen!" Harry said.

"That sounds like a regular battle," Mearns agreed.

Harry held up his hand, and his men stopped. They were happy to do that; it had been an exhausting two days, even if the fact that they were definitely closing on their quarry had been obvious enough. There had been a burst of firing from in front of them, but now it had ceased. "How far, do you think?" he asked Lenzing.

"A mile, maybe a little more. Much more and we would not hear it."

"Right. We'll adopt combat readiness."

Lenzing gave the orders for all packs to be discarded and stacked around the mules, and for two men to guard both the equipment and the animals. As was their practice, the scouts then split into three groups of ten; Harry led the centre, Mearns the right, Lenzing the left. Lenzing and Mearns took their men into the forest; Harry gave them 15 minutes then led his own group forward along the track. He had Robbins with him. He couldn't be sure how many of the enemy were in front of him, but his people all knew what they had come to do.

"Oh, my God!" Constance shrieked, dropping to her knees beside Wishart. Perhaps that saved her life, as bullets were whistling all about her. But Wishart was dead. God, she thought, Oh God! They had simply not expected a counter-attack, had made the cardinal mistake of assuming that after an initial defeat the Japanese would seek to get away.

The firing was over. Constance suddenly sat up and

reached for her rifle, to have it kicked away. Her arms were grasped and she was dragged to her feet, to face a triumphant Ishikawa. Matsumara stood behind him, and behind Matsumara there was Marion Shafter, mud-stained and inelegant, but equally triumphant. The rest of the Japanese were bayoneting the fallen.

"You are guilty of mutiny," Ishikawa told Constance. "You are condemned to death."

Constance turned her head to look for Susan, saw her lying on the ground. And now a Japanese soldier was standing above her, his rifle and bayonet thrusting downwards. Constance's stomach gave a gigantic roll. But Susan was surely already dead. There were in fact only four survivors of the Japanese onslaught, three Indian women and herself.

The four women were each stripped of their *longyis* and tied to trees, while the hungry Japanese ate what was left of the dinner. Constance sagged against the ropes holding her up. She was exhausted, both physically and emotionally, and she ached, and not only in her feet and her shoulders; the Japanese had delighted in manhandling her as they had tied her up.

Now the meal was over they commenced bayoneting the three Indian women, one after the other; their screams lingered in the trees.

Constance closed her eyes. It would be her turn in a few minutes. Surely no more than a few moments of agony, no matter how expert they might be at missing vital organs.

People were standing in front of her. Constance opened her eyes without meaning to. It was Ishikawa, Matsumara and Marion Shafter. In her hands, Matsumara's bayonet was bright with blood. "This will be my pleasure," Marion Shafter said. "But I must warn you, Mrs Brand. I have never used a bayonet before. You must excuse my lack of practice."

273

Constance drew a long breath. She wanted to scream and scream and scream, like the others. But that would only give these people satisfaction. She was more angry than afraid, at having come so close to avenging herself, and now to die like this . . .

She opened her eyes again, to stare at Marion Shafter, who had withdrawn the rifle, but was holding it in both hands, preparing for her first lunge.

"You do her leg first," Ishikawa suggested. "Stick her in the thigh. That way she bleed, but she no die." Matsumara grinned.

"Would you like to say a prayer?" Marion inquired.

"Bugger off," Constance retorted.

"Well, then . . ."

"You no do this."

Their heads turned, and they stared at Ba Pau. He had lost or discarded his rifle, and leaned on a stick, looking every inch the monk in his saffron robe.

"You run away," Ishikawa bellowed. "You traitor. You die!"

"I am monk," Ba Pau said with dignity. "Killing is not for me. Now, you kill this woman, you all hang. British soldiers close by."

Ishikawa stared at the monk, uncertain whether he was telling the truth.

"Rubbish!" Marion Shafter declared, and turned back to Constance. "British soldiers! There are no British soldiers within a hundred miles of us!"

Constance watched the muscles tense, felt her own tighten as she anticipated the coming agony . . . and then watched Matsumara spin round and fall to his knees, blood gushing from his mouth. There had been such a drumming in her ears as she had awaited death that she had not heard the shots. Ishikawa also fell, as did most most of his people.

Marian Shafter remained poised. She could have killed

274

Constance then, but there was always the chance of survival, as she had survived so often, to rely on her charm to enable her to fight another day. She dropped the rifle and raised her hands.

"Don't shoot!" Ba Pau was shouting. "I friend. You remember me, Sergeant!"

Constance could not believe her eyes as she saw the men emerging from the trees behind their rifles and bayonets. They were led by a huge man in a bush hat and a mud-stained khaki uniform. He wore several days growth of beard, and she did not recognise him until he stood in front of her and spoke. "Constance? My God!"

One of his people was using a kukri to slice away her bonds, and another was taking off his own tunic to wrap ground her shoulders. Her legs gave way and she fell to her knees. Harry put his arms round her and raised her up.

"In the nick of time, Colonel," Marion Shafter remarked.

Harry stared at her. A very blonde woman, the headman had said. It had never occurred to him that it could be Marion.

"You want prisoners, Colonel?" Lenzing asked.

"They killed all the wounded," Constance whispered. "You can see." The Indian women still hung in the bonds.

"No prisoners," Harry said.

Ishikawa sat up, and Lenzing shot him through the head.

"I friend," Ba Pau gabbled.

"You are a treacherous bastard," Harry said.

"I save your woman," Ba Pau screamed.

"As a matter of fact, he did," Constance said. "It's her you want to settle with."

Marion gasped, and stepped back, as Harry faced her again.

"She's one of them," Constance whispered. "She's been living and working with them throughout the war. She was going to bayonet me to death."

Harry continued to stare at Marion. "You can't kill me," she whimpered. "That would be cold-blooded murder. I am an Englishwoman."

"Now that's odd," Harry said. "I have evidence that you are actually a Japanese, at least by adoption." He squeezed the trigger.

Lenzing had his men dig a mass grave beside the track. The Japanese were buried without ceremony, but Harry said a prayer over the British and Indians, and the one American.

His eyes were stark as he gazed at Susan's body: she had been so certain they would get together again, some day.

"He was a very gallant gentleman," Constance said, kneeling beside Wishart's body. "But for him, none of us would have survived. But the same goes for Susan. Of course, you met her on the retreat from Rangoon. My God, that seems like another existence!"

"It was," Harry said. "But now you're going home."

Before then, there was a lengthy spell in hospital in Delhi, to be nursed back to health. Constance was still there when Rangoon fell, captured by a lone RAF pilot, who, flying over the city on reconnaissance, was signalled from the gaol that the Japanese had fled, and so landed his machine and took possession. The wheel had swung full circle. Within another month, Hitler was dead and Germany had surrendered. Now the whole might of the Allies would be turned on Japan, and no matter how long it might take, victory was assured.

She was amazed that she no longer felt the joy over that which she had once supposed would be inevitable. She was more happy with the letters Harry brought her, from England, from her parents, from Harry's parents, from Jocelyn Brand, her closest pre-war friend . . . and, best of all, from Mark. Mark was now five, and his carefully guided hand was full of love for the mother he could not remember, and anticipation for their reunion. But Mark seemed almost a creature from another planet. She remembered a baby; she would be returning to a child.

Then what of this planet? For three years she had existed in hell, with only Susan and later Wishart for company. She knew that both Susan and herself had toyed with the *idea* from time to time, simply because they were human beings, and human beings need relationships deeper than friendship. But in their debilitated state they had never possessed the mental energy to become lovers. Wishart now . . . would she had had an affair with him had they both survived?

"I'm to get the DSO," said Harry.

"You'll be sporting a chest like a general," Constance said, touching the purple and white ribbon above his left breast pocket.

He sat beside the bed, wearing uniform. She sat up in bed, wearing a nightdress. They were alone together for only the fourth time since her rescue, and on the other three occasions she had been too ill and exhausted to care. Now . . . "I'm told you'll be out of here in a fortnight," he said. "And there's a passage waiting for you on a ship out of Bombay the week after. You'll be home by midsummer."

"Let's hope it's not as hot as here," she agreed. "Will you be coming with me?"

"I'm afraid there are still some things to be done here," he said.

"Oh!" she said.

There were several seconds of silence. But one of them had to take the lead. "Are you going ahead with the divorce?" he asked.

"Do you want that?"

"Hell, no, Connie! I've spent the past three years dreaming of you. And I think I'm totally cured, now."

"Did you find that out while dreaming of me?" She bit her lip; she knew it was an unkind thing to say. But she had become so used to saying unkind things.

"Touché," he agreed, without seeming upset. "Three years is a long time. But if you'd like to pick up the threads . . ."

"What threads, Harry? Do you know what has happened to me over the past three years?"

"You don't have to talk about it," he said, uneasily.

"If I don't talk about it, then there is no future for you and me, don't you see? I've been raped. I've been stripped naked and whipped. I've been treated like a dog. And I have killed. And I can tell you, Harry, nothing has ever given me greater satisfaction than the killing. I'm only sorry I didn't have the chance to shoot Ishikawa and Marion Shafter personally. You have to know those things, Harry, and think about them, and decide whether I am the wife you wish to have. What you have to understand more than anything, is that the Constance you knew in England, or even in Singapore, simply no longer exists."

"Don't you think I've changed?"

"No," she said. "You haven't changed. You're a Brand. I don't know if you actually killed anybody in Ethiopia. But if you did, I shouldn't think you lost too much sleep over it. It's in your blood."

"Maybe it is," he agreed. "Maybe it's necessary that some of us have it in our blood." He grinned. "As long as we're on the right side." Then his face grew serious

278